Con Living

Also by the author:

Independent Living
Assisted Living
Freelance on the Galactic Tunnel Network
Date Night on Union Station
Alien Night on Union Station
High Priest on Union Station
Spy Night on Union Station
Carnival on Union Station
Wanderers on Union Station
Vacation on Union Station
Guest Night on Union Station
Word Night on Union Station
Party Night on Union Station
Review Night on Union Station
Family Night on Union Station
Book Night on Union Station
LARP Night on Union Station
Career Night on Union Station
Last Night on Union Station
Soup Night on Union Station
Meghan's Dragon
Turing Test
Human Test
Magic Test

Con Living

Book Three of EarthCent Universe

Foner Books

978-1-948691-24-6

Northampton, Massachusetts

One

"Attention all shoppers," the captain's voice echoed through the sparsely occupied food court. "We will be entering the tunnel in ten minutes. Anyone who missed the last shuttle returning to Earth's elevator hub will be charged for passage to our next stop at regular commercial rates. If you don't have a cabin, enter a lift tube and request help. The ship's AI will sort you out."

"I'll drop this stuff in recycling on my way home," Hank told the waitress who was just arriving for her shift at The Spoon. "I shut off the deep fryer, but I left the griddle hot for eggs and pancakes."

"In other words, the usual," Julie said, checking the prepped items in the refrigerator. "You didn't make coffee?"

"I cleaned the pots," the owner's son replied. "You know that I'm only working part-time from now on, right?"

"Your mother told me that you're starting college. She's very proud of you."

"The entrance exam was a snap even though it's been more than a year since I graduated high school. This is the first time the Open University has added a campus that's not on a Stryx station and Flower is recruiting students to make it a success. She's already set me up with a work-study job that will cover all the fees."

"Doing what?"

"I'm not sure yet. Work doesn't start until after the first two weeks of class. Knowing Flower, she'll probably give me a job in one of the ship's cafeterias."

"Knowing Flower, she'll probably give you a job pasting fake authenticity holograms on Grenouthian documentaries to sell in the bazaar," Julie said.

"Anyway, you're our senior waitress at this point, so if you want to take over some cooking shifts, you're first in line."

"Thanks, but waitresses earn more with tips."

"Now you tell me," Hank said with a grin. He slung the garbage sack over his shoulder and headed off for the recycling area of the food court.

"I'll have you know that Open University work-study jobs are carefully designed to ensure that the students can spend at least half of the time studying, ergo the name," Flower's voice said in Julie's head.

"There's a speaker right over the counter," the girl replied to the Dollnick ship's AI. "You don't have to use my implant every time you have something to say. People already think I'm nutty because I'm always pointing at my own ear."

"Are you suggesting that I talk to you too much?"

"No, I'm used to that, but sometimes I think I'm getting too dependent on alien technology. Ever since the Farling doctor cleaned all of those killer nanobots out of my body and gave me the implant, translations are so seamless that I can't even tell whether somebody is speaking English to me unless I watch their lips. I've been sending students to Rinka for her singing school, and she told me the other day that I really need to explain to them that she's an alien so they don't feel awkward when they find out. The funny thing is that I'd forgotten that she's a Drazen, even with her tentacle and the extra thumbs."

"And you think that's a bad thing?" Flower asked.

"I'm just pointing out that having a high-grade implant can get confusing," Julie said. "Am I even speaking out loud now? I can barely tell anymore."

"You've been subvocing, and my infrared imaging doesn't show any more lip movement than I see with Humans who received implants at a much younger age."

"That's what I'm saying. I swear that sometimes I start believing that I'm telepathic and I try to communicate with Bill by projecting my thoughts," Julie said. "I don't realize what I'm doing until he asks why I'm staring at him."

"I could link your implants—"

"NO! Do couples really do that?"

"The manufacturer recommends against it," Flower admitted. "Have you tried the new apple cider donuts?"

"Is that what those are? I thought they were plain. Good thing you told me before the captain stops by for his post-departure inspection tour. He actually likes plain donuts, and speaking of which, I better make coffee."

"Woojin will like these. According to my market research, apple cider is a mature taste for Humans."

"Or maybe you just have too many apples again, and you can't use them all up in Harry's Fruitcakes?"

"You're very young to be so cynical, Julie. Why won't you even consider attending the Open University? We have an excellent program for aspiring writers. Under the Stryx system, your experience from working part-time in the library will translate into advanced placement credit you can use to waive two introductory courses."

"Why not offer me transfer credit for my years at City College?" Julie asked, pouring a measured pot of water into the top of the coffee machine. Then she began topping off the salt and pepper shakers that the waitress from the previous shift had gathered from the tables.

"Because we both know that you never attended City College, it was part of your cover story for the witness protection program. But I could probably get you life-experience credit for the years you spent as a courier for the drug syndicate on Earth."

"Forget it, Flower. I'm just not the school type."

"Are you happy waiting tables twenty hours a week?"

"It's a job, and unlike the library, the pay is decent," Julie said. She picked up the tray with the filled salt and pepper shakers and moved out from behind the diner's counter to the table-seating area. "And look at all the new skills I've acquired," she added, raising the tray high over her head and twirling as if she were working her way through a crowd. "I like to think it translates to my acting work."

"Stand-in work," the Dollnick AI corrected her. "I've explained to you several times that principal animation actors contribute their voice and their likeness as well as providing the vector scaffolding for the artists to flesh out."

"But you ARE using my likeness and my voice."

"Not according to the tests the Grenouthian director ran. He spliced-together dialogue from your Refill character on *Everyday Superheroes* and tried to fool me into believing it was you. I could tell the difference without even trying."

"What kind of test is that?" Julie demanded, checking that the napkin holder on a table was full after setting down a pair of shakers. "First of all, the director has an interest in treating us all as stand-ins because you gave him points in the show. Second of all, if you knew it was a test, of course you'd say you could tell the difference."

"Budgeting is always tight for the first season of a new series. I'll look into your concerns when we start shooting season two next month."

"What if I hold out?"

"I'm sure the animation artists could manage with somebody else providing the scaffolding at this point, and I could always dub your voice."

"So you admit it's my voice."

"I have legal counsel that says otherwise. And you would have to find another team sport."

"Did it ever occur to you that if you paid me what's fair for my acting I wouldn't need this work and then I'd have time to think about things like the Open University?"

"Ah, so now you're negotiating," Flower said. "It happens I have another job in mind—"

"Did we just enter the tunnel?" Julie interrupted. "I felt something, but I didn't even get dizzy."

"Yes, you've gotten used to it, and moving into a Stryx tunnel is less jarring for Humans than jump-drive transitions."

Refill's fifth sense, a skill she didn't even know she had before becoming the stand-in for the waitress-turned-superhero character in Flower's maiden anime production, informed Julie that somebody was approaching behind her. She turned just as a four-armed maintenance bot floated silently up and extended a silver platter with a frosted cupcake sporting a single lit candle.

"What's this?"

"Happy Birthday to you," Flower sang through the bot's speaker. "Happy Birthday to you. Happy Birthday, dear Julie. Happy Birthday to you."

"It's not my birthday."

"First, blow out the candle before the wax melts all over the frosting."

Julie leaned forward and blew out the candle, which sputtered and came back to life. She frowned and blew it out a second time with the same results.

"Ha," Flower chortled. "Trick candle. That one never gets old."

"Fine," Julie said, removing the candle and stubbing it out on the silver tray. "I'll eat the cupcake, but that doesn't mean you're right about it being my birthday, which I don't celebrate in any case."

"Think," Flower said. "We just left Earth and it was your second time back. You've been on board as Julie Gold for exactly one year."

"Oh, I guess you're right. Mmm, tasty. Is that apple cider?"

"Of course it is. I asked Bill to make a special batch for you and he'll drop the rest at your cabin tonight. Don't you think it's about time the two of you got married? You could move into a larger cabin together, and I'll pay all of the wedding expenses as long as you keep it reasonable."

"Don't you think it's time you stopped nagging us about it?"

"Captain on deck," Flower announced.

Julie swallowed the rest of the cupcake in two bites, finished distributing the salt and pepper shakers, and got back behind the counter just as Woojin approached. He was wearing his official captain's hat and supporting an older man, who shuffled forward in slippers and a bathrobe.

"Good evening, Julie," the captain said. "A black coffee for me, plus whatever our guest is having." He helped the old man onto one of the padded stools at the counter and served himself a donut from under the glass bell cover on the old-fashioned pastry stand.

"They're apple cider," she warned him.

"Apple cider vinegar?" the old man asked excitedly. Up close, he looked to be in his nineties, though part of that might have been the stiff white hairs sticking out of his sunken cheeks. His eyes had a watery, unfocused look, and his lower lip seemed to want to hang open. "Cures everything, apple cider vinegar. They kept it from me."

"Why not try it and see?" Woojin suggested, using a slip of waxed paper to extract a second donut. "When's the last time you ate?"

"They put things in the food to control your mind," the man mumbled, but he accepted the donut with a shaking hand, and stared up at the captain as if really seeing him for the first time. "You look like a Chinese George Washington."

"Korean. I'm Captain Pyun Woojin, and the lovely young lady behind the counter is Julie Gold. She'll make whatever you want in full view so you can see she doesn't put anything in it."

"We don't do the regular menu during jumps or tunnel transitions because most people are in their cabins sleeping," Julie said. "I can make breakfast or sandwiches."

A crafty look came over the man's features, and he asked, "Can I have a coffee? They didn't let me have coffee."

"Cream and sugar?"

The old man nodded, and Julie poured him a mug two-thirds full, hoping that would create a sufficient buffer to prevent his tremor from sloshing coffee all over his bathrobe or the captain's uniform. She added just enough cream to change the color, stopping when he raised a hand, and then set the sugar dispenser next to the mug. Julie and the captain watched as the man used both hands to pour what looked like five teaspoons of sugar into the coffee.

"Try the donut first," the captain urged him and made a show of taking a bite from his own donut. "The coffee is hot."

The man broke off a pinch of donut and put it in his mouth, at which point Julie realized that he was missing a good number of teeth. She quickly gave him a glass of water in case the donut proved too dry to swallow. He took a bigger pinch of donut the second time, and then broke off about a quarter of it and pushed it past his lips. The old man's eyes were watering so much at this point that tears were running down his cheeks, and then Julie figured out that he was actually crying, and busied herself looking in drawers.

"Flower?" she subvoced. "I think we may need medical help down here."

"I don't see anything wrong in my thermal imaging other than a lack of digestive activity due to fasting," the Dollnick AI replied. "Try to get him to eat."

"Could I make you some breakfast?" Julie asked the old man. "We have fresh eggs, and I can make any kind you want. There's pancake batter in the fridge."

"You'll make the eggs the way I want?" he asked in a strangled voice.

"Of course. Scrambled? Sunny-side up? Poached? I can even do omelets, though sometimes they come out more like scrambled eggs with vegetables and cheese."

"Scrambled, with white toast," the man said in a strained voice and turned away from her to hide his face.

He put a hand on Woojin's shoulder to steady himself on the stool as his shoulders silently heaved. Julie exchanged a look with the captain, whose lips moved without saying anything.

"Woojin asked me to tell you to make four eggs and four pieces of toast to be sure there's enough," Flower relayed to Julie over her implant. "I suggest adding a bowl of fruit salad on the side."

By the time the toast popped up, the eggs were ready, and the man had recovered himself enough to sit up straight. His eyes were much brighter now, and he managed to take a sip from the coffee without sloshing it over the brim of the mug or breaking any of his remaining teeth. Woojin and Julie made small talk about the stops on Flower's schedule for the three-month leg out to Union Station while the mystery guest demolished the eggs and toast and then started in on the fruit salad. When he speared the last bit of cantaloupe on his fork, Julie got the fruit salad container back out of the refrigerator, but the man waved it off.

"Am I really free?" he asked. "God help me, but even if you're working for them, the meal was worth it. I don't remember the last time I tasted anything as good."

"Everything is grown fresh on the ag decks," Julie told him. She hesitated, exchanged another look with the captain, and then said, "I was hiding out in the witness protection program when I left Earth a year ago, and my boyfriend joined the ship as a stowaway. Even though she's working for EarthCent, Flower is sovereign territory, so you're safe here."

"I'm impressed by your choice of travel clothes," Woojin added. "Looks more comfortable than what I'm wearing."

"This?" the man chuckled slyly and untied the bathrobe's belt. For a moment, Julie worried that she had a flasher on her hands, but it turned out he was wearing an old-fashioned suit underneath. "They watch us all the time so I fooled them with the bathrobe, but then I guess I forgot I had it on."

"Fooled who?"

"The people who ran the place. They would have killed me by now if not for my annuity. The insurance company sends a rep every month to make sure I'm still alive."

"You were held against your will?"

"Do you think anybody would agree to be locked up in a secure ward? It was my ex-wife's kids from her second marriage, never had any of my own. After Sonya died, they started visiting me, people I'd never even met, but they said that their mother told them on her death bed to take care of me." He snorted. "Three visits later, they showed up with an ambulance and a couple of orderlies. They held me down for an injection, waited until it took effect, and then dragged me in front of a judge. It turned out that the spouses of my dear ex-wife's children were actually psychiatrists who the kids hired to railroad me, and after that injection, I couldn't even come up with my name in court."

"What is your name?" Julie asked, and then hastily added. "You don't have to say, but it would be nice to have something to call you."

"Geoffrey. Geoffrey Harstang."

Woojin's eyes lit up. "The author of *Starborn Marines* and the *Galactic War College* series? I read them all when I was in the mercenaries."

"They made an immersive series from my *War College* books," Geoffrey said. "The production values were weak because Earth was only getting started with immersive technology, but it swept the local SciFi awards."

"And your ex-wife's children had you committed?" Julie asked. "Why would anybody do that?"

"For the money, what else? I'm sure they've long since emptied out my assets, and I think the woman from the insurance company mentioned that my so-called family had all left Earth, probably with new names. But the hospital wasn't going to let my platinum annuity go to waste. Fifty thousand e-bucks a month."

"That's nearly ten thousand creds," Woojin said, and let out a long whistle. "Flower will rent you twenty cabins with around-the-clock room service for that."

Geoffrey took another sip of his coffee to wet his throat, and then sang in a cracked tenor,

If you're old, and it's cold,
And you want someone to hold.
Now's the time to visit Flower,
Tours departing on the hour.

"You saw a commercial for Flower's Paradise?" Woojin asked.

"On an ancient display screen, mind you. The hospital was too cheap to put in immersive entertainment systems, or maybe they were worried that we'd start enjoying ourselves too much. When I saw that commercial, something told me it was my last chance. I started fasting to get the drugs out of my system so I'd be ready to make a break for it. Luckily, one of those giant shuttles was scheduled for Pittsburgh your last day in orbit."

"You didn't eat for a week?" Julie asked.

"Nothing but canned beans, and only if I saw Martin open the can. Don't let me forget to send him money. He was one of the decent ones."

"He helped you escape?"

"Inadvertently," Geoffrey said, and made a noise somewhere between a snicker and a snort. "He had a regular thing going with the woman who did the laundry. I slipped in the room and stole his wallet out of his pants while the two of them were making feet for children's shoes, if you know what I mean. The keycard got me out of the locked ward, and the cash was just enough to catch a floater bus to the old fairgrounds where the shuttle put down."

"Why didn't you eat at Flower's Paradise when you arrived?" Woojin asked. "Those tour groups all start with the bazaar and the library, but then—"

"I ditched the tour," the old man spoke over Woojin. "I was dead on my feet so I dropped out at the amusement park. There was an old spaceship ride roped off for repairs, so I snuck onto one of the capsules and slept. My greatest fear has been that the fasting was giving me hallucinations and I was reliving a scene from—"

"*Agent of the Empire*," the captain interrupted him in turn. "I almost forgot you wrote that series because it was more about politics than war, but there were some pretty good chases and escapes."

"Tell Geoffrey I've prepared a cabin for him," Flower said in the girl's head. "Once he's rested up, I'll have somebody from the independent living cooperative come by and give him the tour. And tell him there's free legal aid available."

Julie relayed the message, and the old man shook his head in disbelief. "I guess somebody knew what they were doing when they named it Flower's Paradise," he said. "I wonder if a smart lawyer can get my royalty payments back, though I wouldn't be surprised if those lousy kids sold the rights for a lump sum after the court put them in charge."

"If they really left Earth, that could play into your favor," Woojin said. "We don't have any authority in the Sol system, but EarthCent has limited jurisdiction over humans everywhere else that the aliens don't assert primacy, and we're members of the Inter-Species Police Operations Agency. I'll have our chief of security, Tyrell Hopkins, stop by for a chat tomorrow. Flower can tell him when you're up and about."

Two

"How was class this morning?" Harry asked his assistant.

"I think I'm starting to figure out that algebra stuff," Bill said. "When the instructor goes on about X's and Y's, I just get a headache, but then Flower started explaining everything over my implant using real baking examples."

"I've been a baker for over forty years and I can't say I remember using algebra."

"Well, you could. Like, you know the plum pudding recipe we just released to the factory for production?"

"It's going to be a big hit with the Dollnicks because of the cognac and the cooking sherry. It doesn't use quite as much fruit as my original fruitcake recipe, but Flower loves anything with a long shelf life, and I put in almost as many apples as raisins."

"Right. The test recipes we made all used two pounds of raisins and one and a half pounds of apples. Flower explained how to figure out how many pounds of raisins we'd need for a hundred thousand pounds of apples."

"She wants to make that many plum puddings?"

"It's just an example of using a single equation to solve for one unknown. If you have two unknowns, you need two equations. Like, if I also knew the number of raisins there are in a pound, I could figure out the actual number—"

"Now you're giving me a headache," Harry cut him off. "At the next factory production meeting, don't let me forget to bring up that they're going to need to order vegetable shortening from somewhere unless Flower has enough oil on hand to make her own. The original recipe called for suet, but I substituted."

"So did Flower. When the instructor started giving us all these problems with trains stopping places, Flower substituted the Stryx tunnels and the human communities on our circuit, and suddenly it all made sense."

"What does Julie think of your taking a prep course?"

"I haven't told her so I can make it a surprise when I get into the Open University," Bill said, and began scrubbing the pot he'd let soak in the sink overnight. "Flower told me that Julie went to college before leaving Earth and that she might be hesitating to marry me because I'm not an educated man."

Harry glanced up at the ceiling, suddenly suspicious of the sentient colony ship's motives. "Are you sure Flower isn't just trying to—"

"Am I paying the two of you to stand around and chat all day?" the Dollnick AI blared from the overhead speaker. "Lunchtime is in an hour and I want to make an impression on our latest addition. He's a Sharf."

"You picked up an alien on Earth?" Harry asked. "What was he doing there?"

"Spying, I assume. The same thing he's planning on doing here, since the Sharf have registered him as an alien agent and made the required contribution to EarthCent Intelligence."

"What do Sharf eat?" Bill asked. "I didn't know they were a tunnel network species."

"They're not," Flower told him. "Other than employing Humans on the recycling orbital we stop at and running the second-hand ship dealerships in Earth orbit, the Sharf haven't had much to do with your people. But after an embarrassing incident in which they sold their portfolio of securitized ship mortgages to a criminal organization on Earth and had to buy them all back, they decided to open an embassy there and start paying attention."

Harry pulled his dog-eared edition of the All Species Cookbook down from the shelf and began flipping through the tribute section. It included the recipes contributed by humans who lived on alien open worlds and had created dishes inspired by their host's cuisine.

"I'm not seeing anything for the Sharf," he said, and then flipped back a page. "Hang on, there are two recipes from Maree who lives on that recycling orbital. She called them Steel Toast and Rust Bread, but they look like French Toast and Beer Bread to me. I see she substituted vanilla soy milk for the real thing, and I would have added butter."

"The Sharf are lactose intolerant," Flower informed the baker.

"What will we feed Razood?" Bill asked. "The Frunge don't eat grains."

"I brought back an unused cheese platter from the continuing education lecture at our independent living cooperative last night," Harry said. "It was only out of the fridge for a couple of hours and nobody took the cling-wrap off so he can have that if he shows. We'll make the Rust Bread."

"Why not the Steel Toast?" Bill asked, moving towards the fridge.

"You have to soak the bread in the batter overnight for that one. The Rust Bread is just three cups of self-rising flour, three tablespoons of caster sugar, and a bottle of beer."

"What's caster sugar?"

"Just another name for baker's sugar."

"Got it," Bill said. "What kind of beer?"

"I think there's one bottle left of that homebrew the captain's friend brought him from Union Station. I let Woojin hide it in our fridge, but we may as well use it up before it goes flat."

"Why does the Captain have to hide beer in here?"

"If he left it in the bar fridge out there in the cafeteria, the aliens would drink it, and he didn't want to bring it home. You'll have to wait until you're married a few decades to understand."

"Okay, I've got the beer and the sugar. Where do we keep self-rising flour?"

"We don't, but it's just regular flour with baking powder added," Harry explained. "I usually go with two teaspoons of baking powder per cup of flour."

"What's the difference between baking powder and baking soda?"

"Baking powder gives you a slow expansion, while baking soda needs an acid to do its thing, and then it starts to fizz immediately. We used to make backyard rockets with baking soda and vinegar when I was a kid. Flower could probably give you a more technical explanation if you want."

"Of course Bill wants. You never know what will come up on the Open University entrance exam," the Dollnick AI said, and then launched into an explanation. "Both baking powder and baking soda are made from sodium bicarbonate, but baking powder also includes acidic ingredients such as monocalcium phosphate, sodium acid pyrophosphate, or sodium aluminum sulfate, to extend the carbon dioxide production. Monocalcium phosphate begins reacting and producing carbon dioxide as soon as it comes in contact with water, but the other two ingredients require heat as well."

"Got that?" Harry asked, giving the young man a wink.

"Except for the chemistry part," Bill said. "You're saying that the bread comes out with all the little air holes because the batter is foamy when it gets baked into place?"

"Exactly," Flower said. "One of the reasons that eggs are so common in baking recipes is that their proteins become denatured when exposed to heat, meaning that the molecules unfold and lock into place. When you bake with yeast instead, the gluten proteins hold the bubbles open until the dough is set."

"Mix it up and pour it in this tin," Harry instructed his assistant while handing over a rectangular loaf mold. "It takes an hour to bake, and that's all the time we have."

"So the bubbles in the beer help too?" Bill asked.

"They don't hurt, but that beer is home-brewed with plenty of yeast at the bottom. As soon as it gets mixed with the sugar, the yeast wakes up and starts doing its thing again," Harry explained. "That's what makes beer bread special."

When Bill brought the still-warm Rust Bread out of the kitchen, two aliens were just entering the small cafeteria. The Sharf was as tall as Lume, the four-armed Dollnick spy who ran a soup-and-salad joint for humans in the food court. The Sharf was also the boniest alien Bill had ever seen, with a neck that was perhaps twice as long as the average humanoid type.

"Yaem, this is Bill," Lume made the introduction.

"Pleased to meet you, Yaem," Bill said. "This is the only recipe for Sharf in the All Species Cookbook that we had enough time to make, but if you have any special requests for the future, just tell me and I'll see what we can do."

"You're the cook for this cafeteria?" the bony alien asked.

"Cook's assistant, and Harry is really a master baker. But there are only a few of you who eat here every day, so we just make what Flower tells us."

"Harry? As in Harry's Fruitcakes? I had a slice at our new embassy reception on Earth and started slurring my words in front of the ambassador, which is probably how I wound up assigned here. Why would such a successful entrepreneur be making meals for aliens?"

"The business is Flower's. Harry created the recipe to help use up a bumper crop of fruit and it got named after him. This is also the research and development kitchen for Flower's Foods."

"Some of their premade soup packages for All Species Cookbook recipes are quite nice, and the gluten-free line fits my dietary restrictions," added a wiry Frunge with close-cropped hair vines who had just arrived. "Razood," he introduced himself to the Sharf. "I run the blacksmith's shop in Colonial Jeevesburg."

"Yaem. I don't have a cover job yet because this assignment took me by surprise. Maybe I can set up a little repair business for our old two-man traders that so many Humans buy in the pre-owned market."

"Let me know if you need any custom metalwork banged out," the Frunge said, and then he frowned at the Rust Bread. "I hope that's not all there is."

"I'll bring out a cheese platter, and there's a giant bowl of fruit that Flower had a bot drop off a few minutes ago," Bill told him. "Sorry I haven't been able to help on the bellows lately, but the homework for my new class is taking more time than I expected."

"It's all for the best," Razood said. "A couple of those programmers from Bits who buy weapons from me to model for their games just offered to become part-time apprentices. They're working on a role-playing game and they want to make the crafting option more realistic. Believe it or not, they're paying me for the privilege of doing the scut work."

"Hey, Jorb," Lume called to the Drazen who had just entered the cafeteria. "Come meet the new guy. Flower put me in charge of getting him settled in."

Bill ducked back into the kitchen to get the cheese platter, and by the time he'd brought out the fruit and some reheated leftovers from the previous night's supper, there were seven aliens sitting around the table engaged in an intelligence community name-dropping contest with the Sharf.

"You're telling me that M793qK is here?" Yaem demanded, and the translated voice provided by Bill's implant went up a full octave. "THE M793qK?"

"Most of the Humans refer to him as the Beetle Doctor because they can't remember alpha-numerics," the stunning Vergallian woman informed the Sharf. "You wouldn't believe how easy it is to guess Human passwords. All of my training in breaking encryption is wasted on this species."

"We may as well dig in," Lume said. "Our Grenouthian counterpart isn't going to make it because Flower is keeping him much too busy preparing for the second season of *Everyday Superheroes*."

"I knew you all looked familiar," Yaem exclaimed, his head swiveling around as Harry came out of the kitchen. "You! You're Gerryman," he said to the baker, and then went around the rest of the table in rapid fashion. "Juggler, The Blacksmith, Thinker, Battle Royale, Digger, and Slomo. What a great idea for a char."

"Thank you," the slow-spoken Verlock said. "My real name is Brynlan."

"So we're short Refill and The Producer, who must be the Grenouthian director. It's somewhat ironic. If I had expected to meet any of the *Everyday Superheroes* in a cafeteria, I would have bet on the waitress."

"She works at a diner in the afternoons, though Flower just talked her into giving notice," Bill said. "I don't think she's ever been in here."

"Wait," Yaem said, raising his eyelids almost as high as his brow ridge. "Does that mean M793qK is the evil Farling mastermind?"

"When we can get him to show up," Lume said. "He runs a lucrative medical practice and he has his own stand-in."

"You're not going to believe me now, but I never made the connection between Flower Studios and Flower the rogue Dollnick colony ship. I'm a huge fan of animated dramas, and I originally stumbled into the intelligence business as a location scout for our biggest studio. I'm still a member of the I.A.A—" The Sharf suddenly snapped his jaw shut with a clacking sound and helped himself to a slice of beer bread.

"What?" Lume demanded. "You can't just stop in the middle like that."

"The Interspecies Academy of Anime," Flower broke into the conversation via an overhead speaker grille. "The awards show is in two weeks."

The Sharf started to lurch up from his chair, but Jorb and Razood pulled him back down.

"Spill it," Lume ordered. "You wouldn't be in here if you hadn't signed onto our intelligence-sharing agreement."

"But this is different," Yaem protested. "It's not about the Humans, and you know how much money is wagered on the awards."

"I have a compelling need to know," Flower said. "I already spent a fortune on bribes getting you assigned here. If our production is going to make it to the final round, I'll triple my buy of commercial time during the awards show broadcast."

"Even if I had access to that kind of information, sharing it would put my I.A.A. membership at risk. I'd need something to compensate me for that, and I can tell you right now that my superiors didn't share any of your bribe money with me."

"Free fruit for the rest of your life," the Dollnick AI offered.

"Not going to do it," Yaem said. "The only thing more important to me than anime is my oath to Sharf Intelligence."

"You're welcome to my spot in the cast," Harry said. "I'm getting too old to fight evil."

"*Everyday Superheroes* has enough votes to make the final round," Yaem blurted out before somebody could revoke Harry's offer. "I can play a geriatric Sharf if I have to. Look," he said, jumping up from his seat and then bending halfway over and taking a teetering step. "I even own a sword cane, though it's back home."

"We're going to have to rename the show *Everyday Spies* if this keeps up," Jorb said. "The Humans are the only ones who aren't in the game."

"We can write Yaem into the upcoming season easily enough, but I'm disappointed to hear you want off the show, Harry," Flower said. "I think you should wait until after the con to see if being a celebrity agrees with you."

"What's a con?" the baker asked.

"A con, a convention for fans and industry participants, though primarily fans," Yaem told him. "When is the next AnimeDramaCon? I heard the backers ran into some financial trouble after losing a string of intellectual property suits and it's on hold for the near future."

"I bought the rights and their contact list," Flower said. "Now that I know that our production is a finalist, I'll advertise my con during the awards show and schedule it to coincide with our next stop at Union Station. I really brought you in because I wanted a program director with experience."

"You bribed my superiors to assign me here because of the cons I managed back home?" the Sharf asked in disbelief.

"Forget about setting up the ship repair facility," Flower told the surprised alien. "You're going to love this job so it's win-win. And everybody keep mum about our show making the finals unless it leaks elsewhere. I don't want it coming back to cost Yaem his position in the academy because that could pay dividends going forward."

"Is there really a big enough potential audience on board for an anime con, even adding the people on Union

Station?" Harry asked. "Other than my wife, I don't know anybody who watches our show."

"Aliens are just as likely to attend cons as Humans, and according to my information, there hasn't been one at Union Station in years. Also, cons are destination vacations for true fans, and what better place for that than a Stryx tunnel network hub?"

"And what will you do if a million visitors show up?" Yaem asked.

"A million? I have room to put up four times that many guests and Union Station can easily host a magnitude more on short notice. I'm budgeting to break even on my investment at twenty thousand attendees, but with the contact lists I bought while we were visiting Earth, I'll be disappointed if we don't break forty thousand on Humans alone."

"Who sells contact lists?" Lume asked. "They're the crown jewels of any business."

"Hackers," Flower said. "I was able to purchase the contact information for attendees of every con on Earth that's gone out of business in the last century."

"Aren't you forgetting something, Flower?" Harry said. "Most of those people are probably deceased, and I doubt many hundred-year-olds put on costumes to play their favorite cartoon characters."

"Anime," a number of voices corrected him.

"It came to over seven million names," the AI said. "If I get a one percent response, that's seventy thousand people. Besides, I paid for the lists in fruitcakes and soup kits. Did you think I was running my big shuttles back and forth to Earth for those Flower's Paradise tours with the luggage compartments empty?"

"I'm not in a position to question your ability to make things happen, but I can't just ignore my responsibilities to Sharf Intelligence," Yaem said. "I could give you a few hours a day if you'll let me out of the required calisthenics and community activities Lume was telling me about, but—"

"How often do your superiors expect reports?" Flower interrupted.

"It works out to, let's see," Yaem said, staring off into space and no doubt accessing a calculator on his heads-up display. "Two hundred hours on the Human calendar, give or take some of those funky minute units."

"Lume, you share your reports with him," Flower ordered the Dollnick. "The rest of you can chip in with the occasional tidbit when we visit Open Worlds. Yaem will be too busy with the con to fool around with intelligence work."

"Not to mention acting in the upcoming season of *Everyday Superheroes*," the Sharf reminded the Dollnick AI.

"We're all paid as stand-ins," Jorb informed him. "It's supposedly scaffolding work, even though we say the lines and you recognized us from the chars."

"If we win any awards, I'll put you all on the books as principal animation actors," Flower promised. "I have a good feeling about this."

Three

"I still can't believe I let Flower talk me into quitting my waitressing job," Julie complained to the AI assistant librarian as she helped arrange the books on his shelving attachment. "I've spent the two weeks since I gave notice wondering if I've made a mistake. Why does Flower always have to get her own way in everything?"

"You must have been ready for a change or you never would have agreed to it," Dewey said.

"She's just good at figuring out our weak spots and going for the throat. Is she still pushing you to swap bodies and become an artificial person?"

"Flower correctly pointed out that the library collection has stabilized. For the first few years of the circuit, we were picking up millions of books on each of our semi-annual stops at Earth. This last visit it was just a few thousand paperbacks to replace worn-out copies, plus an abandoned university collection we'll be delivering intact to a Verlock open world for the human community. There's no reason to even unbox those books."

"I thought that after you gained self-awareness during a hack-a-thon on Bits, you designed your body specifically to become a librarian."

Dewey let out a mechanical sigh and his binocular cameras tilted down to look at his shelving attachment. "It seemed like such a good idea at the time, but I'm the only human-derived AI on board, even if my creation was accidental. You're one of the few people I know who doesn't treat me like a bot."

"I guess I never really thought about that," Julie admitted. "Are there many human-derived artificial people in the galaxy?"

"I don't know the exact number, but it's certainly in the thousands by now, and some of the aliens that continue to work with artificial intelligence have their own artificial people as well. I'd be buying a body from one of the other species, as humans haven't achieved that level of manufacturing prowess."

"Do you mean I could come into work one morning and you'll look like an alien?"

"The exterior shell is just aesthetics. Most android manufacturers offer styles for all of the species that create AI, and if I can't afford the price, the Stryx would give me a body mortgage. Flower says that I'm only attracted to working in the library because my creators were trying to build a smart filing system for gaming software modules when I became self-aware. She thinks that I should try a variety of professions before I'm too set in my ways, and the captain told me that there are a group of artificial people working for EarthCent Intelligence."

"You want to be a spy?" Julie asked.

"Maybe an analyst, I don't know. It turns out that the captain's wife was partnered with an artificial person when she started with EarthCent Intelligence, and she said that Thomas is right up at the top of the command structure now." Dewey hesitated for a moment, and then added, "Lynx also said that she and her partner rescued a female artificial person named Chance from a Farling orbital on their first mission and that Thomas and Chance live together."

"Oh. Now everything makes sense. Flower used the same argument on me."

"She wants you to change bodies?"

"I meant dangling relationships. Flower said Bill was worried that I was staying in my waitressing job so I wouldn't make him feel bad about working as a baker's assistant. She implied that I'm holding him back from going to the Open University." Julie wedged a final book into Dewey's shelving attachment. "I'm afraid to tell him that I'm trying to write a book because he already thinks I'm smarter than he is. Bill is always saying I can do anything I put my mind to."

"With the exception of getting to your martial arts class on time," the assistant librarian said. "You're going to have to make a run for it."

Julie checked the time on the old-fashioned clock behind the circulation desk and grabbed her purse. "I was waiting for Bill to stop and pick me up, but I forgot that he was doing some special job for Flower today. See you tomorrow."

When Julie arrived at the dojo, the Drazen instructor was fortunately too busy getting a new group of students oriented to comment on her tardiness. She slipped into the locker room, changed into the traditional sparring uniform, and emerged just as the students began lining up for drills. The forty-five minutes went by in a blink of the eye, and she was almost out the door when a tentacle tapped her shoulder.

"Sorry I was late," she apologized before Jorb could say anything. "That was the first time this month."

"Your month began yesterday, but that's not what I wanted to talk to you about," the Drazen said. "I was hoping to catch you and Bill at the same time, but I guess you can pass along the news."

"What is it? Are you and Rinka engaged?" Julie asked. "I'll have to think of a present to bring her for my next music lesson."

"We haven't even passed the second level compatibility test yet," Jorb said. "How could we be engaged? Anyway, it's been almost ten months since you and Bill started training here, and I want the two of you to transfer to the advanced class that I'll be starting as soon as everybody can settle on a time."

"Does a new class mean that you'll be quitting your job at the Vergallian finishing school?" Julie asked.

"It pays too well, and it lets me keep an eye on Avisia to see if she's recruiting the girls as undercover agents for Vergallian Intelligence."

"I keep forgetting that you're a spy too. There's something weird about the whole setup."

"I think it's brilliant," Jorb said. "Rather than EarthCent Intelligence having to worry about alien spies running all over the place, they collect fees from our agencies to take us around to the sovereign human communities where they can watch us watching you."

"If you say so. I'll tell Bill about the advanced class, and we'll see you and Rinka for dinner tomorrow." Julie was halfway to the lift tube before she remembered that she wasn't going in to work at the diner anymore. "Where is this new job you signed me up for?" she subvoced to the ship's AI.

"You can start by going home for a quick shower and a change of clothes," Flower responded. "I scheduled the first meeting in the common room of the independent living cooperative because several of the staff I've hired for this project live there. I'll have the serving bot save you something for lunch since you won't be getting a shift-meal at work."

"I forgot about lunch completely. You better be paying me enough to make up the difference."

"Don't waste too much time in the shower," the Dollnick AI said as the girl entered the lift tube. "Brenda is already waiting in the common room, and you know how much lawyers charge for time."

"I thought she was giving free legal aid as a retirement hobby and to meet her community service requirement."

"When I realized how much aggravation she could save me I put her on retainer. Now hurry, I expect the others to arrive any minute."

It took Julie just ten minutes to shower and change, a feat that would have been impossible without the alien hair-drying technology that stripped the water molecules down to her scalp. A lift tube whisked her to the independent living cooperative, which was located on a deck closer to the core of the giant cylindrical ship, where the lower radial acceleration dropped her weight to eighty percent of Earth normal.

"To the right," the Dollnick AI instructed over Julie's implant.

"I know where the common room is. Are you finally going to explain to me what this new job is all about, or am I going to have to ask somebody and look like an idiot."

"I already told you that you're starting as the assistant program coordinator."

"You want me to learn programming?" Julie asked. "Like the game designers from Bits?"

"Not that kind of programming. Just be patient another minute, and stop by the steam table for your lunch."

Julie detoured to the cafeteria line where she was the only person taking a tray since it was past the lunch hour. Without asking what she wanted, the four-armed bot gave her a big ladle of fruit salad and a large slice of quiche, which Julie noticed was the last piece remaining in the pie dish. Before she could move away, one of the bot's four arms snaked over the counter and deposited a glass of milk on her tray.

"I didn't want milk," Julie said out loud. "I'm getting a coffee."

"Milk is better for you," Flower said in her head. "Now that you're out of the diner, it's time to start breaking your caffeine addiction."

"If I'm addicted to caffeine, it's your fault," Julie said as she headed for the round table where she had spotted a woman waving at her. "You're the one who keeps talking me into signing up for activities so that my time is scheduled from morning to night."

"Would you rather spend your all-too-short life sleeping?" Flower demanded in response. "Introduce yourself and then we'll have a brainstorming session. It's just ten weeks to Union Station and the con, so we have a lot to accomplish."

"Hi, I'm Julie, and I recognize some of you from the times I went along on your tours," the girl said, setting her tray down at the table. "Flower shanghaied me to be an assistant program coordinator, whatever that is."

"Brenda," the lawyer introduced herself. "We talked at Nancy and Jack's wedding reception."

"Maureen," the next woman said. "I was at the wedding too, and I'm in charge of marketing for Flower's

Paradise. Apparently, I was too good at my job because our AI friend recruited me for her new project."

"How many retired people live here now?" Julie asked, and then took a quick bite of her quiche.

"Just under five hundred with the new batch we picked up at Earth, but we already have three more cooperatives operating on this deck, so the total independent living population is over eighteen hundred and growing rapidly."

"Why not keep everybody in one big cooperative?" Geoffrey inquired as he took his seat. Julie barely recognized the man who had escaped a locked ward on Earth just sixteen days earlier. He looked about two decades younger, his face had filled out, there weren't any gaps in his teeth, and his eyes were bright as jewels. "From what Flower told me, there are over a hundred thousand cabins on this deck."

"We don't discriminate or anything, but most people prefer to live with native speakers of their own language, so we have a Chinese cooperative and a Hindi cooperative. The fourth group is, well, a nudist colony."

Julie choked on her quiche and started coughing, so Brenda reached over and thumped her on the back.

"It's not as bad as you're thinking," Maureen said. "They aren't all nude all the time, they just wanted to have the option. With Flower's willingness to partition off new deck sections, why not let everybody suit themselves?"

"In their birthday suits," Brenda snorted.

"You're the young lady who made the heavenly eggs," Geoffrey said, while Julie recovered her breath. "I'm going to treasure that memory for the rest of my life, and it gave me an idea for a new story. I'm starting to write again." His head jerked around to stare at the latest arrival. "You're a—"

"Sharf," the skeletal alien identified himself via a speaker pendant he wore around his neck. "Yaem is the name, and I'm the program director for the con. Flower informed me that some of you don't have translation implants, so I'm forced to use this external device until I master your primitive tongue."

"I have an implant," Julie volunteered, trying not to stare at the Sharf's impossibly long neck. "Flower made me your assistant."

"Then I look forward to working with you. Before we begin, have any of you attended a con?"

"Hundreds, if not thousands," Geoffrey said. "Primarily on Earth, but I did a few years on the Horten TourneyCon circuit as a Guest Human. Even though their main draw was gaming tournaments, they ran animation and fantasy tracks at the conferences. In addition to my science fiction books, I used to ghostwrite anime dramas."

"Would you take charge of the panel discussion participants?" Yaem asked.

"As much as I can squeeze into five hours a day. Flower has informed me that at the advanced age of seventy-six, that's the maximum number of hours I can work for her under Dollnick labor law. Funny, because I haven't felt this good in a decade."

"I'll get you a list of anime con professionals and ask you to contact them, but feel free to invite anybody you know from your own circles," the Sharf said. "I intend to focus on workshops and screenings, especially previews of coming releases. I'm told that Humans expect a lot of talking heads at cons, but if we're going to attract any of the other species, they'll demand more hands-on activities."

"Since our core team is here, I'd like to start with a brainstorming session," Flower announced via an overhead speaker grille. "I've put an audio suppression field in place around this table, so don't worry about bothering the people who are coming in to watch their afternoon melodrama. Let's start with the name for the con."

"You haven't chosen a name yet?" Yaem asked, and even with the mechanical-sounding translation, his surprise was apparent. "I thought you said you bought the rights to AnimeDramaCon."

"I did that primarily to get their contact list and to eliminate them as a competitor. But I want a catchier name with a broader scope, and all of the ideas I come up with are already taken by one species or another," Flower said.

"AnimeCon?" Maureen suggested.

"Five different species are litigating over the trademark rights."

"FlowerCon?" Julie said, just in case the Dollnick AI was playing hard to get.

"No, the florists have that one locked up."

"Is our main goal here to promote *Everyday Superheroes* and Flower Studios, or is it to maximize attendance?" Yaem asked. "I'll have to plan the program accordingly."

"I want the maximum number of attendees to have the best possible experience," Flower replied. "It's much easier to monetize happiness than disappointment."

"Really?" Brenda said. "I've always thought the opposite."

"That's because you're a lawyer," the Dollnick AI retorted. "Don't take it the wrong way, but nobody seeks legal help because everything is going right in their lives."

"The most successful cons I've been involved with offered something for everyone," the Sharf mused, and then hastily backtracked. "You have to have a general theme, of course, but we can cast a pretty wide net around anime. The background material you gave me about Humans suggests that anime was once associated with a particular geopolitical entity on Earth, but that the term has since evolved to include any animated storytelling with a dramatic arc."

"Which is how the tunnel network species define anime as well," Flower said. "But it turns out that the contact lists I've acquired were for cons related to science fiction, fantasy, and romance."

"Books or immersives?" Julie asked.

"Both. I've been able to recover the programs from some of those old cons on Earth and I'll send copies to all of your tabs."

"I don't have a tab," Geoffrey said.

"There will be one in your cabin when you go home."

"CombiCon?" Brenda suggested. "AniSciFanRomCon?"

"I don't hate it," Maureen said. "It has all the keywords for marketing, and 'Fan' covers both fandom and fantasy."

Yaem shook his head. "I won't even tell you how badly that translated into Sharf. I can't speak for Humans, but if you want any of the other species to buy tickets, come up with something shorter."

"If you're going to advertise and you want to reach a wide audience, I don't think the exact name is that important," Geoffrey said. "Maybe AllCon, or OurCon? Something universal."

"Both taken," Flower said a fraction of a second later.

"How about MultiCon?" Julie suggested.

"No active registered trademarks in the tunnel network database."

"I think it would work well with an advertising slogan," Maureen said. "Multimedia, multispecies, multi-track…"

"Multiverse," Yaem added. "MultiCon it is. Now that Flower has explained that she's open to all possible con activities, we have to decide what to include so that our marketing department," he nodded at Maureen, "can get started on promotions and we can begin putting the program together."

"Will attendees need to see the program before they sign up?" Brenda asked. "Ticket sales are a form of implied contract, and I wouldn't want to deal with tens of thousands of refund requests if the con doesn't meet expectations."

"That's why we should set the parameters right now so that we don't end up making any false promises," the Sharf said. "Anime is obviously in, lots of screenings, plus at least one production track for writers and artists."

"Plan on separate tracks for writers and animators," Flower said. "And my immigrants from Bits will stage a mutiny if we don't have a gaming track."

"Right, I was going to suggest that next. With Geoffrey here, I definitely think we should push books. If you're really planning on large numbers, we'll want a track for aspiring authors and at least one per genre for pure fans. What sort of venues do you have available?"

"I have ten auditoriums with five thousand seats each on my theatre deck, along with an open area equivalent to the size of the bazaar and the amusement park, which we can set aside for an art show and merchandise. There are fifty thousand cabins on the same deck that I'll fill as the guests arrive, and if need be, I'll start putting attendees on the decks above and below."

"Art show?" Julie asked.

"Of course," Yaem said. "We'll want to start taking reservations immediately so we can build-out a proper-sized area, and I'd like you to take charge of communicating with the artists. Will we have trouble finding laborers for the setup, Flower? Most cons rely heavily on volunteers. And when Maureen gets the word out, there will probably be submissions from artists who want to show but can't attend. We should have a mechanism in place for them to pay a little extra to ship their work in for display."

"I can supply all the volunteers we need, though I think I'd rather see if I can tempt some con guests into showing up early," Flower said.

"Filk," Geoffrey suggested. "A good con needs at least one Filk track, with open jam sessions and a songwriting contest."

"Good point," Yaem agreed. "And the art show should have a contest as well. Can we offer prize money?"

"How about prize fruit baskets?" Flower countered.

"As long as there's a purse of creds attached, I'm sure the winner will enjoy the fruit."

"Don't forget a masquerade ball with prizes for skits and costumes," Geoffrey reminded the Sharf. "I can't tell you how many times I won the Best Human Costume award at alien cons I attended."

"Isn't that cheating?" Julie asked.

"If they were willing to offer a prize, I was happy to take the money," the author said. "Besides, I got beat out by Vergallians on more than one occasion, including a face dancer who posed as me."

"How many tracks overall do we want to program?" Brenda asked.

"I've been to cons that seemed to have more tracks than attendees, and I've definitely sat on panels where there were more speakers than audience members," Geoffrey said. "If we're going to push the workshops, let's keep a lid on the number of talking heads."

"But weren't you a talking—, er?" Julie asked.

"And one day I woke up and realized I'd turned into a bore," the author said. "At the time I got locked up, I was planning a colony where creative people could come and work rather than talking about it. I can't help wondering if an interview I gave promoting the idea was what triggered my ex-wife's kids to make their move. They probably didn't know I had money until I stuck my big nose into philanthropy."

"I think that hands-on activities, like role-playing and crafting, fit well with Flower's goal of creating a positive experience for the whole family," Yaem said. "We'll plan on limiting the expert panels for now and see how the early registrations run. Maybe when you start promoting the con to the people on those contact lists you can include a few potential tracks for them to choose from."

"But keep it short," Geoffrey advised Maureen. "If you give them a laundry list, you'll get check-offs on everything. Maybe you could segment the lists and present binary choices at random, so people think they're being asked to choose which of two activities they would prefer for the final open slot."

"Clever," Flower said. "We'll do that."

"How many Human days will the con run?" Yaem asked.

"Three was the norm for cons on Earth, usually with partial programming on Friday and Sunday," Geoffrey said. "There were some mega-cons that ran for a whole week, and I suppose if there's going to be a couple days of travel time involved for most of the attendees, we'll want to make the trip worth their while."

"Are you sure we can pull all of this together in just ten weeks?" Brenda asked.

"You're forgetting who you're talking to," Flower said. "Leave all of the hospitality arrangements to me and just concentrate on early registrations and preparing activities for participants. Are you still a member of any professional groups you can tap into, Geoffrey?"

"I'm a lifetime fellow in the SciFi and Fantasy Authors Guild, and unless it's changed that much since I was away, there are thousands of authors with writer's block wishing they had an excuse to be anywhere other than their home offices. I imagine that live conferencing to Earth costs a fortune—"

"I have an always-on Stryxnet connection, unlimited bandwidth."

"Then I'll ask you to put me in touch with them as soon as I get back to my cabin," the author said.

"Forgive me for asking a stupid question, but I don't understand what you're talking about with programming and tracks," Julie said. "Do you give people schedules they have to follow?"

"Cons are multi-track, meaning there are sessions planned in each track throughout the day catering to a particular interest," the Sharf explained. "A simple example would be an anime screening track, where each session would include a showing of new or classic anime, perhaps with the addition of a brief panel discussion to comment on the work and take questions from the audience."

"But where are you going to find all of those experts on such short notice?"

"Ten weeks is forever in the con business, and the problem is never finding enough experts, it's finding quality experts. You never know how they're going to perform unless they have con experience."

Four

"I'm six," Em informed the Farling doctor. "I'm going to a *real* school now."

"I thought that the Open University had a height requirement," M793qK said. "Climb up on the table and I'll stretch you."

"Nooooo!" the little girl squealed and scurried away to hide behind Lynx. "Don't let Uncle Beetle stretch me, Momma."

"Uncle Beetle is teasing, as usual," the third officer told her daughter, and scowled at the towering alien. "Em's teacher thinks she's having trouble seeing the display board."

"Then why isn't Em's teacher here?" the doctor asked. "I can't fix her eyes remotely."

"The teacher thinks Em is having trouble seeing the display board. She squints."

"You have a squinty teacher?" the giant beetle asked the little girl.

"You're silly," Em scolded. "My teacher says that *I* squint."

"It's your language that's silly," M793qK retorted with mock indignation. "Move the parts of a sentence around and it means something entirely different, not to mention half of your words sounding exactly the same. Here we're talking about eyes, and I'm not sure when you mean your single-faceted viewing organs as opposed to we, ourselves, and I's."

"Try explaining it to him in a civilized language," Flower suggested via a speaker in the ceiling.

Em began to whistle energetically, and the Farling doctor stopped waving his mandibles around and listened. "You're right, Flower," he rubbed out on his speaking legs when the little girl finished explaining her problem in fluent Dollnick. "My namesake is an exceptional child. Climb up on the table, Em, and I'll have a look at your peepers."

Thanks to the gymnastics training Em took for her required team sport, she was able to vault onto the high table without help. The doctor reached towards the ceiling and pulled down one of the alien medical devices attached to articulated arms. "Put your chin in the spoon," he instructed her.

"Are you going to eat me up?" Em asked.

"I'm going to look inside your head and see whether we need to send you back to the Human factory." The doctor adjusted a few knobs on the device to focus the holographic projection of the front-upper quadrant of the inside of the girl's head. "My, what big eyes you have."

"The better to see you with," Em replied immediately.

"It's too many books about the big bad wolf that got you into this fix," the doctor said, and he turned his own unblinking multi-faceted eyes on Lynx. "Your daughter needs glasses."

"Glasses? You can't just wave something and make her eyes better?"

"I don't do eye surgery on growing children for minor issues that can be corrected with glasses. It would be like putting braces on baby teeth."

"I lost my first tooth this morning," Em said proudly and gave the Farling a gap-toothed smile. "See?"

"Did you get a visit from the tooth fairy?"

"Daddy says that where he grew up in Korea, he had to throw the tooth on the roof to get the tooth fairy to come. I asked Flower, but she said our roof is always spinning, so the tooth would go flying through space forever."

"Do you still have the tooth?"

"It's under my pillow. That's what Mommy said to do, but I don't know how the tooth fairy can get into our cabin while we're sleeping. We don't even have a chimney."

"You're mixing up your stories," Lynx told her daughter. "And I would know if we had a store on board that sells eyeglasses, M793qK. I've seen traders in the bazaar displaying reading glasses from time to time, but won't Em need a custom recipe?"

"Prescription," the Farling doctor said, "and I already took the measurements directly from her optical mechanics. Let's see…" He began rummaging through one of the deep drawers under the counter, pulling out all sorts of unlikely prosthetics that might have been intended for aliens, and then removed a small black eyeglasses case. "What's your favorite color, Em?"

"Purple!"

"What a coincidence." He tapped away at a control panel on the case with one of his smaller appendages and it went from black to blue to purple. "Something like this?"

"Can you make it purpler?"

"Purpler isn't a word, honey buns," Lynx told her.

"It is in Dollnick," Em protested. "It rhymes with oranger."

The Farling did something to the case again, and the purple brightened. "Is that good?"

"It's perfect. But where are my eyeglasses?"

The doctor opened the case and used two of his upper limbs to remove the pair of bright purple eyeglasses and place them on the girl's head. "Now, what's the lowest line you can read on the eye chart?" he asked.

Em whistled a few Dollnick characters in keeping with the language displayed.

"She's wasted in first grade," Flower complained over the third officer's implant. "You should just let me keep tutoring her at home and in a few years she'll be ready for the Open University."

"Where she would be the only nine-year-old student?" Lynx subvoced in response. "I don't think so."

The doctor showed Em how she could change the color of the frames using the case's control panel, which was sized just right for little fingers. Then he spent two minutes trying to convince Lynx to eat more green vegetables before throwing all of his appendages up in disgust. "Fine, but don't come crying to me when you fail Flower's new physical for ship's officers."

"You don't want to fail a test, Mommy," her daughter cautioned her.

"Mommy's too big to fail," Lynx said, and then a thought struck her. "How did you happen to have the right prescription for Em on hand, Doctor? Did you and Flower work this out ahead of time?"

"I programmed the lenses after reading the hologram results," M793qK said. "The frames will stretch as her cranium grows, and the prescription will change according to the path I project for her ocular development, though I expect you to bring her in every three months so I can make sure we're on track. These will be the only pair of glasses she ever needs."

"I don't know if I have enough with me to pay for something like that," Lynx said. "What do they cost?"

"Twenty-eight creds. They're actually obsolete Horten technology and I just happened to have a pair."

"That a patient who was done growing and had his eyes permanently fixed left behind," Flower interjected.

"It's called 'recycling' and it helps me offset all of the charity work you have me doing," the doctor shot back. "That last patient Dave brought in needed two replacement hips, extensive kidney and liver repairs, thirteen teeth, plus a double prescription of my best placeboes to wean him off that drug regimen somebody had him on. It's a wonder he could form a coherent thought with all of those trace chemicals in his brain."

"He was committed to a locked ward against his will and they kept him drugged up. Didn't he tell you?"

"I wasn't paying attention. What do patients know about medicine?"

"Are you talking about Geoffrey?" Lynx asked. "As soon as I drop Em off at her gymnastics class, I'm meeting with Woojin and our security chief about him. Tyrell already heard back from EarthCent Intelligence."

"I know, I was listening in, but I won't spoil the surprise for you," Flower said.

Lynx paid the beetle doctor, brought Em to her class, and then took a lift tube to the security chief's office. The officer at the counter waved her through to the conference room, where she was surprised to see Dianne, the Galactic Free Press reporter, and Brenda, the lawyer from the independent living cooperative who had found herself working full-time on Flower's various projects.

"How did it go with Em?" the captain asked.

"Glasses. M793qK gave her a pair that should cover it until she's done growing and can have her eyes permanently fixed," Lynx told her husband. "Is Mr. uh, Harstang coming to the meeting?"

"He gave me the power of attorney to act for him in this matter," Brenda said. "Geoffrey is willing to testify if the local government on Earth will take action against the facility where he was locked up, but he needs to get on with his life, and he doesn't want to spend any more time thinking about his lost decade than absolutely necessary."

"They had him drugged up for ten years?!"

"Almost," Tyrell said. "When I interviewed him, he couldn't remember the dates himself, but the insurance company that paid the annuity was enthusiastic about cooperating when EarthCent Intelligence contacted them. Apparently, there was a long-term-care policy involved as well, so they'll be suing the facility for fraud. The impression I got is that there won't be anything left of that so-called hospital by the time the lawyers finish with them."

"How much of this is on the record?" Dianne asked.

"I think all of it," the security chief said, glancing at the captain for confirmation, "but you should probably double-check with Brenda before publishing anything that mentions Mr. Harstang by name."

"All publicity is good publicity," Flower declared. "Geoffrey has already agreed to let me use his name and likeness in promoting MultiCon, and he has no problems with our spinning his escape from involuntary commitment into a feel-good story about his return to writing."

"I've been in touch with my paper's Earth Syndication Coordinator who deals with the investigative journalists there," Dianne said. "She found a reporter who was already working on a related story, so the Galactic Free

Press is going to publish a whole series about eldercare abuses on Earth. My interview with Geoffrey will run alongside."

"EarthCent Intelligence couldn't find any traces of the ex-wife's children who took control of the assets," Tyrell continued. "It's not that surprising since ten years is a long time to cover your tracks, and nobody seems quite sure about the statute of limitations because there are a number of different jurisdictions involved. Whoever planned the fraud was thinking ahead because they sold Mr. Harstang's future royalty streams for lump sums wherever they could find a buyer."

"And since the buyers were acting in good faith, and the assets weren't stolen in the usual sense of the word, it would require extensive litigation for my client to recover the income he missed," Brenda said.

"How about going forward?" Lynx asked.

"I think a combination of threatened legal action and bad publicity will be enough to get the current rights holders to surrender them back to Geoffrey. We aren't talking about a large amount of money because he hasn't published anything new in over a decade and his backlist sales have been falling steadily."

"My con will change all of that, and we're in negotiations to produce an animated version of his *Galactic War College* series," Flower said. "See if you can work something about it into your story, Dianne."

"I will, but you know that my editor is wise to your trying to get free advertising out of the paper," the reporter replied.

"You can only do your best. Now if Woojin will put his hat on, we have an important ship's issue to discuss."

The captain plucked his tricorn hat off the table and placed it on his head to satisfy the Dollnick AI's sense of propriety. Tyrell's assistant took advantage of the pause to bring in a tray of coffee and cookies.

"I want to join the Conference of Sovereign Human Communities," Flower announced.

"But you're not human," Lynx objected immediately.

"My community is ninety-nine percent Human. Are you saying it's okay for CoSHC to discriminate against artificial intelligence?"

"Alien artificial intelligence."

"There's one of me and well over a half a million of you. According to Kute's Rule, that makes this a Human community."

"Who's Kute?" Dianne asked, making a note on her reporter's tab.

"A famous Dollnick philosopher and mathematician. His rule made modern food labeling possible by defining the level of dilution at which point an ingredient can be considered nonexistent. 'I think, therefore it isn't.' Without Kute's rule, every label would be an encyclopedia of micro-contaminates, including detached molecules from packaging and stirring spoons. Even the Hortens adopted Kute's Rule when they joined the tunnel network, and you know what hygiene freaks they are."

"You're claiming that your presence is diluted by the humans on board?" Lynx asked.

"Precisely," Flower said. "Now, if there are no other objections, I'm requesting that the captain officially look into CoSCH membership. I think it would look better coming from you than from me."

"Which brings us to the sovereign part of the equation," Woojin said. "I'm all for our having representation with

CoSHC, but if they object to our community claiming sovereignty, I would have a hard time disagreeing."

"But I am sovereign," the Dollnick AI said.

"That's the problem. You're sovereign, we're just along for the ride. And I'm saying that as your official hat-wearing captain."

"But they let the Traders Guild join en masse, and they aren't sovereign, or even a real community," Flower argued. "Besides, I consult with you about all of our important decisions."

"After the fact. I'm not complaining, mind you. This is the greatest semi-retirement posting ever, but I think EarthCent had something else in mind when we embarked on our mission."

"Is this really about the morning calisthenics? I stopped counting how many times Humans have complained about stretching when I got to a million, but everybody comes around in the end."

"Maybe we should just try applying and see how CoSHC responds," Tyrell suggested. "I like calisthenics, and I don't have to nag my trainees to stay in shape because Flower does it for me."

"Is there an official application process, or do we just send a delegation to the next CoSHC convention and see what they say?" Brenda asked.

"Good point," Flower said. "I'll want you on the delegation, and—"

"You're doing it again," Lynx interrupted. "The conventions are always on Union Station. Why not just send one of your bots and project your presence over the Stryxnet like you've done when we played poker at Mac's Bones?"

"For some reason that escapes me, my mentor excluded real-time bot control from my free bandwidth package.

When we visit Union Station, I control remote bots using my own transmission hardware, and the Stryx allow the signal through their shields."

"I have a question," Dianne said, half raising her hand. "What's the advantage for you in joining the Conference of Sovereign Human Communities, Flower? They already account for practically all of our stops, and it's not like they're withholding anything from us for not being a member. Besides, what about the case for reinstatement you filed with the Dollnicks, and all of the counter-claims your original owners made? Wouldn't joining a human organization look bad if you ever go to trial?"

"Flower has directed the Dollnick firm representing her to push/pull her lawsuit," Brenda said. "It's difficult to explain because—"

"The sophistication of our legal system," the ship's AI interjected.

"I was going to say because of the peculiarities of your legal system. I've been studying Dollnick law for less than a year, but it seems that the push/pull maneuver dates back to their prehistory when advocates would settle civil cases through wrestling matches. Given that they all have four arms, if one party pushed with the upper set while pulling with the lower, and the other party does the same, it produces a sort of stand-off."

"A compromise?"

"It's more nuanced than that," Brenda said. "Sort of like agreeing to cease hostilities without settling the root causes or admitting to weakness."

"So we'll be able to travel to Dollnick open worlds without the special waivers?" Woojin asked.

"That, and Flower will be able to bank in Dollnick space without worrying about her funds being seized."

"Which is no small thing, given the number of fruitcakes I've been selling to Prince Kuerda's distribution network," Flower said. "My legal position would have been much stronger if I was a member of a tunnel network empire as opposed to an outcast."

"But CoSHC is hardly an empire," Woojin said. "Other than the independent traders and the Tunnel Trips rentals, they don't even have a fleet."

"If I was a member, they'd have a stronger fleet than plenty of young civilizations."

"That's circular reasoning," the lawyer said. "Are you saying that if you join CoSHC and they somehow qualify as an empire because of your membership, you would take your lawsuit off pause?"

"CoSHC is closer to being recognized as an empire than you think, there's a basic definition in the tunnel network treaty that you can look up," Flower said. "How about we just plan on sending a delegation to the next convention and we can discuss who chooses the delegates another time? We have a more immediate problem to deal with right now, namely the awards party."

"What awards party?" Woojin asked.

"That's what I'm saying. I just heard back from my contact at the Grenouthian network and it's a go."

"The awards party is a go?"

"The Grenouthian network is covering the Interspecies Academy of Anime awards show, and thanks to my Stryxnet connection, they agreed to carry live reaction shots from my party if we get any awards. A successful awards show will play back into more work for Flower Studios."

"Which would mean more employment for animators, writers, and production staff," Lynx said.

"And a bigger entertainment ecosystem on board, which will draw more studios," Dianne added, nodding her head.

"So everybody wins," Flower concluded. "The live broadcast begins in nine hours and thirteen minutes, so we don't have much time to prepare."

"That's after one in the morning on Universal Human Time," Lynx pointed out. "Where is the party going to be? One of your big theatres?"

"I think it would be advantageous for various reasons to promote our entertainment community as employing more non-Humans than the facts may currently support," the Dollnick AI said. "I want all of the stand-ins there, and if we hold it in the common room at Flower's Paradise and keep the overall number of guests down, it will create the impression of diversity. Plus it will be easier for Harry and Dave to attend. Most of the cooperative members will be asleep by then and I'll throw an audio suppression field over the whole thing."

"Do you expect the ship's officers to be there?" Woojin asked.

"In full uniform."

"Then you can't blame me for sleeping in and skipping calisthenics tomorrow morning."

"Fine, everybody who comes gets a one-day exemption from their required activities," Flower said. "Can I count on you to write it up for the Galactic Free Press if we win anything, Dianne?"

"It's news even if you don't win," the reporter said.

"Not the kind of news I want."

Five

"All right, settle down," the Grenouthian director shouted in the direction of the production staff, primarily writers and animators who had joined the ship the previous year at Bits. "It looks like the Humans are afraid of the advanced species and you're all sitting too far back." He pointed a fuzzy finger at a Drazen. "Jorb, I want you at a front table with the Human triple-threat, and Razood, didn't you say you have a pair of new apprentices?"

"They aren't involved with the production so I didn't invite them," the Frunge blacksmith said.

"Then this is your big chance to make some new friends," the director said, beckoning the alien forward.

Jorb and Rinka got up and moved towards one of the unoccupied tables just in front of where the Grenouthian director had positioned a floating immersive camera. Along the way, Jorb roped in Zick with his tentacle, getting Renée in the bargain, while Rinka did the same with Julie, drawing Bill along as well. Bill made sure to sit between Zick and Julie.

"Crazy, huh," Zick said. "A year ago I was back on Bits being ostracized as a heretic for wanting to modernize our approach to gaming, and today I'm a writer on an award-nominated multispecies anime drama."

"You're not the only one doing something new this year," Renée reminded him. "Who would have believed that I'd be attending the Open University?"

"I thought you were still working at The Spoon," Julie said. "I wouldn't have quit if I had known you were leaving at the same time as me."

"I dropped a couple of shifts but I'm staying," Renée said. "Flower tried to talk me into her work/study program, but with tips, I earn twice as much waitressing. What does she have you doing?"

"I'm the assistant program director for MultiCon. I still don't have a clue what's going on, but the Sharf I'm working for says I'm doing great and to keep it up. We're all going on a field trip to a gaming con on the Horten open world that Flower is stopping at next. Yaem says there's no better way to learn how to swim than diving right in."

"I'll bet he hasn't seen those Dollnick sharks Flower keeps on the reservoir deck," Bill said.

"I wouldn't advise swimming with any Dollnick fish," the bony Sharf announced his presence, making Julie jump in her seat. "No, you're fine, but I need the two of you to scootch over," Yaem told Zick and Renée. "The director doesn't want four Humans in a row."

"Who's taking the last seat?" Bill asked, pointing at the oversized chair that remained.

"The director—he wants to stay near his cameras," the Sharf replied.

A few steps to the left, Brynlan pulled out a chair for Harry's wife at the other front table. "Please," he rumbled.

"Thank you," Irene said to the bulky Verlock, and then remained standing awkwardly with her knees bent for another five seconds because he was so slow at pushing in the chair. "You can learn a lot about good manners from the advanced species, Harry."

"If I was awake I could learn a lot," her husband groaned. "How can you be so chipper at one in the morning? I haven't been up this late in decades."

"I think it's exciting. You've never been nominated for an acting award before. Besides, you had a four-hour nap."

"I'm just a stand-in," Harry told her. "Maybe if Flower had agreed to make us principal animation actors my character would have stood a chance, but whoever heard of awards for stand-ins?" He paused as a half-naked Vergallian beauty pulled out the chair on his other side. "Avisia. You're wearing your costume."

"Nobody would recognize my char without these," the stunning alien said, adjusting her bosom in the halter top. "I'm hoping to get a still out of this broadcast that I can use in the promo material for my finishing school. Where's Lume?"

"I sent him to fetch M793qK," Flower responded from an overhead speaker grille. "The Farling claims to be busy evaluating patients for sleep apnea, but I know he's just dodging the party."

"So the whole cast is here, and you invited the writers and animators to help fill the room, but what's with all the aliens from the bazaar?" Harry asked.

"I invited whoever I could get to keep it from becoming a Human-fest," the Dollnick AI said. "It cost me a number of one-week waivers from required ship's activities, but it will be worth it if we win any awards and the network cuts to my Stryxnet feed for reaction shots."

"Here we are," Lume announced. The alien was carrying a collapsible chair with one of his lower arms, and a

Dollnick-sized chair with his top arms. "Avisia, could you clear a space?"

The Vergallian got up and showed off her furniture-arranging skills, an elective course at the finishing school. Lume set down his own chair and then unfolded the carbon-fiber-and-metallic chaise-lounge for the Farling.

"This is embarrassing," M793qK rubbed out on his speaking legs as he eased his carapace onto the custom-made lounge. "What if somebody in the hierarchy sees me cavorting with the soft-skinned species?"

"Do they watch anime?" the Dollnick asked.

"No more or less than anybody else," the giant beetle responded. "I was never a fan myself, but I know there's a con for it on our homeworld."

"The Farlings have cons too?" Irene asked. "That's so interesting. I thought that cosplay was strictly a human thing."

"You don't need to dress up in costumes to make a con a con," Avisia said, and then she and the other aliens burst out laughing at Irene's acceptance of the claim. "Humans are so gullible. We all have cons for our entertainment industries and dressing up is part of the fun. I could tell you stories—"

"All right, everybody," the Grenouthian director shouted, stamping his furry foot for attention. "I've got a live link with the control booth on Union Station and the show is about to start. They'll warn me before they use this feed for a reaction shot, so if I do this," he raised a paw and clenched the fist, "I want you all to go crazy like you've been waiting your whole lives to be on camera. Flower?"

"Just a quick word before the ceremony begins," the ship's AI said. "According to my information, we're up for three categories. A win in any of them would allow us to call *Everyday Superheroes* an award-winning show, in which case the network will run the commercials I've prepared. The broadcast will last a little over five hours—"

Harry moaned and dropped his head on his arms.

"—but all of the categories we're up for come at the beginning. Even though it's called the Interspecies Academy of Anime Awards, most of the productions are species-specific, and the Grenouthians tailor the broadcasts for each language feed so that viewers don't have to sit through the awards they aren't interested in. If we were watching the standard Dollnick feed, it wouldn't start for another two hours. Then we'd see the Dollnick anime awards in real-time, followed by a recorded version of the interspecies awards that we're about to see now."

A large hologram flickered to life at the front of the common room, but other than two figures on stools in the foreground, it was mainly empty stage. One of the figures was a Drazen, and he deployed his tentacle to prod his companion, jarring the Horten from his daydream.

"Coming to you live from the Grenouthian network studios on Union Station, it's the two million, three hundred and seventeen thousand, six hundred and thirteenth Interspecies Academy of Anime Awards," the Horten announced. "I'm Poga—"

"And I'm Bunk," the Drazen co-host introduced himself. "We're taking a break from broadcasting the professional LARPing league tonight because the network has us under contract and they didn't allow us a choice in the matter."

"In addition to our studio audience, we'll be checking in with remote locations around the tunnel network where nominees who couldn't make the ceremony are standing by on the Stryxnet," Poga continued. "I'd tell you more about the IAA, but you've heard it all—"

"Two million, three hundred and seventeen thousand, six hundred and thirteen times," Bunk interjected.

"—so without further ado, let's bring out the winner of last year's best director of an interspecies-anime-romance award to introduce clips from the finalists."

"We don't need to see that," Flower said, and the hologram froze. "I'd like to take this opportunity to remind you that volunteering to help with my con will count against your community service requirement, and that includes the dry run we'll be conducting a week before the actual con begins."

"If we work more hours than the community service requirement, will we get paid?" somebody called out.

"I'll let you out of your team sport as well."

"But we never do the team sport while we're stopped."

"You can bank the extra hours," Flower countered. "You should be grateful to get into the con for free."

"Even on the shifts we're not volunteering?" a young woman asked.

"I suppose," the Dollnick AI said after a moment's hesitation, "but only if you come in a costume."

"Is there going to be an art show?" one of the animators asked.

"Of course," Yaem replied in Flower's place. "The art show will include prizes, and if anybody is interested in judging, give Julie your contact info."

"But if we judge, can we still enter our art?"

"You would have to recuse yourself from any category for which you enter your own pieces."

"And can we sell our work?" another artist asked.

"There will be a fee for tables or pegboards to display art that's for sale, but if you're willing to offer the pieces in the charity auction, the fee is waived," Flower said.

"Who does the charity benefit?"

The holographic projection returned to life with the Horten commentator mid-sentence.

"...and the next award is for best interspecies anime stand-in for vector scaffolding purposes," Bunk announced. "The finalists will be read by the last winner, Floppsie Friend, from the hit series, *Dragon Galaxy*."

A Huktra wearing prosthetic wing extensions to make her look a little more like an interstellar-vacuum dragon almost knocked over the Drazen co-host while reaching for the plastic sheet with the names.

"The finalists are, Aaki, the royal Vergallian schoolgirl from *Class Assassins*—"

The projection cut to a clip of immersive anime where a small Vergallian girl with enormous eyes and an even larger sword did a triple somersault and landed in a crouch in front of a group of similarly dressed schoolgirls from a variety of tunnel network species.

"—Sevensie, the Zarent Seventh Apprentice on Koffern from the action/adventure series, *Wanderer Mob*—"

The clip showed a furry octopus brandishing an array of tools racing her unicycle towards a sparking cable dangling from a corridor ceiling.

"—and Mastermind, the evil Farling villain from *Everyday Superheroes*."

The holographic projection showed a giant beetle casually batting away attacks by a tray-wielding waitress, a knife-juggling Drazen, a young man with a shovel, and an underdressed Vergallian beauty.

The Huktra paused dramatically, and then bellowed, "Mastermind, from *Everyday Superheroes*."

"Go nuts," the Grenouthian director shouted as he pumped his fist. The large projection that the partygoers were watching was replaced by a view of themselves staring like a herd of deer caught in the headlights.

Irene was the first to react, letting out an excited scream and grabbing Harry, and then the writers and animators joined in. M793qK rolled off his chaise lounge and ducked behind the Verlock as the floating camera zoomed in on him.

"Looks like we have a shy stand-in," Poga said to Bunk. "How about an instant replay?"

"No time," Bunk said. "Mastermind couldn't be here in the carapace tonight so I'll accept the award in his place. Moving on to the best scream in an interspecies horror anime," the Drazen continued. "The award will be presented by—"

Flower muted the broadcast again. "We did it! *Everyday Superheroes* is now an award-winning anime production. Zick, I believe most of Mastermind's lines were yours."

"I like writing villains, but you know that M793qK was always improvising with those snarky insults," Zick said modestly.

"I think part of the award should go to Dave," Harry said. "He spent as much time standing in for Mastermind as the Farling did."

"I was standing in for the doctor, not for the char," Dave said, though the retired salesman was clearly basking in the shared glory. "M793qK said all of the lines. I just took up space so your characters would have somewhere to point their weapons."

"I'm never going to live this down," the Farling said as he crawled back onto his belly-lounger. "I may as well resign myself to repairing primitive life forms for the next galactic rotation because they're rubbing their speaking legs raw with laughter back home."

"It's the interspecies part of the award show, I doubt any Farlings were even watching," the Grenouthian director pointed out.

"Everybody quiet now," Flower said. "They're running my first commercial."

"Do you have an idea for anime but don't know where to turn for production help?" a voice that sounded like Maureen's spoke over the holographic projection of a hand sketching characters from *Everyday Superheroes*. "Do you have any money or access to grants? Flower Studios, the award-winning producer of *Everyday Superheroes*, has thousands of trained professionals to fit every budget. Check our travel schedule in the Galactic Free Press. Coming soon to a world near you."

"That's the whole thing?" Harry asked. "It couldn't have been twenty-five seconds."

"Twenty-one seconds," Flower said. "You don't want to know what commercial time during a live awards show broadcast costs, even during the low ratings part at the beginning on the Humans-only feed."

"What if we get so much work that we don't have time for our own show?" Zick asked.

"The educational games I have most of your fellow Bitters working on were a stopgap measure to keep them employed while we hunted up paying work," Flower responded. "Those games may make a profit eventually, but it will be decades in the future, and I can't keep all of the designers busy forever doing tech support."

"We're up again, Flower," the Grenouthian called out, and the AI unmuted the feed.

A leathery Thark took the stage, accepted the list of finalists from Poga, and began to chuckle.

"It appears that two out of our three finalists didn't get the memo about waiving licensing fees for award show clips," the Thark said. "I'll just mention their shows for the record. *We Brave Few,* produced by the Interspecies Mercenary Council Studios—wasn't that a recruitment advertisement?"

"A forty-six-minute recruitment advertisement that ran into thirty episodes," Poga informed him. "They probably thought the I.A.A. consent form was a prank."

"And the pirate drama, *Your Ship is Our Business,* produced by Free Republic Studios. Ironic, pirates refusing to grant royalty-free clip usage," the Thark said. "Fortunately, our winner for best new anime production is—"

"Start making some noise," Flower interjected.

"*Everyday Superheroes,* from Flower Studios."

The feed again switched to the scene of the party in the common room, where Irene was so excited that she smooched her surprised husband, earning them both two seconds of galactic fame. The Farling dropped his head below the table in hopes that the top of his carapace would go unrecognized, but everybody else hooted and hollered, pounding the tables and generally looking like winners were supposed to look at awards shows.

The feed cut back to the next presentation, and Jorb asked, "Are you going to keep your promise, Flower?"

"I always keep my promises," the ship's AI replied. "Which one?"

"You said that if we won at the awards, you'd put us all on the payroll as principal animation actors."

"She did?" the Grenouthian director demanded incredulously. "Do you know what scale is for principal animation actors these days?"

"You double-dip," the Verlock who played Slomo pointed out.

"I forgot about my own stand-in work," the director admitted. "I'll have to do the math as to whether I'm winning or losing in the end, since all of your raises are coming in part out of my points in the show."

"I just received offers from a dozen ad brokers trying to lock us in for the next season at the old rates," Flower reported. "Do they think that we aren't watching the awards?"

"Can't blame them for trying," Avisia said. "Am I the only one who's dying for a drink?"

"I'll have the bots start serving as soon as the results for the last category we're in are announced. I wouldn't want a reaction shot going live that makes you all look like alcoholics."

"But it's supposed to be a party!"

"What else are we up for?" Harry asked.

"Best script for an intelligent anime drama series," Flower replied. "According to the schedule, it's on right after the award for the largest production staff."

"They give an award for inefficiency?"

"The I.A.A. tries to encourage employment in the field of interspecies animation," Yaem told them.

"I would have thought that Flower would be a finalist for that," Harry said.

"They only count I.A.A. union employees."

"There's a union we can join?"

"...announce the award for the best script is Hynt, whose *Math For The Masses* anime script has won ten times in a row," Poga was saying as the volume suddenly blared. "The academy wanted to give somebody else a chance, so

Hynt was banned from the ballot this year, but he's being a good sport about it."

A slow-footed Verlock shuffled over to the co-hosts, accepted the list, and tapping his free hand on his chest to speed up his speaking cadence, began to read. "The finalists are, Beeloor, for *Interstellar Ice Harvester*. Multiple writers, for *Everyday Superheroes*. Ruke, for *Open Worlds*. And the winner is—me?"

"Let me see that," Bunk said, snatching the sheet back with his tentacle. "Well, there you have it. Hynt wins again with *Math For The Masses*, even though the show wasn't nominated."

"Rip-off," the Grenouthian director grumbled as the hologram flickered out. "I thought we'd be an easy lock for the best script with the Verlock out of the way."

"Must have been the write-in ballots," Yaem surmised. "There's talk about getting rid of them, but then the awards would all go to insiders."

"Hynt deserves it," Flower said. "I've been using his show in the schools when I substitute teach math and the children love it. Quiet, now. My next commercial is starting."

The hologram flashed to life again, and the word "Multiverse" came zooming forward, followed by, "Multispecies", and stopped on "MultiCon." Then the shot dissolved into a ballroom scene, where the dancers were all dressed as popular characters from various anime dramas.

"Isn't that the same music as the ballroom dancing scene from the Flower's Paradise commercial?" Irene asked Harry, who was nodding off.

"I used the same content and had the animators dress everybody up," the Dollnick AI told her.

"MultiCon, sponsored by the multi-award-winning producer of *Everyday Superheroes*. Includes free tours of our production facilities, discount lodging, and plenty of fruit. Meet Flower at Union Station next cycle for the con of a lifetime."

Six

The president of the independent living cooperative rose to his feet at the front of the giant shuttle's cabin and pulled off his ear-cuff translator, which doubled as a wireless microphone. "Would all the new members of Flower's Paradise who have never been on one of our field trips please raise a hand?" he spoke into the device, and his voice was broadcast over the shuttle's public address system. Nearly a third of the people sitting in the oversized seats indicated that they were new to the experience, and Jack nodded. "That's about what I figured. This is the first time we've stopped at Horten Sixty One, which was only declared an open world last year. The large human community here consists mainly of ex-contract workers from other Horten properties who have accepted Gortunda as their savior and moved here to be together."

"Gortunda?" somebody called out.

"It's called the Old Religion by the Hortens, and don't ask me about the theology because it's a closely held secret. All I know is that they hold regular revivals on Stryx stations and they give converts from other species generous discounts on the tithing requirement."

"So we're visiting a religious community?" a woman asked. "Will I have to cover my hair?"

"If you want to eat in their communal dining hall, yes," Jack said. "It's not a modesty thing, the men have to wear hair nets as well. If you've ever met any Hortens you'll know they're very sensitive about hygiene, and I'm told that the humans who moved here have gone native. The culture is an attractive fit for germaphobes."

"Do we all have to stay together or can we explore on our own?" somebody else inquired.

"Keep in mind that this is an alien world and none of the Hortens will speak English, so if you don't have a translation implant or the external ear-cuff version, it's highly advisable that you remain with the main group. That said, there are nearly three hundred of us along on this trip, so we're planning on splitting into smaller groups once we land and see what day trips are available. We'll be handing out tracking bracelets when you exit the shuttle to make it possible for Flower to locate you from orbit should you get detached from the group."

"Do those of us who aren't with the independent living cooperative get the bracelets?" a young man called out.

"You must be from the group who hitched a ride to go to the gaming con at the spaceport hotel," Jack said. "I don't know if Flower provided enough tracking bracelets for everybody, so I'll ask that you wait for the members of our cooperative to exit the shuttle, and then you can take a bracelet if there are any left."

"Excuse me," said a woman just a row back from where Jack was standing. "I don't want to play the tattletale, but the display flyer for this outing in the common room said that we can't wear perfume or cologne because the Hortens will stick us in isolation. I've been smelling something sweet with peachy overtones ever since we boarded."

"It's fruit," somebody sitting halfway back in the cabin called out. "While we were entering through the front hatch, there were bots shuttling in and out the back stacking crates of peaches and strawberries. Maybe the Hortens like smoothies."

"I'm paying our landing fees with fruit," Flower informed everyone over the public address system. "This results in lower costs for me which I pass on to the cooperative."

"Thank you," Jack said. "Are there any other questions?"

"Do we have to choose a tour, or can we go to the gaming con?" one of the retirees from Bits inquired.

"Uh, if you want to spend your field trip at the spaceport hotel that's up to you, just don't get too caught up playing a game and miss our departure. Flower is leaving orbit tonight, and while she might be willing to send a small ship to pick up stragglers, I wouldn't push your luck."

"Landing in two minutes," Flower announced. "Please return to your seats and fasten your safety restraints."

Near the back of the occupied section of the seats, Julie asked Brenda, "Are you going on a tour or coming to the con?"

"As much as I'd love to see how the human community here is adapting, Flower has already negotiated a deal with the con's legal team to take a meeting with me and Maureen. I think she's paying them in prune juice."

"Don't worry," Geoffrey said from Julie's other side. "I've been to dozens of Horten cons. I'll keep you out of trouble."

"Isn't Yaem coming?" Julie subvoced to the Dollnick AI controlling the shuttle.

"He only sleeps every third night on the Human clock so he headed down with my first fruit delivery fourteen hours ago," Flower informed Julie over her implant. "And please keep an eye on Geoffrey. He didn't get enough exercise for years, and M793qK says that he shouldn't stay on his feet for hours at a time."

"Flower mentioned to me that you're interested in becoming a writer," Geoffrey said as the increasing deceleration pushed them down in their seat cushions.

Julie felt her cheeks turning red. "I'm really just a book addict who works mornings in the library. I've been trying to write in my spare time the last eight or nine months, but I can't seem to finish anything."

The science fiction author turned his head slightly towards her. "How close are you coming? Halfway? Three-quarters?"

"I have a bunch of chapter ones, a few chapter twos, and not many chapter threes," Julie admitted. "I always seem to start strong, but then something just goes wrong."

"Do you work with a plot?"

"Yes, I mean, I think so. I start with an idea that I really like, but it always runs out of steam faster than I expect. Maybe I should be writing short stories."

"Back when I was a twenty-year-old in the mercenaries and realized that dying is a lousy way to make a living, I decided to become an author. I mentioned to a friend that I was having exactly the same problem that you are now, and he asked me to describe my plot. I managed a few sentences about the hero and the enemy he was fighting, and then I realized that I didn't have a plot at all, just an idea. So I sat in the mess hall for a few hours writing one-line chapter ideas on a napkin that took the story from start to end, and two months later, I finished my first novel."

"Was it good?" Julie asked.

"It was a first novel. I eventually rewrote it as a prequel to my *Galactic War College* series but it didn't sell that well."

The passengers burst into applause when the shuttle touched down with barely a bump. Shortly after, a series of accordion-like tubes stretched from the spaceport terminal to seal against the shuttle's hull, and Flower triggered the doors open.

Jack and Nancy positioned themselves on either side of the front exit, handing out bracelets to the members of the independent living cooperative as they shuffled out. "Don't run off in the terminal," Nancy cautioned every other person. "We'll go through Horten customs as a group and Jack will take care of the bribes."

Once all of the retirees were out, the management team for MultiCon rose to their feet, along with a few dozen hard-core gamers from Union Station who had come to compete in a one-day tournament. Julie and Zick spotted each other at the same time.

"Think you can win against the Hortens?" she asked him.

"I'm not here to play," Zick replied. "Flower drafted me to manage a gaming track for MultiCon, though where she thinks I'll find the time is beyond me. I volunteered to run the writing track instead, but she said she already had somebody."

"Me," Geoffrey said, stepping up to Julie's side. "Is this your young man who I've been hearing so much about?"

Julie blushed. "No. Zick writes for *Everyday Superheroes*. I stand in for a waitress named Refill, though Flower promised to upgrade me to a principal animation actor this season since my char ended up looking and sounding just like me."

"I'm afraid I'm not familiar with the show, but I'll ask for it on-demand if there's such a thing on board."

"Flower can get anything for a price, though from what Bill tells me, I'm not sure the money always ends up in the right pockets," Julie said.

"Are you from the generation that thinks there's no difference between anime and cartoons?" Zick asked the old author.

"Anime was big on Earth long before I was born, and the definition has changed radically in the last century," Geoffrey told the scriptwriter. "If it makes you feel any better, I might have watched your show twice a day the last year, but I wouldn't have noticed because I was heavily sedated in a locked ward."

"Sorry, sir. I didn't mean it that way."

"In addition to writing, Zick also created the artwork for Slomo, our Verlock Ninja char," Julie said.

"I'd like to see that one in action," Geoffrey said with a chuckle as they exited into the terminal. "Never had much of a gift for humor myself, though I did write one anime series under my own name and ghost-wrote quite a few episodes for others. Starting with good characters is half the battle."

"What's the other half?"

"Conflict. It doesn't require a lot of imagination, really. It can be an alien invasion, killer artificial intelligence, a child born with a special birthmark destined to fulfill an ancient prophecy and overthrow the kingdom. It's all just a backdrop for the characters to do their thing."

"Where are you going?" Julie asked as the elderly man turned down a corridor before customs. "Oh, right. I'll wait here."

"I don't need the bathroom," Geoffrey told her. "I'm skirting the customs line. I've been to cons at Horten spaceports and those little flashing lights in the deck of this corridor mean that it's the bypass straight to the hotel. Just don't try exiting to the street or security will be all over you. They do everything with cameras and facial recognition."

"I should run back and tell the others," Zick said, and jogged off to catch the group of gamers.

"I guess you really do know what you're doing," Julie said, and then realized it made it sound like she had doubted him. "I mean—"

"I know what you mean," Geoffrey said. "I look my age, but after a decade of institutional living, I'm not in any hurry to move into the independent living cooperative with all the other oldsters. I paid my dues on the con circuit in my thirties and forties. That was back before Earth's space elevators were completed and getting up to orbit cost an arm and a leg if you were footing the bill yourself."

"Who else would have paid for it?"

"Around ninety-nine percent of people emigrating from Earth signed labor contracts before leaving. The aliens provided transportation, usually in their own ships. I got lucky when my military SciFi series began to do well with mercenaries because all of them are employed by aliens and my name got out there. When a Horten con producer invited me to do a circuit as their Guest Human author, I jumped on it."

They stopped at a registration table, and Geoffrey announced, "We're here from Flower. She arranged for passes."

"I don't think they understand English," Julie muttered as the Horten stared off into space.

"She's checking her heads-up display and I wasn't speaking English," Geoffrey said. "That's a pretty good implant you've got if it renders my pidgin Horten into fluent English."

The Horten's skin turned light brown, and she rummaged through a box before coming up with two laminated passes that already had holographic likenesses of the visitors standing out in relief.

"Cool," Julie said. "I've never had a hologram of myself. Do we get to keep them?"

"She wants to know if we get to keep the passes," Geoffrey translated.

"Of course," the Horten woman replied. "Do you think we would reuse them after they've been contaminated by aliens?"

Zick returned with the group of gamers and the rest of the MultiCon team in tow. The Horten found passes for Brenda and Maureen without a problem, but Zick's badge seemed to have been misplaced.

"That's alright," Zick said. "I'll buy a day pass for the competition with all of these guys. What do they cost?"

"Ten creds to enter, twenty creds to participate in a prize tournament."

Zick was the only one who bought a ten-cred pass, and Julie could tell that it had taken him an effort of will to refrain from entering the competition.

Flower must have informed Yaem that they had landed, because the Sharf was waiting just inside the doors, and motioned for the other members of the MultiCon team to huddle up with him.

"We lucked out with this con because they have two tracks for game creators and one includes novel adaptations," Yaem told them as he handed out disposable tabs with con programs. "Brenda, I know you and Maureen are already scheduled to meet with the legal team, but I've been chatting up administrative types since I arrived, and I took the liberty of listing a few managers I think you should talk to. Maureen, I've gathered all of the official marketing materials from the con, but as you walk around, you'll see that the hotel's active displays have all been bought out to upsell attendees into pay-per-play events, including tournaments and a cosplay ball with cash prizes for best costumes. Zick, Flower wants you to take the game physics track with an eye to adding something similar for designers at our con. All of you make sure you grab whatever swag is on offer, whether or not you have a personal interest. We'll sort it all out when we get back."

"What about me and Geoffrey?" Julie asked.

"Flower wants you both in the novels-to-games track, but they only run a session in every other time slot, so you'll have plenty of time to relax or check out the merchandise and art. I'm on headhunting duty for the rest of our stay, but let's meet up for lunch in the food court at twelve-hundred hours, UHT."

"Headhunting duty?" Zick asked.

"I'll be trying to poach some of the con specialists handling events if I can find any who aren't on long-term contracts—or who are willing to do a runner," Yaem added as an afterthought. "If any of you meet a panelist or moderator who you think is a good fit for our con, don't hesitate to throw out a hook and see if they bite. Flower always has room for more, and she said something about not having enough Hortens on board for a balanced still shot to use in advertising."

The group broke up, and Geoffrey confidently led Julie into the crowded main venue, where game vendors were hawking their wares with immersive demonstration rigs. The noise was controlled with some kind of audio suppression technology, and the floor was overlaid with a veritable rainbow of different colored strips that appeared to be indestructible.

"What's with all the colored tape?" Julie asked.

"It's to put conference attendees on their tracks," the old author explained. "See the red stripe at the bottom of the screen on the disposable tabs Yaem gave us? I'm following the red stripe, which will bring us to—over there," he concluded, pointing.

"The Ortha Room?"

"He's probably an ambassador on one of the Stryx stations. Horten hotels are big on naming rooms after their diplomats. I think it has to do with ambassadors being public figures, so they can't make legal claims if their names end up associated with some distasteful event."

"Seems kind of weird."

Geoffrey shrugged. "When you've visited enough alien worlds, you come to realize that half of what they do is an attempt to differentiate themselves from all of the other tunnel network members so nobody can accuse them of copying. The Dollnicks run a big chain of convention centers on Stryx stations and their venues are all named after astronomical phenomena, like galaxies, nebulae, or meteors. The Drazens name their venues after different types of food and the Verlocks use famous scientists."

"Oh, look. There are little red lights in a line on the ceiling as well."

"At my age, it's better to keep an eye on my feet."

The doors to the Ortha room were closed, and a display panel on the wall adjacent showed rapidly changing Horten characters.

Geoffrey frowned. "Well, we got here too late for the panel discussion, but they'll unlock the doors for the question and answer period any time now. We can slip in as soon as somebody leaves."

Julie looked at the program on the disposable tab. "Shape-Shifting Characters in LARPing. I've heard Jorb talk about LARPing on Union Station but I didn't really understand his explanations."

"Live Action Role Playing. It used to be popular at fantasy cons when I was young, people dressing up and fighting battles with foam swords and axes. The main weakness was in casting magic since humans aren't magical, but Flower was telling me that there's a professional LARPing league on the tunnel network now. The Stryx create the immersive holographic environment in real-time, including magic."

"Wow. That would be—"

One of the doors slid open and a young woman slipped out. Julie darted forward and got her hand far enough into the proximity detection field to keep the door from closing, and Geoffrey entered after her.

"...and of course, dragon shifters have been done by so many species that including them in games is seen as a sign of desperation," a pinkish Horten man at the front of the room was saying.

"Are there any other questions?" the heavily made-up moderator asked.

"Why is she wearing so much make-up?" Julie whispered to Geoffrey.

"To mask her emotions," he whispered back. "You can read Hortens like a book by their skin color, so covering up is a common tactic for public speakers." Geoffrey squinted at the name displays in front of the panel members, swore under his breath, and looked down at the program for details. "I don't believe it."

"I have a question for the Guest Human author," a Horten in the audience asked after being acknowledged by the moderator. "I've been assigned to design a game that includes bear shifters, and I want to know if I need to account for their change in mass in our physics engine. When the Humans in your books shift into bears, does their weight increase in proportion to their size?"

A woman who appeared to be in her mid-fifties fiddled with the external translation device she wore around her neck before replying. "Thank you for the question. The main focus in my shifter series is on romance and pack politics, so I don't really get into the physics. But the strength of the shifted characters implies that they have actually become bears, and depending on the type, mature bears on my world would weigh anywhere from two to five times as much as a real hunk."

"Hunk of what?" the Horten followed up.

"Hmm, I think my translation device failed to choose the right word for you in context," the author said. "A hunk is a physically attractive male, preferably of the well-muscled variety."

"Ah, like on the book covers."

"Exactly."

The next question was about a Horten superhero, and Julie took the opportunity to ask her companion, "Do you know that woman?"

"Bianca D'Arc," Geoffrey said. "The Seventh."

"Really? I know her too, I mean, I know her work. I read all of her Jaguar series while I was traveling."

"All three-hundred-plus books?"

"Well, all the recent ones, beginning around two-sixty something, when they start a blood feud with the panther shifters. Are the D'Arcs royalty?"

"What makes you think that?"

"The Seventh. Doesn't that make her like a queen or something?"

"Bianca is a line author. That's what we call writers who pass on a pen name. There must be a dozen line authors working today who date back to the twentieth century, some with thousands of books to their names."

"How about another question for our Guest Human," the moderator suggested. "She's traveled a long way to be here."

"I don't understand the whole vampire thing," a game designer spoke up. "Sometimes they seem to be shifters, other times they're more like undead Humans who don't rot the way that zombies do. How do I model something like that?"

"Thank you for the question," Bianca said. "Different authors deal with vampires in their own ways, but in the vampire romance genre, I wouldn't call vampires shifters at all because the transformation is permanent. There is a parallel tradition in SciFi and horror genres in which some older and more powerful vampires can shift to a different form that's clearly inhuman, but they're so gross that we don't use them in romance, even with glamours."

"Glamours?"

"A type of enchantment that magic-users can cast on themselves to change their appearance."

"I'm afraid that another panel discussion is scheduled for this room in the next session and we need to clear out," the moderator said. "Thank you all for coming, and I hope to see you at the cosplay ball."

"Stay here and grab Bianca when she leaves," Geoffrey instructed Julie. "Find out if she's under contract and offer her a job."

"Where will you be?" Julie asked.

"Hiding," the old author said. "I had a falling out with Sixth, and Seventh won't give you the time of day if she knows I'm involved. If she's interested, have Yaem close the deal, and I'll catch up with you at the next session."

Seven

The students in the prep course clapped politely when the instructor returned the display board stylus to its tray, signifying the end of class. Bill clipped his own stylus to the side of his student tab and noticed that he still hadn't broken the habit of chewing on the end while he was thinking.

"Don't rush off," Flower said in his head. "I have something to show you."

"Is it going to make me late for my job?" he subvoced back.

A young woman who had been about to ask Bill if he wanted to study with her saw him staring at the ceiling and mumbling to himself. She pretended to see somebody she knew at the back of the room and hurried off.

"Did you think Harry was the one putting money in your account?" Flower asked. "You work for me."

"But Harry's my direct manager and he's counting on my help. He's pretty old, you know, and you keep giving him new responsibilities."

"Cooking for the few aliens who use the cafeteria doesn't take the two of you an hour for most meals, and Harry is having the time of his life working for my packaged foods business. He's actually been pushing me to get production up to speed with the current backlog of recipes so we can start testing the market for his all-species frozen pizzas. Now, I want you to watch this while keeping in mind how you would make something similar."

The display board the instructor had left covered with calculations went blank, and then a very solid holographic projection employing a limited color palette filled the entire front of the classroom. A cheerful tune began to play, and then the show's title, *Math For The Masses,* zoomed outward so quickly that Bill ducked in his seat.

The regular cast of animated characters featuring adolescent representatives from ten of the oxygen-breathing tunnel network members appeared. They danced in a circle while holding hands, spinning around faster and faster. Then they all let go simultaneously and their bodies went flying outwards. A funny-looking robot floated into the scene and began deriving the formula for angular acceleration while the animated characters scattered on the ground groaned and rubbed their bruises.

"This is the show that beat us out for best script?" Bill asked.

"Yes, it's very clever," Flower said. "I suspect Hynt originally got the idea from *Let's Make Friends,* but by using animation and an older cast, he can put the characters into dangerous situations to maintain audience interest. The best episode this season explained concepts in probability by having the characters take turns climbing an aluminum ladder in a thunderstorm. The episode about inelastic collisions also won high ratings."

"But you have me taking remedial math," Bill protested. "I don't know enough about anything yet to be making educational anime."

"You're a principal animation actor now and I thought you'd enjoy killing two birds with one stone," the Dollnick AI said. "With the success of *Everyday Superheroes* as our demonstration project, I expect Flower Studios to expand fourfold this year, and that's just the beginning. The future is in entertainment."

"I thought the future was in technology."

"Entertainment is the biggest business on the tunnel network—everywhere else military technology rules the roost. It's the main reason for advanced species to sign the tunnel network treaty and sacrifice some of their sovereignty. Members refer to their savings on military spending as the Stryx Dividend."

"Razood is in the Frunge reserves," Bill pointed out. "And I think Jorb said he has to go for training at some point."

"All of the tunnel network members maintain strong fleets, it's just a question of how much they have to spend. If you think it's expensive to build and maintain ships, try replacing battle losses."

"You know that my ambition is to open a bakery with Julie one day, not to go into the entertainment business."

"Just because I suggested you spend some time shadowing the Grenouthian director and learning about production doesn't mean I'm pushing you into the entertainment business. Don't you think it makes sense to broaden your horizons before you commit yourself to baking cookies for the next five hundred years?"

"It's more like fifty years for us, Flower, and baking worked out just fine for Harry and Irene," Bill said stubbornly. "Every time you start a sentence with 'Don't you think,' what I really think is that you're trying to manipulate me into doing what you want."

"You know that it takes a lot of money to start a bakery from scratch," the Dollnick AI said, adding subtle persuasion to her voice. "Harry and Irene got help from their parents on both sides, and they had already been working full-time for some years. Wouldn't you rather open a nice bakery café than some hole-in-a-corridor with a bread counter?"

"I thought you said you'd lend me the money."

"One pair of hands washes the other."

"Are you talking about me and Julie now, or is that a four-handed Dollnick expression for reciprocity?"

"The latter," Flower said. "Your vocabulary is coming along very nicely. At the rate you're catching up, I think you'll be ready for the Open University entrance exam by our next stop at Earth."

"Julie's friend Renée was telling me that they have a program for the hospitality industry with cooking classes and the kind of business and accounting courses that will help with owning a bakery. I'm doing this for me and Julie, not to get a management job working for you."

"What do you have against working for me?" Flower asked in an injured tone. "I may have had my problems with taking advice in the past, but I've become a very good listener, and I bounce all of my new ideas off of you."

"I've noticed, but I don't understand why."

"Let's just say you're more open-minded about chatting with artificial intelligence than the average Human. Most of the people on board treat me more like a teacherbot than like a sentient being. They're fine asking me questions or telling me to turn off the lights, but they never make the time to just talk."

"They're probably scared of you, Flower. It's like when I was growing up on Earth and people were always going on about giving the mayor or the president of EarthCent a piece of their mind. If they ever had a chance to talk to somebody that high up, they probably would have mumbled something about how it would be nice if the street lights could get fixed quicker."

"My corridor lights have only flickered once, and that's when I was firing my asteroid repulsion batteries."

"I didn't mean it literally. Do I really have to watch the rest of this, or can I go to work?"

"If you're not interested in a career producing anime I can't force you," Flower said, and the hologram disappeared. "I just think you could show a little more flexibility. Take me for an example. I spent the better part of twenty thousand years hosting five million Dollnicks at a time while helping them find and terraform empty worlds. Now I'm working as a glorified cruise ship for Humans. Do you hear me complaining?"

"No comment," Bill said. He headed for the nearest lift tube and Flower surprised him by not saying anything further on the subject. When he arrived at the alien cafeteria, he found there was a meeting going on with the captain, Jorb, Razood, and the bony new alien whose name he couldn't recall.

"Join us, Bill," Woojin said. "We've been discussing a problem and you might be the solution."

"Me?"

"You know about the arrangement we've made with the alien intelligence services to host their agents and ferry them around to the sovereign human communities. Razood has his cover job working as a blacksmith in Colonial Jeevesburg and Jorb runs his dojo. Yaem has started working for Flower now, and the problem is that she needs all his time to prepare for MultiCon."

"And she wants me to work with Julie helping him?" Bill asked hopefully. "I guess if I cut back on my hours..."

"That's not exactly what we had in mind," the captain said. "The problem is that Yaem needs to start showing results for Sharf Intelligence to justify his being assigned here or eventually they'll replace him."

"We've all been chipping in with information, and even ghostwriting intelligence reports to get him off to a running start, but ultimately, the main goal for all of us is recruiting Human sources on the ground," Razood said. "We can't share ours with Yaem because it wouldn't be fair to the sources or to our own employers."

"When you say source, do you mean people living on open worlds who work as double agents?" Bill asked his former employer.

"Just regular Humans who want to earn a little extra coin in return for supplying occasional tidbits of information," the Frunge blacksmith said. "Part of the agreement that allows us to work here precludes our recruiting anybody who's already working for EarthCent Intelligence, so no double agents."

"I haven't known you long, Bill, but I'd be honored if you would be my first Human agent," Yaem said. "In addition to a modest retainer, I can pay a per diem for any trips you take to the worlds we visit, with a bonus for the sources you recruit."

"Let me make sure I have this straight," Bill said, turning back to the captain. "You want me to sign up as an agent for the Sharf so that Yaem's boss will think he's doing a good job. Do you also want me to spy on people when we visit open worlds?"

"You'd be doing both Flower and EarthCent Intelligence a favor," Woojin confirmed. "As to spying, we can supply Yaem with enough information to keep his employers happy, but he needs to show that he's recruiting sources and building a payroll. Traditional intelligence agencies measure success in large part by how much they spend."

"So my job would be visiting the planets we stop at and recruiting people who live there to be sources for Sharf Intelligence?"

"You don't have to tell them that they're being paid by the Sharf," Jorb said. "You know that I'm pretty new to the business myself, but it's common practice for handlers to mislead their sources."

"Intelligence agencies back on Earth used to call it 'false flag' recruitment because the nations all had different flags," Woojin explained. "Some people get involved in spying for the excitement or the money, but others do it out of patriotism or because they're trying to bring about change. If a recruiter for country X knew that a citizen of country Y was really sympathetic with country Z, claiming to be working for Z only made sense."

"I don't know," Bill said. "If EarthCent Intelligence wants me to work for the Sharf, I guess I can try, but I don't want to lie to people."

"You may not have to," Jorb said. "Drazen Intelligence rushed me through a crash course and waived most of the requirements because I was willing to join Flower immediately, but I've done alright recruiting sources just by talking to people."

"And offering them money to spy for Drazen Intelligence."

"It doesn't play out like that at all," Jorb protested. "Take our last stop at the Break Rock mining habitat. I visited the ore processing center, stopped in a few bars, and bought some drinks. When prospectors asked why I was being so friendly, I told them I was interested in anything that might have an effect on the local prices and I could make it worth their while."

"So they didn't care why you wanted the information, and you expect to find the same prospectors when Flower stops at Break Rock again in another six months?" Bill asked skeptically.

"I give them a collect Stryxnet address for tunneling telegrams and tell them to keep it short," the Drazen said.

"Telegrams are a huge savings when you're working with Humans," Razood concurred. "If you let your sources send voice messages, they'll go on talking about the weather for five minutes and you'll blow through your whole budget on nothing. If you can't meet your sources face to face, always have them report in writing."

"Is spying like this everywhere on the tunnel network?" Bill asked the captain.

Woojin snorted. "Industrial espionage is cutthroat in the entertainment industry, but since the tunnel network treaty prevents the members from going to war with one another, they mainly spy on each other to keep in practice for working in the rest of the galaxy. A branch of Vergallian Intelligence made a concerted effort to undermine EarthCent, but they dropped that when the Alts chose the Empire of a Hundred Worlds over the tunnel network."

"I can give you a public Stryxnet address for reporting warranty problems with pre-owned ships which won't put your sources at risk," Yaem told Bill. He handed the young man a plastic chit. "Any messages sent there addressed to you will get routed to my home office and count towards my quota. Your primary goal will be gathering information about the shipping industry. We're especially interested in how Humans are responding to the supply constraint as we run out of pre-owned two-man traders to sell them."

"My information is that your ship dealers are scavenging recycling facilities and old junkyards for shells to rebuild and sell to the Humans," Razood said. "Frunge dealers would happily push into the business, but they just don't have a significant quantity of used entry-level ships that suit the market. The Sharf were lucky to have a large inventory of obsolete small ships available when Earth joined the tunnel network."

"Believe it or not, the basic model was a bit of a disaster when it went into production around a hundred thousand years ago," Yaem said. "Not enough cargo capacity for serious merchants, not enough cabin space for families, no jump capability. The only points they had going for them were the low price and easy maintenance, but those were enough that millions were sold as the poor Sharf's version of a yacht. The replacement model is much more practical, but it's priced too high for the Human market."

"So why don't you start building the old ones again?" Woojin asked. "You know that the demand is there."

"Who would buy ships built to an obsolete design when by stretching out the financing a couple hundred years they could get something so much better?"

"Our traders don't have a couple hundred years to pay down a mortgage, and your idea of obsolete is so far ahead of our state of the art that there's no comparison."

"I'm sure somebody would have thought of it already if it were that simple," Yaem said, though he looked unsure of himself. "Maybe it's a question of factory tooling, or it could be that the shipyard workers would rebel over being asked to build a model that's been out of production so long."

"It's more likely a question of profit," Flower chimed in. "I familiarized myself with the industry when I made my docking bay a refuge for Human traders whose ship mortgages had been foreclosed. There's not much margin in selling used two-man traders, and your dealers made most of their money on upgrades, such as robotic cargo handlers and medical pods. The shipyards building small spaceships are lucky to break even on the economy models. The profits are in the options, financing, and extended service contracts."

"Then I don't imagine that's changed any, but I'll pass the idea along," Yaem said.

"Couldn't you find a factory on Earth and charge them for the plans to build the ships?" Woojin asked. "The labor costs would have to be much cheaper than doing it anywhere in Sharf space."

"Your people don't have the infrastructure or the technology base," Yaem said. "I suppose you could fabricate steel hulls, but the drives and the field generators would all have to be imported, and the Stryx discourage technology transfers that leapfrog the current state-of-the-art for a species, not that Earth could afford the fees. And don't even ask about the fuel packs because we've never licensed that technology to anyone."

"How about me?" the Dollnick ship's AI put in.

"How about you what?"

"I have plenty of manufacturing space available on decks six through fourteen. I also have a complete compendium of Dollnick technology, including an alternative to Sharf fuel packs if the makers are unwilling to supply them at a reasonable price. If Dollnicks had ever developed a ship type that was a good match for the needs of Human traders, I'd already be manufacturing them."

"But you can't just share Dollnick technology with the Humans," the Sharf protested.

"I wouldn't be transferring the technology, I'd be employing Humans in my factory to build the ships," Flower said. "Ask your superiors to check with the intellectual property owners of the two-man trader design to see if they're willing to talk licenses with me."

"If the Sharf don't gear up to keep supplying the Human market, one of the other species will," Razood pointed out. "You've got the first-mover advantage and a large installed base, but the Hortens have a small ship design that's not so different from Sharf two-man traders in terms of capabilities. None of the other species have bothered chasing the Human business because of the glut of used ships you had on hand, but with prices going up the way they are..."

"Got it," Yaem said.

The kitchen door swung open and Harry came out with a tray of freshly baked pastries from the All Species Cookbook. "There you are, Bill," he said. "I was beginning to wonder if Flower had grabbed you for some new job without telling me."

"She sort of did, but I guess it's only when we're at stops, so it won't interfere much with my work for you." Bill rose and hesitated for a moment, then offered the Sharf a handshake. "I guess we'll talk soon."

"I have a handbook for new agents somewhere that I'll get to you as soon as I can have it translated to English," Yaem said.

"I've got something better," Woojin told Bill. "Stop by my cabin this evening and I'll dig it out."

Eight

"Where are you taking me?" Julie asked the lift tube.

"I set up a new office for con management on the theatre deck where we'll be holding it," Flower replied. "It's just three decks in from the library and we've already arrived."

The doors slid open on a cavernous space that could have housed the amusement park. The area in front of the lift tube was completely bare, making the slight curvature of the deck rather obvious.

"What do I weigh here?" Julie asked, stepping out cautiously.

"A little bit over ninety-four percent of Earth normal. The office is around the other side of the spoke."

Julie began to circumnavigate the hollow spoke, the wall of which gave structure for the cylindrical ship, while the interior space provided a shaft for the lift tube. About a third of the way around, she found herself in front of the entrance of what might have been a corporate headquarters from an office building on Earth.

"Miss Gold?" a smartly dressed young man at the reception desk greeted her.

"Yes?"

"The meeting is in conference room three. Can I bring you anything? Herbal tea? Mineral water? Fruit?"

"I'm, um, set for now. Thank you." A sign on the wall showed that conference rooms one and three were to her left and conference rooms two and four were to her right. She turned left and continued a surprisingly long way before she heard familiar voices coming through an open door. Julie entered to see Maureen and Brenda sitting with the Sharf and going over something on their tabs.

"Good morning," Yaem greeted her in raspy English. "Flower suggested I dispense with the external translator if I'm going to master Humanese before the Con. Please correct any errors I make."

"You went from not speaking English to being able to say that since last time I saw you?"

"I started learning your language before I was dispatched to Earth, but I thought I sounded funny when I tried speaking," the Sharf admitted. "Flower assures me that everybody sounds funny speaking Humanese, including all of you."

"I'll keep that in mind next time an alien laughs at me," Maureen said. "Brenda and I were just discussing this meeting's agenda with Yaem, Julie. Did you have any particular concerns you want us to address today?"

"Just that I'm having nightmares about a hundred thousand people showing up for the con and then demanding refunds because we aren't ready," Julie said.

Geoffrey entered the conference room just in time to hear her. "Everything is coming together splendidly," he said. "I've been to cons where the morning of the event it turned out that the main ballroom at the hotel had been double-booked. It's clear we won't have that problem here."

"I set aside this whole deck," Flower confirmed. "I'm planning to employ the early arrivals for the build-out, but if time runs short, I'll just activate enough maintenance bots to get it done."

"You want to use conference attendees who show up early to prepare the con facility?" Yaem asked. "It's normal for volunteers to help with the art show or the masquerade, but I've never heard of paying guests to come a month before the event to convert empty industrial space into a venue."

"We had a much better response than I expected to our early registration offer. We'll start taking guests on board at each stop from here on as they catch commercial transportation out from Earth or their current locations. I would have sent my shuttles back through the tunnels for the first couple thousand but it's too long for Humans to just sit in Zero-G."

"We've had a couple thousand registrations?" Maureen said in astonishment. "Already?"

"Thanks to your expertise in marketing," Flower said. "The promotional material was highly effective."

"I'm a bit confused here, Flower," Geoffrey said. "When you asked me about early registrations, I suggested that a twenty percent discount was standard for Earth cons, but nobody invites the attendees to show up a month early. Are you sure you didn't give them the wrong starting date? I remember a con where that happened and we had to scramble to put together a limited program to prevent the imperial stormtroopers from rioting."

"I added a special offer to Maureen's e-brochure stating that early registrants willing to work this month would receive a travel rebate, free lodging, and paid employment preparing for the con," Flower said. "To be perfectly honest, I was concerned that the contact lists I purchased on Earth had aged out, but one of the smaller lists proved to be pure gold."

"The response rate was nearly a hundred percent," Maureen exclaimed, staring at the new data Flower had just sent to their tabs. "It looks like there are even some apologies from people who said they wished they could register early to help prepare the con but they had existing obligations. It's ironic that the most successful direct marketing campaign of my career would come after I retired."

"Which list was that?" Geoffrey asked Maureen, and then gave Bianca the Seventh a guarded nod as she entered the conference room nursing a cup of coffee.

"A fantasy one, or maybe it's strictly for barbarian role players because they use Conan in the name. 'Conan On', which I guess is another way of saying, 'Conan Forever.'"

"It's not that surprising given that Conan is one of the few Human entertainment franchises to find any traction with the advanced species," Flower said. "I ran all the numbers with the Grenouthian director before we went into the anime business. The barbarian warrior theme is very popular with the Drazens, Hortens, and Frunge."

"I've never heard of Conan On," Geoffrey said. "It must have started after I was institutionalized."

"I can show you their branding from the list Flower purchased," Maureen offered. She tapped and swiped through a few menus on her tab, and then frowned. "Funny. I didn't notice earlier that the logo has a big A instead of a big O."

Bianca sprayed the coffee she had been about to swallow all over Geoffrey. "ConAnon?" she croaked. "You sent invitations to the ConAnon contact list?"

Geoffrey began to laugh so hard he started to wheeze and his face turned red, but he waved off Julie's offer to get him a glass of water.

"I must be missing something," Yaem said, picking up on Brenda's look of shock. "It wasn't a list for fantasy role players?"

"ConAnon is a support group for con addicts, Con Anonymous," Bianca explained. "You know, as in, 'Hi. My name is Bianca and I'm a con addict.'"

"Sounds to me like we got lucky," Flower said. "They must be real experts."

"They're real addicts. They would spend their lives participating in discussion panels or dressing up for cosplay if they could. They prefer the world of cons to real life."

"I've heard Humans contrast living on board my ship with this so-called 'real life' of yours and I don't have a clue what they're talking about. Take it from an artificial intelligence who's been around longer than your people have practiced agriculture. Life is life. There's no real or fake about it."

"I'm talking about work, family, finances," Bianca ticked off on her fingers. "Sure, most of the panelists get comped for the registration cost, and some of the real session troopers get free hotel rooms. But it's only special guests like myself or Geoffrey back in the day who get comped travel plus appearance fees."

"Session troopers?" Julie asked.

"Professionals who are willing to serve on panels about anything," Geoffrey told her. "Con panels aren't workshops, they're more like talk shows. So even though I was best known as a novelist and a scriptwriter, I sat on panels for everything from the art of megastructure construction to mercenary economics. I've even been roped into panels on women's issues as the token male."

"You always wrote a good female lead," Bianca said half grudgingly.

"Comped?" Yaem followed up. "I turned off my implant this morning so I wouldn't lean on it for vocabulary words, but I don't know that one."

"It's a verb taken from complimentary. Cons typically cover some of the expenses for attendees who participate in the panels and other activities that make the whole thing work. It's a common term in the entertainment and hospitality industries."

"So it sounds like I've invited humanity's most rabid con fans to our first outing," Flower summarized. "You're worried about their jobs, families, and finances? I can give them jobs, their families are welcome to come with them, and I have a zero-tolerance policy for debt collectors. You just need to figure out a way to channel their enthusiasm—"

"Addiction," Bianca interrupted.

"—addiction, in useful ways. When life gives you Sheezle bugs, eat your fill."

"Excuse me?"

"That's Flower's way of saying that she thinks something is going well," Julie explained.

"I haven't been to any cons with a large Human contingent so you'll have to fill me in on what negative behaviors we need to plan around," Yaem said. "For example, at Drazen and Horten cons, drunk costuming is often a problem with the youth."

"If you're willing to reengineer the concept from the ground up, I'd like to see if we can do something about session hopping," Geoffrey said. "At the cons I attended on Earth there would always be a group who were never happy with the panel discussion they were attending. Before the moderator even began introducing the speakers, I'd see a few audience members looking at the schedule and second-guessing themselves over whether some other session running at the same time might be more interesting. Five minutes in they'd be slipping out the door. I can't tell you how aggravating that is if you happen to be the person speaking."

"And a minute after that, they're barging into another session," Bianca concurred. "And then the first thing they do after sitting down is to start studying the schedule again."

"How very un-Dollnick," Flower said. "I suppose I could impose martial law, but I know how much you Humans hate being told how to behave. Brenda?"

"You're asking my legal opinion?"

"Surely there must be some rules for Human conduct at cons. Didn't you once tell me about some Robert fellow?"

"Robert's Rules of Order, but they're generally used for well-organized civic societies, not for social events."

"Do cons have security?" Julie asked.

"Some of them give T-shirts to volunteers who get a little training, but back on Earth they mainly relied on hotel security or hiring off-duty police," Geoffrey said.

"It makes more sense to educate all of the attendees to behave properly than to train a subset of them to enforce rules after the fact," Flower said. "We could make training mandatory."

"You mean, put everybody through a course in con etiquette?" Bianca asked. "Not a chance."

"You know, a little training for the panel moderators could go a long way," Geoffrey mused. "We wouldn't have to explicitly call it that. Maybe you could offer a free lunch for all the panel moderators before the first evening of the con and include a little educational entertainment."

"Why are you assuming the con will start in the evening?" the Sharf asked.

"It's just how most Earth cons operate. I suppose given the travel time everybody will put in before meeting up with Flower at Union Station we can pretty much ignore the standard scheduling."

"The official start time for the con will be in the morning," Flower said. "Humans are more attentive in the morning, with the exception of teenagers, and everybody will get a chance to wake up during the mandatory calisthenics before breakfast. I think a banquet for moderators with some stealth training the night before would work best."

"Who's going to be in charge of the training?" Julie asked.

"I can write up some skits or suggestions but I don't want to tire myself out performing the first evening," Geoffrey said. "Best to get an experienced master of ceremonies, both for the banquet and for the big events, like the masquerade."

"Morning," Jorb announced himself. He took the empty seat on Julie's left and playfully reached around and tapped her right shoulder with the tip of his tentacle to trick her into looking that direction. "I hope there's a reason for my being here because I took the morning off from getting beat up by teenage girls at the Vergallian finishing school to attend."

"We've got thirty Human days to the con and we're trying to get the ground rules in place before I start programming," Yaem said. "You'll be in charge of the live-action-role-playing track at Union Station, and Razood, when he gets here, will be running a crafting track on making weapons and general smith skills. I've been to a few Frunge cons, and their blacksmithing competitions are always a highlight."

"I'm twenty minutes early for the time Flower gave me so I assume that means I'm not a core team member," Jorb said. "Should I go out and come back later?"

"We were just talking about having a banquet dinner for the panel moderators so we can give them a little training," Geoffrey said. "I've moderated hundreds of panels so I know all the tricks, but I'd like to find a master of ceremonies who can make my points without offending anybody."

"How about a pair of MCs who will offend everybody?" the Drazen countered. "That way your moderators will be so distracted that they won't even realize that you're telling them they don't know how to run a panel. I could probably get us G.G."

"Grynlan and the Grenouthian?" Bianca's eyes lit up. "They opened the first con of the circuit I was just on. The two of them had the Hortens in the audience changing colors so rapidly that some of the younger ones passed out. G.G. must cost a fortune, though, and I bet that they're booked years in advance."

"I went to the Open University on Union Station with them and it's still their home base," Jorb said. "If they aren't traveling it will be a local gig. They got their professional start doing my going away party."

"Please contact them for me," Flower said. "And make sure they know that the job comes with all the fresh fruit and vegetables they can eat."

"Do you really think that will make a difference?" Julie asked.

"It might persuade the Grenouthian."

"You know, if I could change one thing about all the cons I went to on Earth, it would be the lighting," Bianca said. "Sometimes I suspect that hotels with convention facilities keep the lighting subdued so the guests don't notice the carpet stains."

"It's particularly bad in the common areas," Geoffrey agreed. "And the noise from simultaneous events can be very distracting as well."

"You'll have no problems with lighting at our con, and I'll be deploying audio suppression fields to isolate all ongoing activities," Flower said.

"Including in the merchant areas?" Yaem asked. "I think they may prefer some background noise for a festive atmosphere."

"I'll consult with my third officer who is the point of contact for all of the businesses on board. I'm putting Lynx in charge of the merchant activities. She'll be here any minute."

"So in addition to handling correspondence for the art show, I'm going to be helping Yaem schedule the sessions?" Julie asked. "How are we supposed to know which ones conflict with each other?"

"Having a lot going on at the same time has always been part of the charm at cons," Bianca said. "It's like the difference between ordering one thing for breakfast or going to a buffet. Con attendees like their variety."

"More often than not, it's just bad programming," Geoffrey contradicted her. "I've been to cons where they had three different sessions with galactic empire fiction authors all running at once, and later the same day, there were three overlapping panels on alien lovers in SciFi romance."

"I think I know the con you mean," Bianca said. "Sixth told me about it. They ran a track for paranormal romance against a track for shifter romance and she was actually scheduled for two panels in the same time slot and had to run between them. I mean, if shifters aren't paranormal, what is?"

"Can you give me an example of a strong track for Humans that will keep the same people coming back for more?" Yaem asked.

"Filk," both authors replied simultaneously, and then Geoffrey gestured for Bianca to continue. "Musicians are perfectly happy to spend most of the day playing and composing or just singing along," she said. "They might skip out for a particular crafting class in the costuming track, or to go to a favorite author's signing, but you won't catch them in some session where the panel is dissecting AI in fiction before the Stryx opened Earth."

"What if we applied Vergallian rules?" Yaem asked, scanning the faces around the table for a reaction. Jorb groaned, Geoffrey opened his mouth and then didn't speak, and Bianca looked thoughtful.

"What are Vergallian rules?" Julie asked.

"Some of the biggest Vergallian drama cons feature over a hundred tracks. They've been making dramas for at least a million years, and there are probably fans out there for every show that made it through a hundred seasons."

"A hundred seasons as in a hundred years?"

"Vergallian years, but, yes. It's a funny culture," the Sharf continued. "Most of the planets in their Empire of a Hundred Worlds enforce tech bans, but they usually allow entertainment systems, though I've heard that some queens put strict limitations on how much children can watch. And when I went to a Vergallian con maybe fifty years back when I happened to be visiting a Fleet world, the thing that struck me was the tracked passes."

"The con management kept tabs on everybody?" Julie asked.

"Probably, but what I meant is that attendees registered for a particular drama track and the pass was coded for it. I was signed up for 'Fleet Scout', a drama about interstellar exploring that must be in its ten-thousandth season by now. I'm not a big drama fan," Yaem added, "but I used to play a game based on the show so I thought I'd check it out. The first session I attended was all about the psychology of solo-scouts. I was ready to fall asleep after ten minutes, so I slipped out and tried to go into the screening across the corridor. My conference badge almost choked me."

"I had that happen once myself," Bianca said ruefully. "The Vergallians program them so you can only enter rooms in your track."

"And they choke you otherwise?" the lawyer asked. "I don't like the potential for liability."

"Actually, you choke yourself," the Sharf said, rubbing his neck with the memory. "The Vergallians simply run a filtering field at the door of every meeting room and it's set to pass everything except a badge that's not coded for the track. It's rather like finding yourself pulled up by a leash."

"The Vergallians can get away with something like that but I doubt we can," Maureen said. "Besides, I'm not sure that restricting attendees to a single track is fair if that's not what they're used to."

"How about a single room per session?" Jorb suggested. "Lots of magical effects we use in LARPing have a cool-down period so you can't spam some awesome spell over and over again to win every battle. Flower could program smart badges so that after you enter a room and sit down, it changes color, and it's only good for that one room until the next session."

"What if somebody goes in the wrong room by mistake?" Julie objected.

"Don't badges guide you to the correct room?" Flower asked.

"Not at any con I've ever been to," Yaem said, and the two authors nodded in agreement.

"But that would be a simple add-on, and it would allow us to make last-minute room changes based on demand," the ship's AI said. "In fact, if I make smart badges out of miniature display panels, we can integrate the schedule, and then attendees can choose where they're going and I can make sure they get there. Of course, I'll have to hand off control to the station librarian if any of them go to Union Station for the LARPing studios."

"Won't badges like that be too expensive?" Brenda asked.

"Wait a second," Geoffrey said. "Could you make the badges so that the visitors can enter their own names, Flower? That would save a tremendous amount of time spent waiting in the registration line."

"You mean the preregistered attendees could just swipe their personal ID to prove they paid and then take a blank badge?" Bianca asked. "That would also make it easier to deal with guests paying at the door because we wouldn't have to print badges for them."

"You see?" Flower said over Julie's implant. "Everything is developing according to plan and we're going to have the best con ever."

Nine

"Flower expects you to turn this whole area into a market in less than four weeks?" the captain asked his wife. "It must be the same size as the amusement park and the bazaar combined."

"You're looking at the empty end of the deck. Our offices for the con are back that way, then the theatres, and then empty residential cabins. Flower has bots working around the clock to reconfigure the Dollnick sleeping nests as beds."

Woojin shielded his eyes from the bright lights glaring off of polished metal surfaces. "So everything from this ring of spokes forward is going to be filled with folding tables for merchandise vendors?"

"There's the art show too, though Julie is in charge of that," Lynx said. "We have to decide whether it's better to separate art from merchandise all around the deck's circumference or to have a sharp division between the two."

"If you're asking my opinion, I would prefer to see a clear boundary between art and commerce," Woojin said. "I just hope Flower isn't putting too much of a load on Julie with managing the art show."

"You know what it's like working with Flower. Sometimes I suspect that the only reason she gets us involved in these projects is to have somebody to tell what to do."

"Go ahead, talk about me as if I'm not here," the Dollnick AI said over their implants. "And I'll have you know I keep a close eye on Julie's digestive activity to make sure she isn't stressed. Infrared imaging works as well for troubleshooting Humans as it does for spotting electromechanical problems before they develop."

"Do you really expect enough merchandise vendors and artists to fill the whole circumference of the deck, or are you planning to leave a big bare section?" Woojin asked.

"Once we have the final numbers for how many merchants and artists are showing up and how many tables and vertical pegboards they'll need, I'll turn whatever's left over to the Bitters to set up a gaming space," Flower said. "If there's not enough room, we'll just break gaming into multiple locations. I'm told that out of all the con participants the gamers will be the least mobile, since once they start playing, they don't move for hours on end."

"How about bathrooms?" Lynx asked. "You're going to need hundreds of toilets in this area for the number of people you're expecting, and with the Union Station crowd, we could get a lot of aliens with, er, special requirements."

"All of my decks are fully plumbed, and I have enough modular toilets in storage to equip five events like this," the Dollnick AI replied. "I'll direct the maintenance bots in setting them up once you determine the basic floor layout for the show."

"I thought you were planning to use early registrants to do the setup work," Woojin said.

"Plumbing for all-species facilities is a specialty. Our con workforce will be busy enough putting up partitions, preparing conference rooms, and decorating."

"The conference rooms are going to be on this deck as well?"

"It makes more sense than having people running in and out of lift tubes around the clock," Flower said. "The next section of deck, where I set up the con offices, is also practically empty. We'll partition it into conference rooms and workshops. On the last day of the con I'll have my bots break everything down to open the area for a grand ballroom."

"Aren't you forgetting about food?" Lynx asked. "Unless you're planning on everybody going back to their cabins and eating takeout, the lift tubes are going to be packed with people leaving the deck to eat. Either way, it would take a lot of time out of the day for guests."

"I've already asked all of the main food court vendors to set up temporary service here, and I'm going to halt production of prepackaged soups for the week and have my factory workers prepare and serve hot soups instead. I'm told ramen noodles are very popular at cons. If the turnout exceeds my expectations and the current food workers can't meet the demand, you know I have ten times as many kitchens on board than I'm using. Have you forgotten the machine I showed you before I set up the original fruitcake baking lines?"

"I remember a giant oval with the conveyer belt. You said it could do everything from baking cakes to shelling nuts and making ice cream, not to mention washing the dishes. But I thought you only used machinery to prepare food in an emergency."

"If there are more guests than we can feed without using the machines, it's an emergency," Flower said. "Bill just got in a lift tube for the docking bay and I'm going to divert the capsule to your location. I'd appreciate it if you could give him a pep talk, Captain, before he heads down to the planet's surface with the independent living tour group."

"Note that when she wants something, I'm the captain even if I'm not wearing the hat," Woojin said to his wife as he turned back to the lift tube. "Are you all set here, or do you want me to return after I talk with Bill?"

"I'm going to meet with Julie and Yaem to sketch out a floor plan on a long roll of paper, and then we're going to tape the ends together to make it a cylinder so we can stick our heads inside and see how it really works," the third officer said. "Don't forget to pick up Em on your way home."

The lift tube doors hissed open and Bill stumbled out, looking puzzled. "This isn't the right deck," he said out loud.

"Flower added an unscheduled stop," Woojin told him. "Did you trip over your own feet?"

"I already activated my magnetic cleats because I thought I'd be exiting on the docking deck, Captain."

"Did you read that book I gave you?"

"Yeah, but I don't know how much of it really applies," Bill said as they entered the capsule together. "I hope I won't be doing anything with dead-letter drops or one-time pads, and the whole section on disguises was intended for undercover agents. I just plan on trying what Jorb said, talking to people I meet and asking if they ever get to the spaceport. If they do, I'll tell them I work for a Sharf who's interested in the used ship market and he'll pay for information."

"Honesty is the best policy when you can get away with it," Woojin concurred. "Are you going to stick with the tour group the whole time? Jack told me they'll be heading for

Floaters, a factory town that I visited with Lynx on our honeymoon tour. Flower will put the shuttle down near the town, but the main spaceport is probably a few hours away."

"Do they have public transportation?"

"Floater buses, but if you decide to go off on your own, you'd probably do better by renting a floater. That way you'll have time to spend a couple of hours at the spaceport before you have to return to catch the shuttle back up to Flower."

"I've never driven anything in my life," Bill admitted. "I guess I'll stick with the bus."

"Dollnick floaters are perfectly capable of navigating themselves," Flower interjected. "You just need to tell it where you're going. If you get in trouble, shout for me over your implant. I'm maintaining a geosynchronous orbit and I'll keep an antenna pointed your way."

"I meant to ask you why the high orbit," Woojin said. "Is it just so you can stay in one spot and keep an eye on everybody?"

"It's part of my new deal for visiting Dollnick space," Flower said. "I'm staying in one spot so they can keep an eye on me."

The capsule stopped and the lift tube doors opened on the docking deck. Bill shuffled out, letting his magnetic cleats maintain contact with the deck.

"Break a leg," the captain called to him. "Let me know how it works out."

A minute later, Irene nudged her husband and said, "Look, Harry. Bill just got on the shuttle. He must be joining us for the day trip to Chianga."

"Over here," Harry called to his assistant. "Why didn't you tell me you were coming with us?"

"I just found out last night," Bill said, taking the seat next to Irene. "Julie told me that she used to enjoy tagging along with your independent living tour group."

"I swear that Flower is working that poor girl too hard," Irene said. "All of the volunteer greeters and information desk helpers for the bazaar and the amusement park have been offered paid shifts if we work at the con. Julie met with us yesterday to talk about the art show and she looked a bit frazzled. When Harry and I were growing up, everybody understood that young people need lots of free time to find their way."

"Fiddlesticks," the Dollnick AI said privately over Bill's implant. "I'm sure that Irene was as miserable as all Humans her age before she got married and settled down."

"We're visiting the factory city called Floaters, so you can guess what they make there," Harry told Bill. "We used to spend half of our time on these trips trying to recruit new cooperative members, but we're growing so rapidly at this point that we stopped handing out flyers."

"Except for me," Dave said, plopping down in the seat next to Bill and handing the young man a colorful sheet of paper. "What do you think of this?"

"Osteoporosis special," Bill read. "Free bone density testing this week only at the walk-in clinic on Flower. Stop by while you visit the library."

"Turn it over."

"Trouble reading that library book? If you've got cataracts, we've got the solution. Twenty creds an eye includes permanent correction of most vision problems. Forget about primitive lasers and weeks of messy eye drops and get repaired the Farling way."

"I had my cataracts done and I was in and out of the doc's office in eight minutes," Dave boasted.

"He doesn't do one eye at a time?" Irene asked.

"When I mentioned that, M793qK asked me, 'Would you bake one cookie?'"

"I guess he has a point there. Are you getting anything for all the business you send his way?"

"I used to take it out in trade but I'm running short of problems for him to fix. I just bank the extra credit now since I'm not getting any younger and I'll need to get more work done sooner or later."

"Aren't you going to fold down your footrest, Bill?" Harry asked. "Your feet are dangling."

"Oops, I guess they are," the young man said, and reaching under the seat, folded down the footrest intended for Dollnick children. "I usually fly with Dewey on the bookmobile when I leave Flower and that's set up for people our size. How long will it take to reach the surface?"

"Normally around an hour once we get going. Flower accelerates halfway there and then spins the seats around and decelerates the rest of the way so we have some weight."

"You look like you must have been up all night dancing with Julie," Irene added with a wink. "Why don't you take a nap and we'll wake you when we arrive."

Bill couldn't tell her he stayed up late reading *Espionage for Humans* without blowing his cover, and while he was sure that he'd never get to sleep, he leaned back and closed his eyes. The next thing he knew Dave was shaking him awake.

"Let's go, sleeping beauty," the retired salesman said. "You looked so peaceful that I let you snooze until everybody else disembarked."

"Wow, I guess I really was tired," Bill said, undoing his safety restraints. He rose from the seat, folded up the footrest, and followed Dave to the front exit, where Jack and his wife Nancy were handing out tracking bracelets.

"Will you be joining us for the tour of Floaters?" Jack asked.

"I think I'll just snoop around a bit on my own," Bill replied.

"Snoop?" Dave inquired with a grin. "That sounded like a Freudian slip if I've ever heard one. Don't tell me that your cafeteria crowd has roped you into spying for them."

"It was Flower," Bill blurted out. "She told me I'd be doing everybody a favor if I helped the new Sharf make his recruitment quota, and the captain approved it."

"Did they give you any training?"

"Just a book. It had lots of helpful hints and little pictures of spy stuff, but after reading the whole thing, I don't feel like I know anything more about recruiting sources than when I started."

"Why don't we team up?" the old salesman offered, and gave the surprised neophyte spy a wink.

"Do you mean…?"

"M793qK stands out like a, well, like a giant alien beetle, so I've been doing a little recruiting for him on our field trips. It's an old sales trick, really. If they aren't interested in a medical procedure, I hit them with the 'Do your best for Humanity' pitch."

"Isn't that from the EarthCent oath?"

"Do you think I tell the people that I work for a Farling? How many sources do you think I'd be able to recruit?" Dave took hold of Bill's arm as if he was using it to steady himself, but he applied surprisingly strong pressure to steer the young man away from the tour group. "Doc is mainly interested in finding out which aliens have been visiting Chianga so I'm going to grab a taxi for the main spaceport."

"A taxi? Won't that cost too much?"

"Doc covers my expenses," Dave said, and waved to an attractive young woman who was standing next to the open door of a low-slung floater. "Spaceport?"

"Are you talking to me?" she asked, taking a quick look around to see if there was another vehicle parked behind her.

"We want to visit the spaceport but we need to be back before our tour group leaves at the end of the day. Can you make us a special rate?"

"Fifty creds and I'll wait while you look around and guaranty getting you back on time," the young woman offered with a predatory grin. "I only take cash."

"I'll have to do a withdrawal from my programmable cred at the spaceport," Dave said. "Is that okay?"

"No problem, hop right in."

"I'm Dave and he's Bill." the old salesman said, getting in the back seat.

"Sephia," she introduced herself. "So you guys are visiting from Flower?"

"We're with the independent living cooperative," Dave said from the back.

Sephia glanced at Bill in the front passenger seat. "You look a bit young to be retired," she said.

"I just tagged along to, uh, keep an eye on Dave."

The floater lifted off the ground to about knee-height, and then it accelerated gently away from where the members of Flower's Paradise were boarding floater buses for the factory tour. Then Sephia flipped a red switch on the dashboard and an artificial voice announced, "Safety interlock disengaged."

"Uh, is something broken?" Bill asked.

"If you're going to spend any time looking around the spaceport we can't dawdle," the driver said. "Fortunately for you, I race floaters for our factory, and I'm currently the top driver on the circuit."

"My apologies," Dave said. "I assumed this was an unregistered taxi."

"No, but I have a little business at the spaceport I've been putting off taking care of," Sephia said. "It's not the most exciting place to visit," she added. "Chianga is a relatively new world, and between the Dollnicks and us, there are just over two hundred million inhabitants. All of the cities have their own landing areas for shuttles like the one you came on."

"Isn't there a space elevator?" Bill asked, trying to stifle a yawn.

"Too slow," Sephia said. "It's cheap, but it takes over a day to get up to orbit. The elevator gets all of the freight traffic, and most of the Humans going on long trips use it to save money because if they're going to be gone for a month, an extra day or two doesn't matter."

"How far is it to the spaceport?" Dave asked.

"On a floater bus, a bit over two hours. With me driving my special rig, maybe forty minutes. I have to keep it under the speed of sound or the Dollnick cops will be after me again. If my dad wasn't the mayor of Floaters, they probably would have kicked me off the planet years ago," she added, flashing a grin at Bill. "Hey, are you actually falling asleep while I'm driving?"

"Nerves of steel, that one," Dave said. "Either that or he has his eyes closed because he's terrified, but the ground here is so flat that it's hard to tell how fast we're going."

A soft snore proved that Bill had indeed fallen asleep again, and after Sephia found out that Dave had lived his entire life on Earth before moving to Flower, she spent the whole trip peppering him with questions about the motherworld. Thirty-eight minutes later, she dropped them both at the main spaceport terminal and promised to return in four hours to take them back to Floaters with ample time to make the shuttle.

Bill finally began waking up once they entered the air-conditioned building, but he was at a loss for what to do next. Dave recognized the young man's hesitation, and taking his arm again, led the way to the nearest pub.

"But it's barely noon on their clock," Bill protested. "The place will be empty."

"Spaceport bars are never empty, and the posted menu looks pretty good so they probably get a big lunch crowd. See?"

The young man had to admit that his guide was correct because it seemed that there were more people crammed into the pub than he had seen in the whole terminal building on the way there. The seating was all Dollnick style communal tables, each of which sat a dozen people per side. Dave spotted two open chairs at the center of one table and half-dragged Bill over.

"Are these seats taken?" Dave asked.

"Help yourself," a large man wearing coveralls with 'John' embroidered over the breast pocket replied. "We were just joking around about keeping two open seats to see if we could catch a couple more meal tickets like last night."

"Big spenders?"

"Aliens down from the rogue colony ship that works for EarthCent. We couldn't figure out if they were spies or just kidding around."

"What kind of aliens?" Bill asked.

"There was a Drazen, with the extra thumbs and a tentacle, and a barky looking fellow with vines in place of hair," a woman directly across the table replied. "Funny names. Lorb and Kazoo."

"You drank one too many free beers," John said. "It was Jorb and Razood. They kept buying drinks and asking questions about the local entertainment industry, like anybody in here would know anything about the glitterati."

"I told Jorb about that Horten crew that came through surveying locations for a historical colonization drama, and he slipped me this and told me there would be more if I reported anything else," another man said, displaying a thin gold wafer. "I mean, I'm a hundred percent loyal to Prince Drume, but if a Drazen wants information about the Hortens, that's just good business."

"The barky one was also asking questions about Weavers, the factory town that makes fireproof blankets for export, but you could tell that his heart wasn't really in it," John said. "Then I mentioned that I was beat because I spent the day trying to straighten the bent forks on a cargo stacker, and he insisted that I sneak him into the maintenance shop to give it a go. That Frunge looked wiry but he swings a mean sledgehammer. Straightened those forks out so you'd think they were new."

"He's a blacksmith," Bill said. "I used to be his apprentice."

"Apprentice blacksmith or apprentice spy?" the woman asked, and everybody at the table had a good laugh.

"Uh, right," Bill said. "I'm trying to get into the used ship business with a, uh, friend, but I'm just starting. If anybody, er..."

"You're supposed to buy me a drink before you start asking questions," the woman teased him. "It's lunchtime, though, so I'll settle for dessert. Are you on an expense account?"

"I'm working for the—"

"Don't tell us," John interrupted. "It takes all of the fun out of guessing after you're gone."

Ten

"There's fresh-squeezed fruit juice in the fridge," the ship's AI suggested hopefully over Julie's implant.

"I've been dealing with correspondence about art show display space for the last three hours," Julie replied out loud as she filled her cup. "Coffee is a must. If you want my production to fall by half, send a bot to take the machine away."

"Don't even joke about that," Yaem said, setting down his own mug for a refill. "Before I got assigned to Earth, I never even heard of caffeine. I can't believe how addictive the stuff is. It's surprising the Stryx don't isolate your world for being a bad influence."

"I've heard that coffee is one of Drazen Food's biggest exports, right up there with hot peppers," Julie said. "How are you coming with the program that I'm supposed to be helping you create?"

"You're more valuable right now doing exactly what you're doing," the Sharf said. "With you taking care of the art show and Lynx handling the merchants, I can concentrate on the schedule grid for sessions and activities. Geoffrey's help has proven invaluable too, but Flower keeps making him take breaks because of his age, so I'm putting off sleeping until after the con."

"You can do that?"

"With enough of this stuff, I could probably postpone sleeping for a year," Yaem said, taking a sip of the steaming coffee. "I'll catch up eventually. Life is too short to spend it all in bed."

"How long do Sharf live?"

"In your years? Let me see. Divide by seven, carry the three. Around nine hundred?"

"No wonder all of you aliens are so fanatical about entertainment," Julie said. "You have a lot of time to fill."

"Humans will get there eventually, longevity just takes time," Yaem said, and then held up a finger while trying to figure out if his last comment had made sense in Humanese. "Well, I have to get back to work."

Julie returned to her own cubicle, snorted at the bowl of fresh grapes that had materialized while she was talking with Yaem, and sat down in front of the display. The con staff all worked with their personal choice of office technology, and Flower seamlessly handled the necessary connections and conversions required for collaboration. Rather than using voice and gesture, Julie stuck with the old-fashioned wireless keyboard that Zick had found for her back when she mentioned that she was trying to write a book. Being from Bits, Zick had insisted she start with a typing exercise game, and within a month, Julie was tapping away like she'd been born with a keyboard in the cradle.

"Where was I?" she asked herself, scrolling through the list of open correspondence on the over-sized display.

"Rosen," Flower said over her implant. "The one with the T-shirts."

"Right. I tried to hand him off to Lynx, but he said that he wants to show his book cover T-shirts in the art show. I wrote back to ask if he painted the covers himself, but it turns out that he hired an artist. So I asked Brenda what to do, and she created a legal form for the artist to authorize the author to represent the work at the art show and accept payment from the auction. Then Rosen wrote back and said he doesn't want to sell the T-shirts, just show them and maybe win a prize."

"What does he do with the T-shirts if he doesn't sell them?"

"He wears them, and he said if people want copies, they can order their own from any print-on-demand T-shirt place with access to the content database. So we got all of the paperwork out of the way, he submitted the fee, and now he's asking about our pegboards."

"What does he want to know?" Flower asked.

"Whether he needs to bring hardware to hang the T-shirts. I wrote back that we'll supply a variety of metal hooks for the pegboards, and then there are those clip things that Lynx found, but he also wanted to know about lighting. He said that the last time he did this, the lights were really dim in the hotel ballroom where they had the show. All of the artists had to rush out and buy battery-powered spotlights to attach to the tops of the partitions."

"Tell him that my lighting is fully customizable and I can employ phased lobe steering to create any number of highlight spots."

"What if he wants to know what that means?"

"I'll explain it then," Flower said. "Who's next?"

"If you want to handle all of the art show correspondence yourself, I can go help Yaem with the program," Julie said testily. "Sometimes I think you only hire us all for window dressing to impress your Stryx mentor that you're providing employment."

"I'm just trying to be helpful while you get settled into the job. In a couple of weeks, you'll know more about managing art shows than anybody else on board and I'll have nothing to add."

"In a couple of weeks the con will be over and you'll be explaining a new job to me," Julie retorted. "At least when I worked in the library, Bea and Dewey waited for me to make mistakes before explaining what I was doing wrong."

"Don't you think it's possible that's why Humans are so far behind the rest of the tunnel network species? You're the only sentients I've encountered who take such pride in doing everything wrong the first time."

Julie was careful not to say or subvoc anything as she dealt with the next message in her queue, which was all about how to fill out the auction bid sheets for the items on display. The message after that was a request to swap some reserved tables for pegboards, and then she replied to an artist who had already paid the extra fee to have her works displayed without personally attending. The woman was having trouble choosing between shipping services, so Julie laid out all of the options she had learned about over the last few weeks.

"You know, I was skeptical about that keyboard interface when you started using it, but you actually type faster than you speak," Flower said.

"Not when I'm working on my novel. I spend most of my time staring at the screen trying to figure out what happens next."

"Knock, knock," Bianca announced herself as she entered the cubicle. "I didn't mean to eavesdrop, but it sounds like you're having trouble plotting. I was going to ask you a favor, so maybe we can trade off. Have you had lunch yet?"

"No, but I was thinking of just getting a salad at Lume's. He's a Dollnick, so Flower gives him the best produce."

"Not true," the ship's AI protested through an overhead speaker. "Lume goes down to the ag decks every day to pick his own. He has a very discerning eye, and of course, four arms don't hurt when you're harvesting in a crowd."

"It sounds good to me," Bianca said. "I've been on a diet for, oh, about thirty years now."

"Just let me send this quick before I forget," Julie said. Fingers flying over the keyboard, she typed out a disclaimer stating that the risk of damage to poorly packed items was assumed by the sender. "I wish there was a way I could avoid having to retype the same bit over and over again."

"There is," Flower said over her implant. "I'll show you how after lunch."

"You type faster than me and I've been at it for longer than I've been dieting," Bianca commented as the girl rose. "Did you take a special course?"

"A training game. There was a timer involved, and I swear the keyboard sent little shocks through my fingers if I didn't keep up," Julie said. "And what you said about plotting, Geoffrey told me the same thing. I just have trouble coming up with a whole story in one shot."

"You don't have to get the whole plot done in one sitting," the seventh author in the D'Arc line said with a smile. "And I'm surprised Geoffrey offered even that much help. He used to be a real jerk to new authors."

"Really? He's been so nice to me. Geoffrey even offered to read what I have so far, but I was too embarrassed to send it to him."

"Maybe having his freedom taken away taught him some humility. He was a bit famous in his day, and when he and Sixth were together, he made her feel like he was doing her a favor. It's quite a story, really. She even wrote a fictionalized version of it under her own name."

"You mean, not as Bianca D'Arc?"

"Right. After she passed me the torch, she started writing children's books, of all things, and she's been quite successful. She's even had a special guest appearance reading one of her books on *Let's Make Friends*."

"Wow, she must have sold like a trillion copies," Julie said as they entered the lift tube. "Food court."

"Nobody sells a trillion books, not of a single title," Bianca said. "Well, I guess quite a few Vergallian classics have sold more than that if you count back far enough, but they've had interstellar travel for millions of years, and there are over a trillion of them. Have you ever read 'The Little Princess?'"

"This is a Vergallian book?"

"Yes, it made me cry. It makes everybody cry."

"I'll check if the library has it in translation," Julie said, leading the way out of the lift tube capsule and into the maze of the food court. "Do you write books under your real name?"

"Not since I took over from Sixth. My children had just started school and my ex is a chef, so my time was tightly budgeted."

"I'd have thought that being married to a chef would have saved you time," Julie said.

"A professional chef. He barely went into our kitchen at home. The restaurant business requires insane hours, and when I would suggest that he slow down, he'd always say that he was working for me and the children and there would be plenty of time to relax once the restaurant was established. After the children were grown and we divorced, he married a waitress half my age and finally found the time to smell the roses."

"Oh, I'm sorry."

"I like to think I got his best years, even if they were barely average. But the kids turned out wonderful, and I have my own career. Someday I plan to write under my own name, probably historical fiction, but first I have to find a replacement and train her up."

"Refill," Lume greeted Julie by her char name as she stepped up to the counter. "The usual?"

"Yes, and whatever Miss D'Arc is having."

"Bianca," the author introduced herself, eyeing the towering Dollnick's chest. "Could I ask you something crazy?"

"It can't be any crazier than the questions I get every day."

"Could you flex for me?"

"Okay, I guess it was crazier," Lume said, but he put down his chef's knife, the carrot, the grater, and the mixing bowl. Then he rolled up his sleeves and balled all four fists in a bodybuilder's crab pose. "I can't take off my shirt behind the counter because of Flower's health code."

"You could be the cover model for 'The Trillionaire Prince's Third Wife.'" Bianca said. "You look just about the right age and—it is you, isn't it?"

"I might have agreed to do a bit of modeling last time we stopped at Union Station," Lume said modestly. "The publisher who bought the translation rights to the Trillionaire Prince series lives there. She's one of the founders of InstaSitter, and she funds Eccentric Enterprises, which officially operates this ship."

"Blythe Oxford, I met her at a romance con," Bianca said. "Small galaxy."

"What can I make you?" the Dollnick asked, rolling his sleeves back down. "I picked some lovely watercress and arugula this morning, and the olive trees Flower had transplanted from Earth recently started producing. It took them a few years to get over the shock."

"Do you have something like a Mediterranean salad?"

"That's what I always order," Julie said. "I love the salty cheese and olive oil."

"I'll have them out in a minute," Lume said, and gestured towards the common seating area. "Anything to drink, Bianca?" he added, giving the author a sly wink.

"Distilled water," she said with a grimace. "I'm counting calories. Aren't you getting something?" she asked her companion.

"Milk," Julie said. "Lume and Flower are thick as thieves. He brings me milk no matter what I order."

"Milk builds strong bones," Lume called over his shoulder, proving once again that Dollnicks enjoyed superior hearing. "M793qK told me that Human females lose bone density faster than males as they age so you should at least start from a good level."

"Are all of the aliens on board so protective of humans?" Bianca asked Julie as they took their seats.

"Well, Lume is one of the stand-ins, I mean, principal actors in the anime production Flower talked me into for my required team sport," Julie explained. "I guess they're all pretty nice, actually. I take singing lessons from a Drazen girl named Rinka, and she's the reason that Jorb—you know him because he's handling the LARPing track—joined the ship."

"How romantic. Have you considered working it into a plot?"

"I don't really know enough about Drazen culture. I'd get something wrong and everybody would think I was just faking."

Bianca laughed. "Alright, I see we have some work to do. First of all, I didn't mean to put your friends in a book as themselves. And even if you were writing about them as Drazens, you'd want to change the details so that nobody would know who you're talking about. Is there some reason you couldn't take their story and make the characters humans?"

"Well, there's a lot of romantic tension in their relationship because Drazens don't fool around, at least, the women don't. Rinka told me that they usually have arranged marriages set up by the families, and there are all sorts of tests and stuff they have to take."

Bianca nodded. "Most of the advanced species have elaborate courting rules that involve chaperones, matchmakers, and various aptitude and compatibility tests. I was on a panel with Blythe, the publisher of the alien romances in translation who Lume and I were talking about. She said that the biggest challenge for her editors is making sure that they explain the cultural references without turning the novels into academic treatises on alien sociology. Often times, if a subplot is too complicated, they just edit it out."

"But if I made Jorb and Rinka into humans, the fact that his family are major stakeholders in a consortium and are pushing him to marry into another consortium family to consolidate their holdings doesn't mean anything. And from what Rinka tells me, her family almost disowned her when she told them she was moving to Flower to start a remedial choral school for humans. They all expected her to return to the Drazen homeworld for advanced training in composing and conducting large choral groups. The Drazens take music really seriously."

"Jake, the billionaire scion of the Las Vegas city-state's top casino family, meets Reba, the daughter of backwoods alien-deniers, who learned how to play fiddle by ear and is now competing for a spot in Earth's top music conservatory."

"Wait, wait," Julie said, pulling her personal tab out of her purse. "Let me take a few notes."

"You've read romances," Bianca said. "You tell me what happens next."

"Well, they'd have to feel an attraction to each other at first sight, but he's used to sophisticated party girls, and she thinks that he's a spoiled rich boy. Then they, I don't know, something happens and one of them saves the other one. Maybe Jake's family is mixed up with organized crime, or her family is making illegal drugs up in the mountains? How about they meet at a charity event where he's a donor and she's one of the poor musicians brought in to entertain them, and then kidnappers coming for one of them end up grabbing them both? It would work better if they were actually shifters, but one of them doesn't know it yet."

"Everything is better with shifters. And if they're different types, that gives you another obstacle for love to overcome."

"Oh, I have to think about this now," Julie said. "How am I going to get any work done this afternoon?"

"It's best to let plots simmer for a while and work on adding new levels of complexity," Bianca said. "Jorb, I mean, Jake, could be getting pushed into marriage with the daughter of another casino owner, and Reba could have a loyal friend from childhood who she just never thought about romantically. And then there's the whole plotline about whether or not she wins the spot at the conservatory—"

"She could hurt her hand helping Jake in a fight," Julie interrupted. "And their families have to hate each other, maybe her grandfather was originally a partner in the casino and his grandfather stole the share." Julie looked up from her tab. "Wow, I may have to split this into two books to fit it all."

"Now you're getting it."

"Ladies," Lume said, placing their salads on the table with his lower set of arms, and the milk and distilled water with the upper set. "Are you looking forward to our new season, Julie?"

"I forgot about that completely," she said with a groan. "We have a script meeting this week, don't we?"

"I'm sure Flower will make sure we're all there."

"He really is quite the charmer," Bianca said after the Dollnick returned behind the counter. "Kind of like a big teddy bear with extra arms."

Julie leaned forward and whispered. "He's actually a spy, and deadly. When I was working at the diner and an assassin came on board to find me, Lume killed him. Flower was giving all of the aliens bonuses to protect me."

"That's another plot right there! I think I've held up my part of the bargain, so let's talk about my problem."

"Mmph," Julie nodded, chewing on the first mouthful of savory salad.

Bianca speared an olive, started to raise it to her mouth, and then said, "Flower made me an offer I can't refuse to be her positive experience coordinator for the con. I've been running the D'Arc line long enough to understand something about business, but I don't understand her budgeting at all. Last night, right before I fell asleep, it occurred to me that con visitors from Earth might like to get a tour of the outside of this ship and Union Station while we're there. Flower said it was a brilliant idea and that she'd make the tours free for anybody who spent the full week at the con. I can't imagine how much something like that would cost."

Julie swallowed her salad and said, "Flower's idea of economics is weird. She hires people to do everything we're capable of, but she has a seemingly unlimited number of maintenance bots that could probably do most jobs better and faster at no cost. She's supposedly making a fortune selling fruitcakes, but she spends another fortune employing immigrants from Bits to keep them on board. A year ago she seemed to worry about every cred, but then the Stryx gave her a huge bonus for reaching a population milestone. I think now she's shooting for getting a million humans to live here."

"So Flower isn't necessarily trying to make a profit on the con?"

"I think she is. I mean, she could have made everything free otherwise, but I guess the fees we're charging for the art show and the vendors are in line with other cons. But Flower takes a long view of things, I guess most of the aliens do, and she really wants the con to be a success for the visitors. Maybe she figures that it's all good advertising for her anime studio business. I wouldn't be surprised if it turns out that her real goal is finding more talent to hire."

Eleven

"Not taking the bookmobile down to the surface?" Bill asked Dewey. "I thought you usually left as soon as Flower reached orbit."

"She asked me to stay on board and help out with the early arrivals today," the assistant librarian replied. His binocular cameras spun in the direction of the lift tube. "Good morning, Third Officer Pyun."

"How many times do I have to tell you that it's Lynx," the captain's wife said as she joined them. "Something's different about you today, Dewey. You look naked somehow."

"I left my shelving attachment home," Dewey told her. "Flower thought it would just get in the way. I gave myself a tour of the residential section of this deck on my way here, and there are hundreds of maintenance bots floating in and out of the cabins like giant bees."

"They're still changing out the bedding," Lynx guessed. "Flower hasn't ever hosted humans on this deck before, and sleeping in Dollnick nests gives most people a backache." She removed three handheld scanners from her shoulder bag and placed them on the table. "And how come you're not down on the planet yourself, Bill? Woojin tells me you picked up a part-time job recruiting intelligence sources for Yaem."

"You know about all the spies too?"

"I was the first agent EarthCent Intelligence ever hired, the first human agent, I mean. Are you grabbing the shuttle to the surface later with the independent living tour group? These Drazen worlds are quite interesting."

"Flower said that around a quarter of the people who took her up on the early arrival offer are coming from open worlds, so it would be more efficient for me to stay here and watch for potential recruits. If you guys see any likely candidates, send them to me."

"What exactly are you looking for in a spy?" Dewey asked.

"I guess anybody who lives on an alien world with a sovereign human community, though it would be a bonus if they know anything about the small spacecraft industry since that's what the Sharf are interested in," Bill said. He checked the battery status on the scanner. "Did Flower explain to you guys what we're doing?"

"Scanning IDs, answering questions, and handing out programmable badges," Dewey said. "It will be just like working at the library, except with smart badges in place of books."

"Here comes the first batch," Lynx announced, as a half-dozen humans rushed out of the nearby lift tube and mobbed the front of the table.

"Are we the first?" a breathless young woman asked. "Did we beat the lines?"

"Yes you did," Dewey told her, and held up one of the portable scanners that Lynx had brought. "Your ID please?"

The young woman presented a plastic card of some type with her picture and Dewey scanned it. The man on her left held up his ID for Lynx without being asked, while the novice intelligence recruiter attempted to strike up a conversation with the first person to approach him.

"Where are you from?" Bill asked.

"Earth," the man said, handing over a programmable cred which doubled as an ID. "Do I get a prize for coming a long way?"

"Just curious." Bill scanned the coin and got a green light, which meant the owner had in fact registered and paid. "Here's your con pass," he said, handing the man a smart badge on a lanyard.

"Did you charge me for the lanyard?" the man asked suspiciously. He dipped in a pocket and pulled out a flat cord with promotional printing on it from some other con. "I brought my own if it's not free."

"We don't charge for the lanyard, and it actually doubles as an external antenna for the smart badge and increases the range if you should go on any off-ship activities," Bill said.

"How do I get it to show my name? Is this thing turned on?"

"You have to push the button on the bottom and then it walks you through the setup. It works by voice or touch screen, but you might want to find a quiet corner to do voice."

The man looked around the gently curving section of deck devoid of any partitions or furniture other than the registration table. "I don't see any corners."

"You'll work it out," Bill said. "Next?"

A person who looked like Jorb when the Drazen martial artist was tired and his tentacle was hanging limply stepped up to the table and presented a crystal. The alien ID was pinched between the man's real thumb and the opposing prosthetic that brought his finger count up to six per hand. "My Two Mountains passport," he said. "Can you understand me?"

"Uh, yes. You're speaking English, aren't you?"

"Drazen," the young man said. "You must have an implant."

"I do. Cool costume, but don't you speak English at home?"

"My family speaks Drazen," he said proudly. "They make us learn English in school but it sounds funny to me."

"Here's your smart badge," Bill said. "You have to—"

"The button, I see it," the young man said impatiently. "Is this the whole registration?"

"The badge will lead you to your room, and if you come back after lunch, we'll be ready to start assigning jobs. Hey, you don't happen to work in a shipyard or know anything about two-man traders?"

"I'm strictly into mining."

A middle-aged woman with a shoulder duffle stepped up in place of the faux-Drazen. "The lady on the end told me to talk to you."

Bill glanced over and saw that Lynx and Dewey had already processed the first batch of guests, though another group was just exiting the lift tube.

"Did you get your badge?"

"Right here," the woman said, fishing it out of her pocket. "I'll put it on once I get it programmed. The lady said you were involved in the shipping business and might have something for me to check on when I return home."

"Where's that?"

"Tzeba. It's a Frunge open world. We're famous for our semi-metallic cloth exports, and we also do a big business in craft goods, so we have independent traders coming and going all the time."

"I actually work for a Sharf who is trying to gather information about the shipping business," Bill said, producing one of Yaem's chits with the contact information. "He's really interested in the market share of the used two-man traders that his species sells to humans. He'll pay for the kind of information that you can't just read in the Galactic Free Press."

"Is he some kind of spy or something?"

"Maybe. How did you guess?"

"This isn't my first con, kid. They're hotbeds for recruiting casual sleeper agents. I make decent money as a pattern consultant, but I couldn't afford my lifestyle without bringing in side jobs. I'm signed up with half the species on the tunnel network to keep my eyes open for this and that." She noted his expression of disbelief and added, "I wouldn't sell any information that would hurt the Frunge, of course, but once I got a nice bonus from the Vergallians for reporting about a Horten dance school that opened up on Tzeba."

"I see," Bill said, somewhat taken aback by her matter-of-fact attitude towards spying for aliens. "So the contact info is all on the chit there, and I guess you know how to get paid."

The woman winked and sauntered off to program her badge in quiet.

"Cool costume," a young man said to Dewey as he handed over his ID. "You must be pretty cramped in there, though."

"It's my body, I'm artificial intelligence."

"Are you competing in the costume contest? I was hoping to find enough stuff to fabricate a robot costume in the crafting track, but it will be a complete waste of time if you're entering."

"I heard that species won't be allowed to compete as themselves, but I haven't read the rules because I'm not an attendee," Dewey said. "I'm just here to help out with registration."

Lynx handed a smart badge to the man she had just processed and then joined the conversation. "People can compete as humans, but it can't be their whole costume."

"You mean I can cosplay as a mercenary, but I can't just show up in a T-shirt and jeans to compete for Best Human," the young man said, nodding in agreement with his own analysis. "That makes sense. I've been to cons back home where aliens who happen to be working on Earth show up and sweep all the prize money without putting any effort into it."

Two hours later, Bill handed one of the last smart badges in the box to a woman in her early thirties. "You wouldn't happen to know anything about small ships, would you?" he asked her casually.

"My father builds sailing craft if that's what you mean. I grew up in the lofting room."

"Like, boats for the ocean?"

"Or big lakes," the woman confirmed. "I heard that Dollnick colony ships have a reservoir on the outermost deck that goes all the way around. Is there any wind?"

"Not that I remember, and there were catwalks all over the place, so I don't think sailing would work," Bill said. "You can rent a scull though, and rowing qualifies as a required team sport for residents."

"Then why did you ask me about boats?"

"I work part-time for a guy who's interested in the small spaceship market."

"Well, I don't know anything about the economics, but I tried a Frunge sunboat on vacation last year. As soon as I got back to Earth, I started designing a hull that would be compatible with those magnetic envelope masts they use."

"Hire her," Flower said over Bill's implant.

"What?" he asked out loud.

"Magnetic envelopes," the woman repeated. "You know, to catch the solar wind."

"If she knows how to loft a hull and she's designed her own sunboat I want her for my shipyard," Flower said.

"You don't have a shipyard," Bill protested, looking back and forth between the woman and the ceiling.

"It's my father's shipyard," the woman said, though she was starting to sound a little put-out. "You don't believe me?"

"Just repeat what I tell you," Flower said. "I'm speaking for the ship's AI and she wants to offer you a job."

"I'm speaking for the ship's AI and she wants to offer you a job," Bill said, looking back at the guest. "I have an implant and she's talking in my ear. Sorry, I forgot to point."

"Your ship wants to hire me? But I'm already committed to working here the next month helping to set up the con."

"This is different," Flower said. "You know what I want, just explain it to her."

"This is different," Bill repeated. "Flower, uh, she's always starting new businesses, and I heard she's trying to license the old two-man trader design from the Sharf to put them back into production. I think she figures a shipyard will employ a lot of people."

The woman looked from Bill, to the ceiling, and back again. "I don't know anything about Sharf ships."

"Flower says if you can loft a hull for a sailboat you can learn."

"Tell her I know all about magnetic envelopes," the Dollnick AI added in Bill's ear. "More than the Frunge, anyway."

"And she says she can teach you all about magnetic envelopes," Bill repeated. "Can't you just give her an external ear cuff and talk to her yourself?"

"Who?" the woman asked.

"Tell her to hold her smart badge up to her ear," the Dollnick AI said. "I don't want everybody hearing this."

"Uh, Flower wants you to hold your smart badge to your ear so she can talk to you in private," Bill said.

The woman looked at him skeptically, no doubt wondering if it was all part of some elaborate gag. Then curiosity got the better of her and she pressed the badge against her ear and listened.

"How did you know that?" she demanded thirty seconds later. "No, not you," she said to Bill and began walking away from the table. "How much? That's three times what my father pays me. And all the fresh fruit I can eat?"

"Sounds like Flower's hooked another one," Dewey said to Bill. "I think the rush is over, so why don't the two of you break for lunch and I'll handle any stragglers."

"Sounds good to me," Lynx said, and pointed at her ear for a moment. "Flower confirms that's it for this morning. She's had four hundred and sixty-one badge activations and that's how many people were on the first shuttle. The next group won't be here for another three hours, so we can all take a break."

"It's probably best I stay in case anybody has a question and doesn't realize they can just ask out loud," Dewey said. "Go ahead. I have a lot of thinking to do, and this is a good a place as any."

Bill followed the third officer into the lift tube, and Lynx requested the food court.

"Is Flower really serious about this shipyard business?" Bill asked her. "Yaem mentioned it to me as a cover story for when I try to recruit sources for him, but it's got to be more complicated than setting up to sell fruitcakes."

"I own a two-man Sharf ship myself," Lynx said. "I was an independent trader before I was recruited by EarthCent Intelligence, but I bought it back when used ships were still cheap and you could pay down the mortgage in ten years if you worked at it. I don't know if Flower could manufacture every part, but I think she just wants to build the hulls and customize them for our independent traders, which is something you could do in any space that's big enough."

"But wouldn't she need to hire far more experts than would be willing to come and live on board?"

"It's the drive and the fuel packs that are complicated. Well, the navigation system and the controller are probably the most high-tech, but those are mainly supplied by the Verlocks, who manufacture them under license from the Stryx."

"You mean a single person working alone could really build a spaceship?" Bill asked.

"I'm sure Flower plans to employ more than just the one woman you hired for her. And the funny thing about spaceships is that if you don't care about landing on planets, almost anything that holds air can be fitted out with a propulsion system that will get you around the tunnel network. The Sharf stopped building the type of two-man ships that independent traders want because they were never that profitable and the styling aged out. Do you have an interest in the ship-building business?"

"I never even thought of it before," Bill said. "No, I still want to be a baker, but it depends on what Julie wants too."

"You really are smitten," Lynx said with a sympathetic smile.

When they returned after lunch, there were around fifty people listening as Dewey filled them in on Flower's way of doing things. A couple of minutes later, Yaem and Julie showed up.

"And here's the con's program director, who will be telling you about the work opportunities," Dewey concluded his speech. "Yaem?"

"Where are the rest of the people we registered?" Bill whispered to Dewey.

"Flower broke them into ten groups and she drafted greeters from the bazaar to take them on tours of the ship," the assistant librarian explained. "It will also make things easier for Yaem and Julie."

"Right," the Sharf said, finishing his silent head count. "If anybody has experience managing a labor crew, please step forward."

A few people hesitated, and then a man in his forties separated himself from the crowd. "Don Harper. I ran a framing crew for almost twenty years."

"Humans need a crew of workers to frame a picture?" Yaem asked incredulously. "I realize that the corners are tricky, but there are plenty of specialized tools."

"We framed houses, not pictures," Don said. "Ranches, mainly. Don't they have wood houses where you come from?"

"Not that I've ever heard of," the Sharf said. "We like to keep our trees on the outside. When I visited Earth, I thought the individual dwellings were made out of plastic."

"Vinyl siding, it goes over the wood."

"I see. Well, if you can frame a house, I'm sure you can put up pre-built partition walls."

"Do you have prints?"

"Why is he back to framing artwork?" Yaem whispered to Julie in his scratchy voice.

"I think he means blueprints," Julie said.

"What difference does it make what color the prints are?" the Sharf asked plaintively, and then thrust his tab in Julie's hands. "The basic layout for the merchant sections is on there and you can check with Lynx if you have any questions. According to the questionnaires submitted through their smart badges, most of the early registrants claimed to have been panelists at previous cons, so I have to get back to the office and start sifting through it all."

Julie watched in dismay as Yaem hurried back to the lift tube, and then she turned and offered the tab to Don. "Does this make any sense to you?"

"The layout is clear enough, but what are those dimensional units? Pliffs?"

"Flower?" Julie subvoced. "Can you remotely translate the units on Yaem's tab?"

"Done," the ship's AI said, and Don grunted in satisfaction. "I'm sending bots with the partitions now. The group you're addressing are the ones who didn't claim to have any special con skills. If anybody doesn't want to help with the build-out, send them back to their cabins and I'll find something else for them to do."

"Got it," Julie said, and cleared her throat self-consciously. "The partition materials will be here any minute, but if anybody doesn't feel up to physical labor, if you return to your cabin, Flower will find something else for you to do today."

"How heavy are the partitions?" a woman asked.

"According to this, they're honeycomb aluminum with Dollnick closed-cell foam, so they should be pretty light," Don said. "It looks like all of the hardware is attached so this will be a breeze. Does anybody have experience with layout?"

"Do you mean measuring and marking?" a woman asked. "I'm a stagehand when the union has work and I'm not off at cons. I've set up lots of props."

"Perfect, you're my foreman. Anybody else with construction experience?"

A few more people admitted to having worked on occasion, and Don quickly organized those who didn't head back to their cabins into six crews of four each. Then a pair of maintenance bots guiding a train of floating dollies piled high with partition panels arrived. One of the bots approached Don and handed him an ear-cuff translation device.

"Like this?" He placed it over his right ear, listened, and then laughed. "All right everybody, this is going to be even easier than I thought. The ship's AI can tell exactly where we are by tracking our badges, and since the panels are all the same size and they lock together, we won't have to do any measuring after placing the first one. And she wants a person on each corner of the panel when you lift them. They feel light now, but wait until you've put up a couple hundred and you'll appreciate the help."

Twelve

"I can't stay for the whole meeting because I have to get to theatre practice," Harry informed the other board members as he took his seat. "And I'm sorry I'm late, but I met Irene for an early dinner at the food court because she's doing an extra volunteering shift today."

"We were just discussing the potential for recruiting new cooperative members at the con," Jack told him. "Flower has a plan in motion to promote the independent living deck that I have to admit isn't half bad, but I'll wait until Dave gets here so you don't have to listen to it twice."

"Dave's not going to make it," Maureen said, setting down her coffee. "I ran into him in the corridor and he said it takes him an hour to get prepared for if he has to stand in for M793qK."

"An hour?" Harry asked. "I had a disastrous fling with method acting in college. I hope he's not standing in front of the mirror trying to get inside the Farling's head."

"It's his new costume. I think it just takes him that long to get dressed. I'm going to go back and grab a Danish. Flower has me working so hard that I need the sugar."

"Bring one for me if there's anything good left," Brenda said, looking up from where she and Nancy had their heads together over a large tab.

"Really?" Nancy asked, pointing at a sentence in the fine print. "All presentations and lectures become the property of the con unless otherwise negotiated?"

"I made Flower put that in the contract," Brenda said. "She wants to record all of the sessions and be able to publish a transcript, and without the intellectual property clause, the speakers could take her to court for copyright infringement. Laws vary across the different species, but everybody agrees it's safest for the promoter to do a rights grab."

"And what if any of our presenters want to reuse something from their con sessions in a book? Does that mean they need to license the rights back from Flower?"

"Dollnick law states that the right to publish always remains with the creator unless there's a specific contract proving it was work-for-hire, like if Flower employed you to write an instruction booklet about, I don't know, living on board."

"So two parties can end up holding the copyright to the same material?"

"More than two under Dollnick law, but they're restricted to different publication domains. For example, the rights Flower takes under this contract are limited to verbatim reproduction of the sessions for educational purposes, and snippets up to ten seconds for promotional use."

"Last cheese Danish," Maureen said, setting a plate before Brenda.

"So let's get started and I'll fill in Dave when I see him at lunch tomorrow," Jack said. "Maureen? Do you want to explain the lists?"

The marketing director for the independent living cooperative, and now MultiCon, washed down a bite of her apple Danish with a swallow of coffee. "Basically, Flower got conned, if you'll pardon the pun, when she bought attendee lists for defunct cons on Earth. It turns out not to matter because she also ended up with the Con Anonymous list somehow and that in itself was enough to make up for all the duds."

"You mean the people from those other cons aren't interested in SciFi or anime anymore?" Harry asked.

"They're mainly deceased," Maureen said. "Half of the opt-ins dated back to the first couple decades after the Stryx opened Earth. We segmented all of the lists aside from ConAnon, and burned around twenty percent of the names before we realized that the low response rate wasn't a fluke. I finally figured out that the average age of the people who were still alive is two years higher than it is here in Flower's Paradise."

"So they're probably all retired and have time for traveling," Harry said. "It doesn't cost that much, relatively speaking, to take the elevator up to orbit and catch a commercial spaceliner from Earth to Union Station."

"The problem wasn't with the cost, it was with the pitch," Maureen said. "Most people our age can't get excited about traveling halfway across the galaxy to dress up like aliens when they can do it at home. So Flower and I came up with the idea of staging an ElderCon and running it at the same time. The response rate jumped through the roof."

"So let me get this straight," Harry said. "In addition to fixing up a whole deck for MultiCon, Flower wants to duplicate the effort with a con dedicated to growing old? What can she possibly gain by hosting both cons at the same time?"

"We're actually going to do a mash-up," Maureen explained. "All of the ElderCon sessions will be available to MultiCon participants who are of retirement age, and everything at MultiCon will be open to ElderCon attendees, though Flower insists on a health screening for seniors who want to try the LARPing studios on Union Station."

"We're hoping that the ElderCon attendees will spend most of their time on the con deck, but I told Flower we could manage a couple of tracks here by repeating the lectures and classes we've already put on for our cooperative members," Jack told Harry. "Nancy will be in charge of the programming, and we're hoping that you'll be available to talk about your work on *Everyday Superheroes* and in the fruitcake production business."

"I've barely been retired a year and I've never worked so hard in my life," Harry complained. "What else are you going to offer them?"

"I'm going to run a track on elder law, and M793qK is going to move his pop-up clinic to one of our classrooms during business hours for the duration of the con," Brenda said. "I'm going to ask your wife if she'll participate in a session about selling a small business and retiring to space."

The five board members batted around ideas, agreed to let Flower handle all of the details and not to overwork themselves, and then Harry had to grab his sword cane and get to the theatre. He was relieved to find he wasn't the last to show up, even though he was almost five minutes late.

"Where's M793qK?" the Grenouthian director demanded. He made a quick circle around the stage as if he expected to spot the Farling hiding behind the props box.

"The writers will be arriving at a quarter past for a script walk-through. I can't believe the Farling would be late for the first rehearsal of the new season."

"I can go get him," Dave volunteered, his raised hand also lifting the appendages on the right side of his new beetle costume.

"No, we'll need you to stand in if he doesn't show up," the director said and gave the old salesman an approving nod. "Your costume looks much more realistic than the pillowcase you used to wear."

"Flower suggested I get help from some of the con addicts who arrived early. They're working on multi-faceted eyes for my head so I should have it by next week. They really know their stuff."

"I'm glad somebody does. Now before we—there you are," the Grenouthian interrupted himself when M793qK appeared. "What's your excuse this time?"

"Flower picked up the crew of a Horten ice harvester that had been drifting without power or shielding for two cycles," M793qK rubbed out on his speaking legs. "I had to thaw them out and start them on radiation protocol, not to mention trimming all of their nails, which continued to grow out in those cheap emergency stasis pods. Then on my way here, I encountered a young man in the corridor with acute appendicitis, and using his pocket knife as my only—"

"All right, we've heard it all before," the bunny cut him off. "As I was telling the cast members who arrived on time, today we'll be doing a script walk-through with the writers. I know you all must be feeling pretty good about yourselves after we won two awards, but I can tell you from experience that making a splash your first season is easy. Sustaining audience interest after the novelty wears off is hard."

"You've directed anime drama before?" Harry asked.

"Well, not anime, but the same holds true for stage productions. Everybody wants a new theatre company to succeed when it opens, but selling season tickets the second year is the real challenge. Now, before the writers get here, do you have any questions about your promotion to principal animation actors?"

"Do we have to join a union?" Julie asked.

"Excellent question," the director said. "The anime actors union is particularly strong with the Hortens and Drazens, but the other species generally run open shops. Unless Flower Studios grows by an order of magnitude, the fees and overhead for starting a local chapter for actors would likely cost us more than we earn by providing voices and motion scaffolding for the animators. I'll vote against union membership myself, but I can't dictate to the rest of you."

"It costs money to be in a union?"

"Setting aside payroll deductions for pension benefits and such, which aren't really costs, the interstellar parent organization charges a basic fee for setting up a local chapter and requires contributions to the strike fund, etcetera. It really doesn't make sense to fund the local infrastructure, elect officers, and appoint a business agent for just a dozen members working a few hours a week."

"Are we going to get paid the union rate?" Bill asked.

"You'll earn the prevailing wage for principal animation actors working in space, which amounts to almost the same thing. I know, you're all thinking that I have points in the production so I profit from keeping costs down, but check the math with Brynlan if you don't trust me."

Bill turned to the Verlock who played Slomo, and the bulky alien shrugged. "For the two evenings a week we're working, it really doesn't make a difference," he said slowly. "But if you plan a career in animation acting, every hour counts towards the pension."

"Which doesn't vest until you reach five thousand hours," the Grenouthian added hastily.

"Five thousand—that would take almost fifty seasons at the rate we're going," Bill calculated.

"Very good," the Verlock complimented him. "Your math really seems to have improved since the last season."

"Yaem will be joining the cast today," the director continued, "and the animators have worked up a char for him. So let me introduce the newest member of *Everyday Superheroes*—Skeleton."

The Sharf strode onto the stage wearing a skin-tight black body stocking that was printed with a wrap-around skeleton. Between the alien's naturally protruding bones and the costume, he really did look like a skeleton.

"I can't tell you how excited I am to be here," Yaem practically gushed. "I've watched anime all of my life, and to take part in a production is a dream come true."

"Do you have a special superhero skill?" Harry asked.

"I fall apart, but I can put myself back together. The animators showed me a rough draft of the sequence, and the sound that my bones make collapsing in a pile is spot on."

"How is that going to help us win battles against the evil Farling mastermind?" Julie asked.

"The writers had an idea for sneaking me inside M793qK's null-space compound. When I'm broken down, I fit in a box no longer than my thigh bones. Zick said they plan for your Refill char to take up cello because the case will have room for my skull."

"Do you have any musical talent?" the director asked Julie.

"I've been taking voice lessons with Rinka, but singers don't need equipment."

"You could lug around a karaoke setup," the Vergallian who played Battle Royale suggested. "Then you could infiltrate the mastermind's compound and even get a chance to perform."

"I just sing for myself, I don't think I could manage in front of the immersive cameras," Julie said nervously.

"Don't worry, the animators will make you look confident and Flower can fix your voice," the director told her, clearly taken by the idea. "We could even get Rinka to dub."

"She'd like that," Jorb said.

"But if Refill is already infiltrating, what's the point of smuggling me past security in her equipment case?" Yaem asked.

"You could stay behind after she leaves and do your mission behind enemy lines," Lume suggested. The Dollnick sat down in his stage chair with his lower arms holding his knees and his upper arms supporting his chin in the modified 'Thinker' position that invoked his planning superpower. "Yes, that should work."

"Skeleton will never make it out of the secret lair alive," M793qK boasted. "My minions might be fooled by a waitress who moonlights as a karaoke singer, but we have procedures in place to prevent superhero exfiltration."

"Yaem won't walk out. As soon as your minions catch him, he'll collapse in a pile of bones and they'll dump him with the trash," the director said.

"I'm not sure that's in keeping with the dignity of—" the Sharf began, but he was interrupted by the writers trooping onto the stage.

"It's bad enough the Farling makes up his own lines," the head writer complained. "We heard you plotting scenarios for the new guy and it sounds like you're trying to put us out of work."

"I just want to smooth the way for you, Jeanie," the director said diplomatically. "I'd like to introduce you to Yaem, our new—"

"We know Yaem," Jeanie said. "He recruited us all for panels in the anime track for MultiCon. It's going to be awkward writing lines for somebody who has the power to schedule our sessions against stiff competition."

"As long as I do get lines and don't spend the whole season as a pile of bones in the corner," the Sharf said. "But if you can avoid having me escape as trash..."

"Did you bring the latest scripts?" the director asked.

"Zick," the head writer said, and the young writer/animator began handing out printed sheets of stiff thermal plastic to all of the actors. "After reading your feedback from last season, we've started showing all of the lines on every actor's script, rather than the shorthand of 'Slomo speaks' or 'The Blacksmith groans.'"

"Speaking of The Blacksmith, did you figure out how to rescue me from that block of ice that M793qK froze us into at the end of the last season?" Razood asked.

Jeanie frowned and pointed to one of her group of writers. "Continuity," she barked.

"In the final scene, The Blacksmith and Refill were helping Gerryman escape from the genetically engineered turtle guarding the sewer," the continuity editor said. "The evil Farling mastermind flash-froze them using his thermal whatsit."

"My thermodynamic vision," M793qK said.

"But this script starts with all of us back at headquarters talking about a suspicious increase in criminal activity in the Orion sector," Razood pointed out.

"Then you must have escaped the ice during the offseason," Jeanie said. "Now, if you'd all read your lines in turn, we'll get a feel for the rhythm and produce the finished script for Episode One by Thursday."

"What's the point of tracking continuity if you aren't going to proceed in a linear fashion?" the Frunge objected.

Jeanie spun on the director. "I knew this would happen when Flower made you all principal animation actors. If your actors keep trying to tell us our jobs, I'm going to file a union gripe."

"You're in a union?" Julie asked.

"The Interspecies Academy of Anime Writers Guild."

"And I'm in both the Writers Guild and the Animators Guild," Zick added. "I don't get overtime if I split my daily hours between the two, but it all earns pension points in the same system."

The director sighed and explained to the glowering actors, "The writers and animators work full time on our production. You're working five hours a week for twenty weeks a year."

"Yeah, being a principal actor for anime scaffolding sucks," the continuity editor commented.

"Now that everybody is here, I have an exciting opportunity to talk about," Flower announced over the public address system. "The early con arrivals have all been asking me about *Everyday Superheroes* and I thought it would be fun to let them come and watch a behind-the-scenes production session. Does anybody have any objections?"

"Yes," a dozen voices said all at once.

"I guess I should have asked earlier because they're already on their way. Besides, it will be good practice for you to work in front of a live audience."

"Practice for what?" Bill asked. "We're just here to make the work easier for the animation artists. It's not like we ever have to perform live."

"Yaem has scheduled the production for two public recording sessions during the con," Flower said, as people started trooping down the aisles. She activated the public address system for the full theatre. "Come, sit up front. We don't have the immersive cameras out today because it's just a walk-through, but we're planning tours of the studio where you can see the animation artists at work."

"I can't believe she's doing this to us," Julie grumbled to Bill. "Flower knows I get nervous in front of crowds."

"There's nothing to be nervous about," Harry told them, giving his sword cane a jaunty twirl. "You've both been through a lot more harrowing experiences than reading a few lines in front of a crowd that's predisposed to like you."

"If it makes you nervous, I can hide the audience with a hologram of empty seats," Flower offered over Julie's implant. "I can polarize the light so they won't even know it's there."

"Let's just get this over with," Julie said. "Where did the director go?"

"I'm back," the Grenouthian replied, hurrying onto the stage. He was now sporting a silk 'Director' sash that he had left off wearing at the start of the previous season. "It will help keep the audience from getting confused about who's in charge here. And the first line is Jorb's."

"I don't think the audience will find you all standing around talking about the Orion sector that interesting," Flower said before the Drazen could even begin. "Why not skip forward to an action scene?"

The director groaned, but he flipped forward a few sheets in the script. "Will you throw up an audio suppression field and translate for the audience, Flower?" he requested. "I'm going to start by framing the action for everybody. The evil Farling mastermind," he pointed at M793qK, "has kidnapped a group of orphans with the intention of using them as test subjects for unspeakable genetic experiments. One of his minions has hypnotized the children into believing that they're all on a field trip to a natural history museum. The Thinker," here the bunny gestured in Lume's direction, "has determined that the children have been stashed on an ore carrier that's scheduled to depart for Orion Prime through—a wormhole?"

"What's wrong with a wormhole?" the chief writer demanded.

"Just that they're inherently unstable and nobody has actually tried using one for interstellar travel in about a hundred million years. It stretches the suspension of disbelief beyond the breaking point."

"As opposed to the Stryx allowing the evil Farling mastermind to take a ship full of kidnapped orphans into a tunnel?"

"Why an ore carrier?" M793qK asked. "I would have brought a jump-capable ship, probably armed to the teeth."

"Fine!" Jeanie barked and made a notation on her plastic script with a thermal pen.

"So the Farling's ship is about to leave the elevator hub, but The Blacksmith uses his sledgehammer to jam the docking coupling, and the evil Farling mastermind emerges alone from the ship to face our *Everyday Superheroes*," the Grenouthian director said. "Positions, please. I believe I have the first line."

M793qK moved to one side of the stage, and the other actors all gathered together, brandishing their makeshift weapons. Jorb stood a bit apart, juggling a glittering arc of knives. The director, who also played The Producer, drew an abacus out of his pouch and began calculating their odds of victory.

"Fifty-fifty," the Grenouthian proclaimed in his char's thunderous voice. "Attack!"

Jorb acted first, gathering in his juggled knives and tossing each in turn at the Farling, but M793qK either batted them away or let them bounce harmlessly off his hard carapace. Razood charged forward, swinging his hammer, but the Farling excreted a spray of light oil from a gland in his lower body, and the Frunge lost all traction and skidded by.

"Surround him," Lume ordered, standing up from his chair to better coach the team. Bill went left, brandishing his shovel, and Harry unsheathed his sword from the cane and carefully skirted the oil slick to the right. M793qK rubbed out the Farling equivalent of a maniacal cackle and spread his wings.

"Now, Refill," Thinker shouted. "Throw the acid!"

Julie hesitated for a moment and then brought her glass coffeepot with the orange decaf handle forward in a practiced motion to slosh the imaginary contents over the evil beetle. M793qK retracted his wings to protect the delicate membranes, and Harry and Bill simultaneously closed in, leading with the business ends of their respective weapons. Just before they came within reach, they both appeared to be stuck in place, and Bill's left foot came out of his sneaker.

"Cut!" the director shouted, and stuck his abacus back in his pouch. "What's going on, M793qK? The script called for your slippery goo, not the glue."

"I've improved the goo so it turns into glue after a thirty-second delay," the Farling said modestly.

"How come I'm not attacking?" Yaem asked.

"You're offstage with Battle Royale, freeing the orphans," Zick told him. "You can't break the hypnosis, but the children think you're an interactive anatomy exhibit in the museum collection and they're following you to safety as the Vergallian deals with the minions."

"There's no glue in the script," Jeanie said, scowling at the Farling.

"As the only winner of an individual Interspecies Anime Academy award on the stage, I thought you'd appreciate my improvisation," M793qK said. "Now I have to get back to my clinic and check on those irradiated Hortens, but do what you want with the script, and I'll be here for the scaffolding shoot. The glue should have lost its strength by now. Dave?"

The retired salesman in his beetle costume waddled forward and exchanged places with the alien doctor, who exited backstage without another word.

"Alright," the director said. "Let's take it from, 'Throw the acid!'"

Thirteen

"Attention all hands, this is the captain," Woojin announced over the public address system. "We have arrived at Union Station's large-ship parking area. Thanks to Flower's decision to use her elective stop to extend our stay, we'll be remaining within a fifteen-minute taxi hop of the station for the next twelve days. Flower has also asked me to remind you all that unpaid work at either MultiCon or ElderCon will count against your volunteering requirement, but contrary to a rumor going around, morning calisthenics are NOT waived for the duration of the cons."

Julie stopped typing for long enough to listen to the announcement, and then realizing that she had lost her train of thought, went back to the start of her reply and read it out loud.

"While your performance piece titled 'Long-distance runner fleeing from alien invaders' struck a chord with our staff, we regret to inform you that your request for a marathon-length course without any turns is beyond the scope of our facilities. Perhaps you could display a hologram of yourself running a course on Earth, or provide a series of still images? We have a limited number of tables and pegboards still available, and—" she started typing again where she'd left off, "we will be accepting reservations for the next five days."

"Why don't you just let her perform live?" Flower asked.

"Because you aren't twenty-six miles long," Julie replied, chiding herself for having spoken out loud and giving the Dollnick AI a chance to horn in. "She explained in her request that it's important to flee in a straight line because any turns would give her alien pursuers a chance to make up the distance."

"Does a circle have an endpoint?"

"What does that have to do with it?"

"She can run around my circumference a few times without turning."

"But running from imaginary aliens isn't really art," Julie protested. "Anybody can do that."

"Anybody can do it, but not everybody can think of it," Flower said. "You should be more open-minded about art. Just because it looks silly to you doesn't mean nobody else will appreciate it."

"So how much do I charge her? Do we need to cordon off an area all along her route? That would be expensive."

"She can choose a route when she arrives, and if there happen to be people in the way, that will just make it more realistic. Charge her for one table so that after the run she'll have somewhere to sit and answer questions."

"Knock, knock," Bianca said, leaning into Julie's cubicle. "I'm heading over to Union Station to meet with the publisher who's interested in licensing alien translation rights to my new series. Any interest in coming along and posing as my assistant?"

"Would that really help you?" Julie asked.

"One of the first business strategies Sixth taught me is that the more people you bring to a negotiation, the more seriously the other side takes you."

"Go," Flower told Julie over her implant. "It will be a good learning experience."

Bianca glanced down at Julie's feet and bobbed her head in approval. "Good. You're wearing your magnetic cleats."

"I was planning on spending some time in the docking bay later today. We gave artists who can't attend the con the option to ship us their work for display. It made more sense for everybody to direct their packages to a temporary holding area on Union Station rather than trying to time deliveries to meet us at our stops along the way here. Dewey is going to bring it all over in the bookmobile."

"Flower certainly seems willing to draft all hands on board to help with the cons," the author said. "She's not like any other artificial intelligence that I've ever encountered."

"I've heard that before, but Flower was the first I'd met, so I guess she always seemed normal to me," Julie said, following Bianca into the lift tube. "How are we going to get from here to Union Station? Should I see if Dewey is ready to leave so we can hitch a ride?"

"The publisher is sending a ship to fetch us. Have you ever read anything from Abs House?"

"Abs House?" Julie tried not to laugh, but in the end, she couldn't help herself. "As in six-pack abs?"

"Dollnicks have twelve-packs and A. B. S. officially stands for Amor Besotted Species. Up until now, they've translated alien romances into English, but they're ready to start going the other way. The publisher said that they've actually been getting requests for my first Gryphon shifter book from Huktra and Vergallian distributors."

"I don't think I ever saw your Gryphon series. Did it come out in the last year or so? I've mainly been reading old library books since I joined Flower."

Both women activated their magnetic cleats and shuffled out of the lift tube capsule into Flower's core. Julie couldn't help flinching when she looked up and saw tiny people loading packages into a shuttle on the opposite side of the cylinder's interior surface. They looked upside-down in her frame of reference, and the primitive part of her brain expected them to rain down on her head.

"The first book in the series came out just two months ago, and it's been my best launch since I took over from Sixth," Bianca said. "I was beginning to worry that I wouldn't have a hit of my own while writing as Bianca D'Arc, but maybe it's better this way. If I had struck gold with my first new series, I might have felt bitter about not publishing it under my own name. But I've made a good living as a line author thanks to all of the Biancas who came before me."

"So there are other species with gryphons in their mythology?"

The author smiled. "Art imitates life," she said. "I never would have had the idea if I hadn't met a couple traveling with a Tyrellian gryphon that treated the two of them as if they were her pets. We spent a week together at a Horten con, and Semmi, that's the gryphon's name, tried to click-train me."

"Gryphons are real? As in winged lions with beaks? Who would bring one to a con, and what's click-training?"

Bianca pointed at her ear, nodded, then said, "The taxi will be here in a minute. Yes, gryphons are real, a winged lioness in this case. The people traveling with her were posing as merch vendors, but the woman was really a freelance journalist working for the Galactic Free Press, and her husband was wearing a standard-issue poison detection ring, the kind EarthCent Intelligence gets from the Drazens. What was the last part of your question?"

"Click-training?"

"My parents had a parrot when I was growing up and he was very intelligent. My mother used a clicker to teach him tricks. I noticed that Semmi was watching me like, well, like a gryphon, and she would click her beak when I started doing something she approved of, and again when I completed the action. By the end of the day, I realized I was giving her treats and she was rewarding me with clicks."

"How did that work exactly?" Julie asked.

"It was one of those outdoor cons the aliens love, with lots of medieval role-playing. John and Ellen camped next to me and we shared a lot of meals together. Every other time I stuck my fork in something Semmi liked, she would click her beak and look at me expectantly. If I gave it to her, she would click again, and if I didn't, she gave me this sad-eyed gryphon look that made me feel like I was starving her. I learned pretty quickly to just share."

"That's really cool. Did you use it in your book?"

"Let's just say there was a different type of positive reinforcement training going on. Oh, will you look at that!"

A small craft with a full-ship advertising wrap printed with "Bianca D'Arc" in what must have been a hundred different fonts, sizes, and languages, settled to the deck about fifty steps away from them. Before they were half-way there, a Horten girl popped out and came to greet them.

"Hi, I'm Marilla," the alien introduced herself. "Blythe hired me to pick you up and show you how this ship operates. It will be at your disposal for the length of Flower's stay at Union Station."

"I'm Julie, the assistant. She's Bianca," Julie said.

"So you're not a taxi driver?" Bianca asked.

"I'm a part-owner in Tunnel Trips, the only Human ship rental agency on the tunnel network," Marilla replied proudly. "You don't have any baggage?"

"We're only coming for a meeting today," Bianca told the Horten. They followed the alien back to the ship and in through the hatch. "You know the owner of Abs House?"

"Is that what Blythe decided to call the new imprint?" the Horten asked, and politely covered her mouth so they wouldn't see her teeth as she suppressed a laugh. "I went to the Open University with her daughter, Vivian, and Tunnel Trips was started by Vivian's fiancé's father and step-brother. It's been a real eye-opener for me how rapidly entrepreneurial Humans can do things. Hortens like to study a business for fifty or a hundred years before we put any money at risk, but Humans want to be first-movers, kind of like the Grenouthians."

"Are you looking forward to reading romances translated into Horten?" Julie asked out of curiosity.

Marilla's skin began to change to a very strange color, but she seemed to be able to battle it back with an effort of will. "My mother made me promise not to read any of Blythe's books until I get married, especially the ones translated from Dollnick," she said. "Have you seen the covers?"

"If they're anything like regular alien romance covers, I know what you mean. Hey, how come it feels like we still weigh something?"

"This close to Union Station, Gryph, the Stryx who owns everything, handles all of the small ships traveling in the area with manipulator fields. It's safer for everybody this way, and he'll keep accelerating the ship until we're halfway there, and then flip it around and decelerate. The weightlessness will be so brief that you'll barely notice. That reminds me. I was going to show you how to operate the rental."

"It doesn't sound like we need to learn if this Gryph actually does all the work," Bianca said. "Do you know Mrs. Oxford well?"

"Not that well, though I've been a member of her focus group from the start. She buys lunch in an expensive restaurant for a bunch of us girls from advanced species once a cycle to get our input on books she's interested in translating to Humanese." The Horten paused for a moment as she replayed Bianca's question in her head, and then she brightened. "I get it. You're curious because I keep referring to Blythe by her first name. I haven't really noticed what she does around Humans, but when she's with the rest of us, she only uses the one name."

"I should start doing that myself," Julie said.

"When you come back from your meeting, I'll give you both the standard orientation as if you were renting," Marilla said. "You might want to pop through a tunnel to somewhere since Flower is here for almost two weeks. Did you like the ad wrap?"

"It's very distinctive, and it certainly made clear that you were there to pick us up," Bianca said.

"We usually use the wraps to advertise Tunnel Trips, but Blythe thought you would enjoy it. You can keep it after the rental and use part of it for a tablecloth the next time you do a book signing. It's a nanoweave that the Sharfs use to protect new ships from interstellar dust when they're parked at orbital dealerships. If you ball it up it will fit in your fist, but the wrinkles come out with a shake."

"That might actually work out well," Bianca mused. "The shows I go to usually supply a plain tablecloth for the folding tables and fans are always coming up and asking me to sign books that are written by one of the other line authors."

"Are you an author too, Julie?" Marilla asked.

"Not really. I've started on a few books but I've never actually finished anything."

"I tried writing a novel before I went to the Open University, but my friends all teased me until I gave up."

"I never knew that Hortens looked down on authors," Bianca said. "I actually had the opposite impression."

"It's complicated," Marilla said. "Famous authors are some of the most respected members of high society. But my friends were always asking, 'Who are you to write a novel? What have you ever done?' And that made me think about all of the books I'd ever read. The authors had obviously lived much more exciting lives than I have, with the wisdom of hundreds of years behind them. It made me feel like I was some kind of fraud."

"Your friends were idiots," Bianca told her. "All books are a cheat of sorts. Succeeding as an author depends on craft, not life experience. I used to love reading the biographies of famous people before I started writing novels. After I learned how a plot is put together, I realized that all of those supposedly true stories were just too dramatic to be real."

"What if they have footnotes and references?" Marilla asked.

"Years ago, a biographer writing about a famous writer who I won't name asked me for my memories. I gave him a bunch of quotes for the funny and insightful things that Rob—I suppose it doesn't matter—Robert Anglish said in my presence. Later that day I realized that none of the quotes I gave her were actually Robert's. I was subconsciously borrowing them from other authors I knew, including myself. Maybe I did it to show off to the biographer or because I wanted to be a footnote in history. I don't understand it myself."

"But that doesn't mean that books are all a cheat," Julie said. "Sure, biographers cherry-pick what they include to make their subjects interesting and sell more copies, but true romance—"

"The emotions are all true, nobody would read my books otherwise, but that's not what I'm talking about," Bianca said. "The big cheat in fiction is that authors cram all of the highlights of a life or a relationship into sixty or a hundred thousand words that a real romance fan can swallow in a lazy afternoon. And I'm not picking on my own genre because it's the same for all novels. The minute-to-minute progress of a normal life isn't interesting for art."

"What about immersive documentaries?" Marilla asked.

"Puh-lease," Bianca said. "They usually take a life or a whole culture and squeeze it down into a few hours. In my experience, people who expect their lives to be an unending series of highlights end up addicted to drugs before they ever have a chance to accomplish anything."

"My father reads thrillers and I always thought they were pretty unrealistic," the Horten girl said. "They start with some pirate or crime lord kidnapping the daughter of a retired intelligence agent or fleet officer, and then they all go chasing around the galaxy and a lot of stuff gets blown up. I had a lecturer at the Open University who said that the key to writing bestsellers was to keep raising the stakes to get readers emotionally committed to the outcome and flipping the pages."

"I've grown out of reading books that keep me on the edge of my seat," the romance author said. "If I want an upset stomach, I can just order fast food."

"You told me last week that the key to writing a good romance is to keep placing obstacles between the two main characters," Julie reminded Bianca. "Would anybody want to read a book about a couple who meet on an arranged date in the last chapter, get married that night, and live happily ever after?"

"No, but I think I've explained myself poorly," Bianca said. "It's the sheer concentration of events that's unrealistic. The idea that every bit of dialogue or action has to move the plot forward is copied from scriptwriters who don't want to leave the audience time to think too deeply about what they're seeing. Characters that only exist to serve the plot are the very definition of one-dimensional. It's not about how well you describe them or how full you stuff their back story with traumas—if you want your characters to come alive, you have to let them live their own lives."

"Thank you," Marilla said. "I thought that I was going about it all wrong when I tried, but now I'm going to start writing again."

"It's funny, but you sounded just like Jorb when he's teaching martial arts," Julie told the author. "He always stresses that the most important part of fighting is what comes in between all the strikes and blocks."

"You know Jorb?" Marilla asked. "He went to the Open University with me and my friends. Is he still chasing that pretty choral teacher?"

"Rinka, I take lessons from her. And he's caught her, kind of, but I guess they have a lot of dating rules."

"Not as many as the Frunge," the Horten girl said, and that seemed to remind her of something. "How about world-building?" she asked Bianca. "How do you balance between going on and on describing the settings and only providing as much information as the plot demands? I've read detective novels where it seemed like every object the author took the time to describe turned up later as a clue or a murder weapon."

"One-dimensional objects can be easier to spot than one-dimensional characters because they don't have any lines to distract you from their purpose," Bianca said. "On the other hand, the only writer I ever heard of who described every part of life with equal weight was a crackpot autobiographer who recorded his waking hours for decades. Do you think anybody wanted to read it? He thought he would leave an invaluable record for future historians, but I can't imagine they'll have any interest in somebody who sat around all day writing about how he felt about writing."

"We're here," Marilla declared suddenly. "That didn't feel like fifteen minutes at all."

"I visited Union Station the last two times Flower stopped here," Julie said. "Are we at the main travel concourse?"

"The rental agency is in Mac's Bones, that's where you should tell the lift tube to bring you when you're ready to leave. I'll point you in the right direction, and you can either ask for Abs House or Blythe. The station librarian will know who you're talking about and have the lift tube bring you to the right deck."

Apparently, the station librarian also alerted Blythe they were on their way, because the publisher was waiting in front of the lift tube when Bianca and Julie exited.

"Thank you for coming, Bianca, and you must be Julie," Blythe greeted them. "I sort of have the advantage of you, Julie, because my husband is the director of EarthCent Intelligence and your name came up quite a bit around a year back."

"Thank you for all the help," Julie said. "The captain told me that you sort of financed EarthCent Intelligence and Flower's mission."

"EarthCent Intelligence, yes, though it's almost profitable at this point, but Flower is heavily subsidized by the Stryx," Blythe said. She made small talk about their trip in the rental and led them down a corridor and past a guard into a small conference room. "There, we're in a secure meeting room, which means only half of the alien intelligence agencies on the station have the technology required to eavesdrop. Can I get either of you something to drink? Did you think about my proposition, Bianca?"

"The advance offer was quite generous, but the devil is in the details," the author said. She seemed a bit flustered by the fact that Blythe was alone. "I don't want to sound paranoid, but do you have a team of lawyers somewhere ready to pounce?"

"I don't blame you for thinking about publishers that way," Blythe said. "Translating books by human authors for alien readers is a new business for Abs House, so I thought I'd start by asking a few of the authors we're approaching what you'd like to see in your contracts. I'm not offering you carte blanche," she added hastily. "The economics on our side are largely constrained by what alien publishers are willing to pay since we're using a partnership model to get distribution, but we have plenty of room to discuss subsidiary rights and the like. Your English rights obviously stay with you."

"Action figures? Immersive rights? Anime adaptations?"

"Some of the alien publishers we partner with require audiobook rights in their languages, but that's about it," Blythe said. "They initially asked for more, but I pointed out that they don't give up any of the other rights when we translate their books into English, and that sort of shamed them into cooperating for the time being."

The conference room door slid open, and a tall man walked in explaining the shortcomings of the room's security over his shoulder to a younger man, who turned out to be Bill.

"Sorry," the tall man said. "I didn't know you were using the secure room."

"My husband, Clive," Blythe introduced him to her guests. "This is Bianca and Julie. The witness-protection-program Julie."

"What are you doing here?" Julie asked Bill, who had followed Clive into the room.

"Can I tell her?" he asked Clive.

"Go ahead. I don't imagine she's a security risk," the director of EarthCent Intelligence said with a smile.

"I'm here to be debriefed," Bill said. "The captain didn't mention that when I agreed to work for the Sharf, I would be expected to report to EarthCent Intelligence. I guess I'm kind of a double agent now."

Fourteen

"They seem to have put us next to each other," Bianca said. She stared balefully at her name card at the head table on the raised platform at the front of the banquet hall. "Just because I agreed to work with you doesn't mean you're forgiven."

"What did I ever do to you?" Geoffrey demanded.

"You hurt Sixth is what you did to me, and you ruined her bestselling series. You were her model for the soldier-poet in *Mercenary Hearts* and she couldn't write it anymore after you walked out."

"But I didn't even do a full hitch in the mercenaries, and I certainly would have remembered if I had ever saved an empire or even just a princess. What was the hero's name again?"

"Abraham," Bianca said. "He was strong, yet vulnerable, handsome without being pretty. After being orphaned and raised by pirates, he had enough conflicts to make him interesting, but he was loyal to a fault and he never would have walked out on Ophelia. After you left, Sixth ended the series with Abraham forced to abandon ship in one of those lifeboat stasis pods. The lifeboat's transponder was defective, and since she never wrote another romance, he's still out there floating around interstellar space in suspended animation. It's lucky she had already recruited me or the D'Arc line would have died out."

"Abraham wasn't a man, he was an ideal that I couldn't live up to," Geoffrey protested. "I used to get up every morning and do a hundred sit-ups just to try to recover the shadow lines between my abdominal muscles. You think that was fun for a man in his fifties?"

"And you didn't know that Sixth starved herself to fit into those stylized Vergallian fashions you always admired? It's a lot harder for a woman to keep her figure than a man."

A bot dressed in the ship's livery floated up in front of them and inquired, "Chicken or beef?"

"No fish?" Bianca asked.

"I got so many requests for vegetarian meals that it's all dressed up tofu tonight," the bot replied in Flower's voice. "I can shape it like a fish if you want."

"Beef is fine," she said.

"You don't have to dress it up for me," Geoffrey said. "I take my tofu straight."

"You're doing it again," Bianca complained as the bot floated off. "That's so like something Abraham would have said. Sixth really loved you."

Geoffrey flinched, and for a moment, he looked almost as old as he had on his first night on board Flower. "Maybe I got scared," he finally admitted, struggling to meet Bianca's eyes. "You need to keep your edge in the writing game and Sixth was making me soft. She was too good for me, and then when the royalties for *Mercenary Hearts* started flowing in—"

"You asked her for money?" Bianca looked shocked.

"No! The opposite. I had overextended myself trying to produce a game based on my *War College* series, the dumbest thing I ever did, and she offered me money. Offered ME money! I used to be the top author in the

Space Marines genre and she was bringing in more money than I was." Geoffrey stopped suddenly and put his hand to his forehead. "Gods, was I really that stupid?"

"Apparently you were. Did you actually leave because you couldn't stand being with a woman who was more successful than you were?"

He took a sip from his water glass, and Bianca couldn't help but notice a tremor in his hand. "You know, I had a lot of time to think about all the mistakes I made in my life while I was locked up. It was more like reliving those years in an unending dream sequence, thanks to all of the drugs they were putting in my food. But even then I couldn't be honest with myself about the biggest mistake I ever made. It was just my stupid pride. That's what ended my first marriage too, when it turned out my stint in the mercenaries had left me sterile."

"Why didn't you just talk to Sixth? Why did she have to wake up to a note on the dresser?"

"Would Abraham have told what's-her-name that playing the consort role to her princess was making him feel small?"

"Ophelia, and don't try to worm out of it." Bianca glared at the old author, but either he was a better actor than she remembered, or he was already beating himself up more than she could. "Let's just drop it for now," she said with a sigh. "You have to do the intro after dinner and I don't want you weeping on the microphone."

"First rule of being a military science fiction author," he said, dabbing at the corner of his eye with his suit sleeve. "Never let them see you cry."

Another bot floated past the table ladling fruit salad in the bowls that were part of every place setting and not taking 'no' for an answer. Soon after the main course arrived, followed by apple pie with a choice of frozen yogurt or vanilla ice cream for dessert. Then the lights over the floor of the banquet room dimmed slightly, and a spot illuminated the lectern placed to the right of the head table.

Geoffrey moved slowly to the lectern, adjusted the old-fashioned microphone he had requested, and blew into it, causing the audio engineers in the audience to flinch. "Testing. Of course, it works. I don't know what I was thinking."

"You were thinking of NewCon," somebody called out. "I saw you give the keynote there thirty years ago, and when you touched the microphone, the fire alarm went off."

"Ah, yes. And a noisy fan in my room's ventilation system kept me from sleeping, but that's what you get at those old New York hotels. I hope you all enjoyed your vegetarian meals," Geoffrey continued, "and for those of you who are wondering, there is a cash bar, but it won't be open until after this evening's entertainment."

"Where have you been the last ten years?" somebody else called out.

"Let's just say I was on a retreat, but now I have the big guns on my side and I'll be advancing again."

"Are you moderating any sessions?" somebody closer to the stage asked. "I want to see you roast some newbie butt."

"I don't do that sort of thing anymore," the old author said. "I learned quite a few things about myself in, er, on retreat, and I'm trying to put the old Geoffrey Harstang behind me. I'll no longer be pointing out to new authors that the seasons in the southern hemisphere on Earth run opposite those in the northern hemisphere, or that diving a ship into a black hole is not a reasonable method of escaping pursuit."

Geoffrey waited a moment for the brief round of laughter and snorting to die out before taking a hand-written index card out of his pocket.

"MultiCon is proud to present Grynlan and the Grenouthian, just back from their second galactic tour. We were lucky—"

"You can sit now," interrupted the fast-moving alien who looked like an enormous bunny. The new arrival used a gentle belly bump to move the old author away from the lectern. "I'm the Grenouthian, and he," the bunny pointed dramatically at a Verlock shuffling slowly across the stage, "is Grynlan. Normally, the last place the two of us would want to spend our time off is talking to a bunch of Humans, but—"

"Money," the Verlock bellowed.

"—the money was so good we couldn't refuse. In the interest of getting this over with as quickly as possible, I'm going to skip the bit about how we're glad to be here, which we aren't, and jump right to the jokes. A mathematician walks into a bar and gets into an argument with a physicist about the shape of the multiverse membrane. The bartender says—what now?" the Grenouthian broke off when his partner finally drew near and poked the bunny in the shoulder.

"Humans," Grynlan said in a slow stage whisper. "They don't get math humor."

"Then what are we going to do for an hour? I suppose I could dust off the old 'How many Humans does it take to...' jokes that I tell to the other species. If these people get offended, that's their problem."

"'How many Humans' requires math," the bulky Verlock pointed out to his partner.

"Then it's going to have to be improv. Can I get some volunteers up here? How about everybody sitting at table number three? You're all funny-looking, so at least we have that going for us."

"Do we have to come up on the stage?" a woman at table three asked.

"Unless you have a personal holographic projector. No? I didn't think so. Hop to it," the bunny demanded, stamping his foot to speed them up. "What do you think, Grynlan? Have you ever seen a less-likely looking bunch of panel participants in your life?"

"Poor material," the Verlock concurred as the guests took the stage and stood facing the audience. "Moderator?"

"Right. I'm going to have you people form a panel discussion for our little improv because I doubt you know how to do anything else. We're going to need a moderator so how about you?" the Grenouthian asked, pointing at the woman who hadn't wanted to get on stage.

"I've moderated over a hundred sessions at—"

"A simple 'yes' would have been sufficient," he interrupted. "Now what is the panel going to be about?" he asked, massaging his furry chin between his thumb and forefinger.

"Artificial Intelligence," the Verlock suggested.

"Perfect. Artificial Intelligence. I'm sure you all know as much about AI as you do about whatever you normally talk about on panels, which is to say—"

"Nothing," Grynlan interjected in a gravelly drawl.

"—nothing, so here we have our panel discussion on AI, and," the alien made a show of squinting at the smart badge of the woman he'd chosen for moderator, "Miss Smut is going to introduce the panel."

"Smith!" she corrected him indignantly.

"Sounds like a fake name for a love-hotel registry to me, but I won't go there," the Grenouthian said. "Introduce your panel."

The woman proved to have an excellent memory and was able to name the table companions she had met over dinner. She gave each a chance to say a few words about themselves, but when the third man began talking about an award he'd received decades ago, the Verlock shouted "Time!"

"Excuse me?" the man said.

"Time," the bunny picked up on his partner's criticism. "Your time, my time, our time. You can waste your time talking to the mirror at home, but don't waste my time or our time in a pathetic attempt to justify your presence on the panel. The civilized galaxy has long since settled on the maximum time for speakers to introduce themselves at cons, and it's—"

"Twenty-seven seconds," the Verlock said slowly.

"Twenty-seven seconds," the Grenouthian repeated. "Next, please, and I'm counting."

The rest of the introductions went by in a flash, and then the moderator turned to the pair of aliens to see what they wanted her to do next.

"Well, start moderating," the Grenouthian said.

"Do you want us to have a panel discussion or just go straight to questions from the audience?"

"What does it say in the program?"

"We don't have a program," the man who had gone over time on the introduction protested.

"It's improv," the Verlock bellowed. "Improvise!"

"I have this," the moderator said confidently and pretended to be reading from the small screen on her smart badge. "Today we'll be talking about artificial intelligence in science fiction versus the real thing. What's scarier? Our imaginations, or the reality of the Stryx?"

"The Stryx don't exist," somebody in the audience shouted. "Everybody knows they're just a bogeyman the aliens made up to keep humanity down."

"Well?" the Grenouthian asked the moderator. "Aren't you going to do something?"

"What do you mean?" she asked.

"That man is a heckler. Are you going to let him interrupt your panel at will?"

"I'm sure the other people in the room will tell him to stop interrupting," she said uncertainly. "What would you have me do?"

"Tomato," Grynlan declared.

The Grenouthian pulled a bright red tomato out of his belly pouch, wound up, and threw it so hard that the heckler failed to duck out of the way even though he saw it coming. It splattered on impact with the man's forehead, spraying the people around him with bits of tomato. "The next loud-mouth gets a Dollnick tan tuber in the noggin," the bunny threatened the audience, and then turned back to the moderator. "Carry on."

"So, who wants to get us started," she said nervously. "Eleanor?"

"Well, I was a writer on *Lost in the Horsehead Nebula,* and in order to make the story believable, we intentionally didn't include any AI characters because they never would have gotten lost."

"Wrong," a younger man on the panel said in an obnoxious voice. "That may be true for most alien artificial intelligence, I couldn't say, but I've met human-made AI that's no smarter than any of us."

"If you believe that, Bruce, then I have a space elevator on Jupiter for sale," Eleanor retorted.

"You always get snarky when you're wrong," Bruce shot back.

"If I was trying to be snarky, I would have said something about your suit."

"Isn't your nose half the size it was the last time we were on a panel together? Surgery much?"

"Enough!" the Verlock shouted.

"Were you going to let them trade insults all night?" the Grenouthian asked the moderator.

"I watch the audience response during back-and-forths to see how long I should let them go," she replied. "Everybody seemed to be enjoying it."

"I don't remember two idiots insulting each other being in the program description you read."

"I guess not." The moderator spotted a raised hand in the audience and pointed in that direction. "Yes?"

"Could everybody speak louder?" the older woman who had raised her hand asked in a surprisingly strong voice. "And when the panelists talk, I notice they're looking at each other rather than the audience. They should be looking at us."

The Grenouthian reached in his pouch and handed the moderator a large potato.

"What's this?" she asked.

"That is a Dollnick tan tuber, and she," he indicated the old woman in the audience who had just complained, "is a troll."

"Peg her," Grynlan ordered.

The moderator jumped at the Verlock's voice coming from behind her and tried to heave the heavy tuber, which barely made it off the stage.

"Pathetic," the bunny said. "You throw like a Human."

"A Human girl," Grynlan added, and the two aliens shared a belly-bump, apparently well pleased with their joint put-down.

"That's two strikes," the Grenouthian told the moderator. "Are you going to get somebody on your panel to say something interesting about AI, or are you giving up?"

"Why are we doing improv anyway?" she asked.

"You can't spell 'improve' without improv, and somebody clearly needs to improve."

"Hey, are you trying to tell us how to moderate?" the panel's loud-mouth demanded. "I'll have you know—"

"Strike three," the Verlock drowned out the objection, jerking his thumb like an umpire moving in slow motion. "You're out!"

"Let's have a round of applause for Table Three," the Grenouthian said, clapping his furry paws and taking advantage of his mass to hip-check the nearest "volunteer" into motion. "That's right, they're finally doing something they're good at—sitting down. Let's get Table One up here and see if they can do any better."

"Or not," one of the men at Table One said, getting up from his chair and heading towards the exit rather than the stage. The three sliding doors at the back of the banquet hall slid open at the same time, and three aliens, each brandishing a poleaxe, stepped into the room. The doors slid shut behind them, and they simultaneously slammed the butt ends of their weapons into the deck.

"Nobody walks out on Grynlan and the Grenouthian," the bunny growled. "Get up here with your tablemates, Mr. Moderator."

The man cast an uncertain gaze at the armed Dollnick who was blocking the closest way out, and then at the Frunge and the Drazen covering the other two exits. His confidence withered, and he followed the others from his table onto the stage.

"We're going to do something a little different this time," the bunny announced. "Our group of volunteers will serve as the panel, but Grynlan and myself will be the whole audience."

"Won't be the first panel I've done for a two-member audience," the moderator said, and the others from the table all nodded their heads. "I once ran a group discussion about interstellar drives and the only audience member was a ten-year-old Horten boy."

"And did he explain interstellar drives to you?" the Grenouthian asked facetiously, and then exchanged another celebratory belly-bump with the Verlock.

"It was about interstellar drives in science fiction," the moderator mumbled. "You don't have to rub it in."

"Alright, so let's do a little improv. What's the session description in the program guide?"

"Uh, the economics of space elevators in fact and fiction. Why everybody buys them from the Dollnicks."

"Boring," Grynlan declared, and began to shuffle off the stage.

"I guess it's just me now," the Grenouthian told the moderator. "What are you going to do to keep my butt in the seat?"

"I'm going to stick to the program," the moderator said indignantly. "If you don't like it, you can leave with slowpoke."

"Ten points," Grynlan announced, turning back and pointing at the man. "You just beat Table Three."

"You see," the Grenouthian told the audience. "Running a panel isn't multiverse physics, you just have to stick to the program guide. Now show us how you take a question for your panel from the audience."

"Uh, does anybody have a question?" the moderator asked the two aliens.

"I do," the Grenouthian said. "Why doesn't the elevator stalk and its giant counterweight make the planet wobble?"

"I know," a woman on the improv panel spoke up. "Because there's always another elevator on the opposite side of the world to balance it out."

"But what if they aren't on the equator?"

"Who would build a space elevator anywhere else?"

"Uh, Peg?" said her husband, giving her a nudge. "Earth's elevators aren't on the equator."

The Grenouthian bowed to the audience with a flourishing arm movement and said, "I rest my case." It got a laugh from the sprinkling of aliens in attendance.

Fifteen

"The final step is to add—be careful with that!" Harry interrupted himself to warn the young woman, but she already had the lid off, and her eyes began to stream. "Quick, Bill. Get her to the rinse station."

Bill vaulted over the counter where he had been helping a middle-aged couple with the Dollnick mixer and half-carried the young woman to the emergency eyewash sink. He pulled her hands away from her eyes, yanked the chain, and ensured that her head was properly positioned for the dual fountains of water.

"Try not to blink," Bill told her. "Are you okay holding this position yourself?"

"Yes," she choked out, her hands gripping the edges of the sink. "What was that stuff anyway? I thought the label said it was hot sauce."

"It is hot sauce, but that's the special jar we keep for Jorb, a Drazen who eats in our cafeteria," Bill explained. "I had to stick my whole head in the bar sink once after serving him. By my next shift, Flower had the emergency eyewash station installed."

"How long do I have to rinse?"

"I'm not sure. Flower?"

"If she got the sauce directly in her eyes, fifteen minutes is the minimum," the Dollnick AI responded over Bill's implant. "If it was just a few airborne capsaicin molecules, then she can stop as soon as she's not in pain."

"I guess if it doesn't hurt anymore you can stop, but if your eyes start burning again, I'd keep rinsing them out," he told the young woman.

The woman reached blindly for the pull chain, tugged it to turn off the water, and straightened up. "Who would have thought that cooking for aliens could be so dangerous?"

"Thank you for that lead-in," Harry said. He clapped his hands to get the attention of the other participants who had signed up for the workshop. "You all listed professional kitchen experience on the con questionnaire so I'm not going to give you a lecture on safety. The key point here is that just because the aliens can eat most of our foods doesn't mean that some of their foods aren't dangerous for us to even handle."

"I thought aliens could eat everything in the All Species Cookbook because we share some of the same genetic stuff," a man said.

"I'm not sure if that's been proven one way or the other, but I do know that the only alien food we can safely eat without elaborate detoxification methodologies is Vergallian vegan."

"How can you detoxify a food if it's poisonous on the chemical level?" the young woman with the watering eyes asked as she attempted to dry her hair with a dishtowel.

"Thank you for that question as well," Harry said with a grin. "People are going to think that you're a paid shill. Our final recipe for the day is a quick-baking flatbread using flour that comes from the cassava root, which contains cyanide before processing."

"And that's poisonous to the aliens as well?"

"Drazens eat raw cassava root while they're drinking, and I think Jorb mentioned that the Verlocks like it as well," Bill spoke up. "And that hot sauce was an Earth product exported by Drazen Foods, but you won't meet too many humans who can tolerate it."

"So you're going to teach us how to detoxify cassava roots?" the first man asked.

"I'm afraid that takes too long because there's a lot of soaking involved," Harry said. "We grow cassava and manufacture the flour on board, though it's primarily used for tapioca, one of our many dessert exports."

"If you can get away early, Razood is asking for help," Flower told Bill over his implant.

"Are you all set, Harry?" Bill asked. "Apparently Razood is running into trouble with his workshop."

"Go ahead, the cassava bread is dead easy," the baker told him. "I'll see you later when we battle the evil Farling."

"I forgot that was tonight," Bill groaned, taking off his apron and tossing it in the laundry bin. He slipped out of the kitchen, through the empty cafeteria, and into the nearest lift tube. "Colonial Jeevesburg," he requested.

"The workshop is on the con deck," Flower said. "There was nowhere near enough room in his blacksmith shop for the number of people who registered."

"Con deck," Bill corrected his instructions, even though he knew that the Dollnick AI would take him where she wanted. "I thought Razood said he found a couple of new apprentices."

"He did, but there are over four hundred aspiring weapons smiths signed up for the track, and this workshop on crossbows turned out to be very popular. One of his new assistants caught a finger in a firing mechanism, and the other one is taking the injured man to M793qK for repairs."

"So Razood wants me to load," Bill surmised, rubbing his wrist in anticipation of the soreness he'd be feeling later. "Couldn't the Frunge come up with a high tech solution for cranking back the drawstring? Maybe a battery-powered motor?"

"That would be an anachronism," Flower told him.

"Are you feeding me vocabulary words for the Open University test again?"

"You'll remember better if you learn words in context rather than memorizing from a list. Do you know what an anachronism is?"

"Something that doesn't fit the purpose?" Bill guessed.

"Close. Something that doesn't fit the time period. A good example would be a recent Earth production about colonial farming techniques that featured draft animals, period costumes, and in the background, the space elevator stalk."

"How could they have missed that?"

"It happens quite frequently in historical immersives. Since the production crews are living in the present, they can forget that some monument or technology which is always there in the background of their lives postdates the period they are attempting to recreate."

The lift tube doors slid open on a madhouse of activity, and the Dollnick AI told Bill, "Razood has a partitioned-off space up on the right, just about where the merchant area gives way to the art show."

Bill began jogging through the crowd, dodging around people wearing alien costumes and aliens wearing human costumes. He was about to ask Flower how far he had to go when a woman ran past him shouting something. It took a moment for his brain to process her warning to run faster or the aliens would get him.

"Uh, Flower?" he said.

"Yes, Bill," the Dollnick AI replied in his ear.

"A woman just ran past me yelling about being chased by aliens."

"She's an artist doing a performance piece. I tried to talk Lume into chasing her for a lap, but he said that he did his running in the army."

"Does anybody else know that she's doing art, or is it just the four of us?"

"Julie knows because she processed the application. And I've been contacted by a number of Good Samaritans reporting that there's a woman with mental health issues fleeing imaginary aliens on the con deck, so the word is getting around," Flower said. "It's the next partitioned-off area on your right."

Bill dropped to a walk so he wouldn't be out of breath, and against his will, he found himself glancing over his shoulder to see if any aliens were closing in on him. "I guess art is more powerful than I realized," he muttered.

"Performance art often has an effect on the subconscious even when the audience laughs."

The workshop was packed, and Bill had to skirt the crowd to get to where Razood was standing on a low platform. The Frunge blacksmith was currently demonstrating a variety of lock mechanisms that allowed crossbows to remain cocked until it was time to fire, one of their main advantages over the longbow.

"This one," Razood said, nodding at Bill as he slipped in behind the table, "is a Horten design from about six hundred thousand years ago. The Hortens went through a period where they made every part of a crossbow from steel, including the string, which is really a braided wire. Although steel obviously has higher tensile strength than many traditional crossbow materials, you still end up with a weapon that weighs more than some species want to be bothered with, not to mention corrosion issues."

"How do I craft a crossbow in *Legions of the Dark Moons*?" somebody dressed as an elf warrior called out.

"Is that a game?" Razood asked.

"It's THE game," the elf replied indignantly.

"I only build real weapons and I've never played it," Razood replied. "Isn't there a help forum?"

"Are you telling me that the siege crossbow on the stand behind you isn't from a game?" a girl demanded. "It looks like you'd need four arms just to load and cock the thing."

"Which is why I requested my former apprentice come and lend his help. And I can understand why you would mistake it for a siege weapon, but it's actually a full-scale replica of a standard Dollnick crossbow from their Princely Wars period."

Bill helped Razood lift the giant crossbow from its stand, and then he held it steady from the front while Razood put his feet in the stirrups and exerted his appreciable strength to pull the cord down over the lock mechanism. Then he gestured for his assistant to come around and install the windlass in the socket, and the two of them took turns cranking until the bow was at full cock.

"Can I get a volunteer to hold the target?" the blacksmith asked.

"Are you nuts?" the girl who had spoken up before demanded. "I don't want to be on the same deck if you're actually going to fire that thing."

"Just a little weapons-crafting humor," Razood said. "Actually, we're going to demonstrate how to rate a crossbow for draw. Bill, hang onto this a second while I get the testbed set up. Any of you who brought your own crossbows today can check the draw after we demonstrate, and if one of you crafted a crossbow that draws even half as much as this Dollnick beauty, I'll let you take it home."

The Frunge rapidly unfolded a device that looked a little like a hammock frame crossed with a bicycle, and then together with Bill, he lifted the Dollnick crossbow into place and extended an attachment with two hooks to grab the bowstring. Next, he tied a string around the trigger, motioned for Bill to step back, and pulled. The whole testbed assembly jumped like a bucking horse, but the magnetic clamps on the anchor chains kept it from moving far. Razood leaned in and read the result off the sliding scale. "One hundred and sixty-four."

"Is that it?" a burly looking man asked in disgust. "I can draw a longbow at one-seventy."

"One-seventy whats?"

"Pounds. Were you talking metric? That would be like three-sixty."

"It's in Plizars. To convert to pounds, you multiply by, uh, Flower?" Razood asked.

"Nine point seven four," the Dollnick AI replied by way of the speakers inside the workshop area.

"Just under sixteen hundred pounds," the Frunge calculated in his head. "But I'm feeling generous, so if any of you brought a crossbow that manages seven-fifty, you win."

None of the aspiring weapons smiths attempted to claim the prize, but many of them did have crossbows they wanted tested. After finding the third one cocked and ready to fire a bolt that the owner had forgotten was loaded, Bill understood why Razood insisted on a double inspection before testing the draw.

"Were you really apprenticed to that Frunge?" a teenager asked Bill. "They're the best medieval weapons smiths in the galaxy."

"Maybe because they make apprentices pump the bellows for seven years before allowing them to swing a hammer," Bill replied. "Aren't real weapons kind of overkill for a costume?"

"I'm in the junior LARPing league and we use real weapons when it's a raid against NPCs."

"NP whats?"

"Non-player characters. They're actually just bots wrapped in holograms so there's something solid to hit, but when we compete against real players, we have to use noodle weapons."

"I've heard of those," Bill said. "They're rigid when they contact another weapon but they flop like a wet noodle if they hit clothes or skin. But wait a second. What's to keep a bot wielding a real weapon from killing a player?"

"The league's Live Action Role Playing studios are all on Stryx stations," the teen explained. "The local station librarian controls all of the bots. If they can use a bot to do neurosurgery, they can manage a sword fight without killing anybody. Besides, somebody told me that the NPC weapons are all dull."

"Not terribly sporting, beating up on poor bots who are only armed with dull weapons," a familiar voice joined the discussion.

"Dewey," Bill greeted the AI. "Did you come to help with the workshop?"

"I don't know a thing about medieval weapons," Dewey said. "If I'm ever forced to fight, I'll go with a plasma blaster or something a little more modern. I'm here because Flower's paying me to be the official con photographer."

"But where's your camera?"

Dewey raised and lowered the mast carrying the binocular cameras that served as his eyes.

"I forgot you could do that," Bill said. "But why didn't Flower just use her own imaging?"

"Most of it is infrared, and the maintenance bot optics aren't optimized for still images," Dewey explained. He hesitated a moment, and then added, "She said something about how I should take advantage of the opportunity to study the human form for in case I decide to purchase a body and become an artificial person."

"Are you really considering it?"

"You won't laugh?"

"You're my friend, Dewey. I won't laugh at you."

"Lynx put me in touch with the artificial people she knows on Union Station, and, well, the local broker is having a sale."

"A sale on artificial person bodies?"

"Specifically the core bipedal platform humanoid models. I'm thinking of buying one, and if I don't like the face, I'll take my time to think about it before ordering a custom overlay."

"You mean the skin is sold separately?"

"Unless I stick with the off-the-shelf model, but then there could be other artificial people walking around somewhere who look just like me," Dewey said.

"You know, it works that way with people too," Bill pointed out. "Back on Earth, there was a kid in my neighborhood that people kept confusing with me, and he was always in trouble."

"I'll keep that in mind," the assistant librarian said.

"Bill, could you give me a hand with this ballista?" Razood called to him. "I should have specified that we would only be testing crossbows with tension prods, but the siege team from Bits dragged a torsion arm thrower all the way here from their workshop, so the least we can do is try."

The rest of the session was spent testing a bizarre array of bolt-launching devices, with the Frunge blacksmith providing the makers with pointers about design features that various aliens had developed or abandoned millions of years earlier during their own early fumbling with weapons. Razood kept Bill busy right up until they both had to run for the theatre to prepare for the *Everyday Superheroes* shoot.

Flower concealed the audience behind a holographic projection of an empty theatre, and the Grenouthian director omitted reminding Julie and Bill that they were performing live. Miraculously, both the scaffolding and preliminary voiceover work for the half-hour episode were completed in just over a hundred minutes, at which point Flower dropped the hologram and the audio suppression field, revealing a packed house of cheering fans.

"Someday I'm going to find out where you live and kill you," Julie subvoced to the Dollnick ship's AI.

"You see? You're developing a flair for dramatics," Flower replied over her implant. "Now take a group bow with the others and then meet your public."

A dozen maintenance bots carrying folding tables and chairs streamed onto the stage behind the actors, who lined up for the obligatory hand-holding bow. Then the

Grenouthian director's voice was routed to the public address system, inviting the audience to meet the cast. People began forming a long line in the aisles, and Julie and Bill found themselves shepherded to the tables by the other actors who refused to let them flee. The bots had also placed a number of felt-tipped markers at each seat, all of them printed with, "Vote for Larry, Phil's son."

"How much are we charging?" Jorb asked the others as they took their seats behind the tables.

"What are you talking about?" Harry asked the Drazen.

"For autographs. We should decide on a price and not undercut each other."

"One cred is fine by me," Avisia said. "But if any more young men ask me to sign their body parts, it's ten creds."

"Did that really happen?" Julie asked the Vergallian, whose Battle Royale costume did nothing to conceal her curvaceous figure.

"More than once," Avisia said. "It's better than catching them sniffing my shoes."

"You can charge for autographs and posing for selfies another time," the Grenouthian director told them. "You're all still on the clock as principal animation actors for the next half hour and Flower advertised this event as gratis."

"We really need to join that union," Julie muttered to Bill, who nodded in agreement as the first fans reached the tables.

"Could you sign my tab?" a young woman asked Harry, holding out the device with the screen side down.

"I'd be honored," he said and scrawled his name.

She inspected the signature and her smile dropped. "Who's Harry Bloom?"

"There's an eraser on the other end," Dave whispered to the retired baker. "I think they want our char names."

"Sorry," Harry said, taking back the tablet. He flipped the marker around and erased his signature. Then he slowly wrote "Gerryman," being careful not to leave out any letters. The young fan beamed at him before moving on to the next actor.

"Tell them about the opportunities for anime production on board," Flower encouraged Bill over his implant.

"Who should I make this out to?" he asked the woman who had passed him an autograph book to sign.

"You mean you'll write more than your name? I'm Darla."

"To Darla," Bill said out loud as he wrote. "Have you ever considered working in the field of anime production? Ask our ship's AI about available opportunities. Digger."

"And we have open positions in animation and scriptwriting," the Grenouthian director was telling a couple who were dressed as bunnies as he signed the smooth spot on the back of the wrists of their costumes. "If you brought any examples of work you want to show me, I'll certainly look at them as well."

Sixteen

Julie forced her way between the two groups of feuding women and brandished her management badge at anybody who looked her direction. She channeled her Refill character's waitress-taking-control voice and ordered, "All right, break it up. Just step away from each other and act your age. Now somebody tell me what the problem is."

"Isn't it obvious," a middle-aged woman in an ankle-length dark dress with long sleeves and a black bonnet demanded. "Just look at them!" She pointed dramatically at the opposing group of women, who were dressed in revealing silk wraps that left most of their skin showing. "It's scandalous. The only reason they could possibly have for attending our session is to provoke us."

"Which panel is it?" Julie asked.

"Amish Romance," the woman replied, at the same time that one of the scantily-clad women said, "Alien Abduction Romance."

"It appears that there must be an error in the program," Julie said. "Please wait a moment while I check." She pointed at her ear and subvoced, "Flower? Can you get me Yaem?"

"What's wrong now?" the Sharf's voice inquired in her head. "My hands are full here trying to deal with some clown who brought an organ to a Filk session."

"Organs aren't allowed?"

"Fairground pipe organs aren't. Apparently he borrowed it from a Libbyland attraction on Union Station. It runs on steam."

"Oh. Well, I have two groups of fans waiting for the door to open for a session that starts in a few minutes. One group thinks the panel will be discussing Amish Romance, and the other group is here for Alien Abduction Romance."

"So what's the problem?" Yaem asked. "We agreed not to have a dozen romance sessions running at the same time to cut down on room-hopping, and both genres came at the start of your alphabet. It's about time that Humans learn how to share."

"But the two types of romance are as incompatible as you could possibly get!"

"It's really not my thing," the Sharf said. "Check with Bianca. I have to—Do not fire that boiler!" The connection broke off.

Julie managed a nervous smile at the waiting women. "I'll just try somebody else." She pointed at her ear again and subvoced, "Flower? Can you get me, Bianca?"

"I'm right behind you," Bianca said in her ear. She stepped past Julie and inspected the opposing groups with amusement. "I see that our alien program director has played a little joke on all of us. I imagine that you," she gestured at the conservatively dressed women, "are here to see Marcy Planter, Judith Wood, and Melody Sawyer, while you," she turned to the other group, "came for Alyssa Steel, Xena Star, and Venus the Fifth."

"You're Bianca D'Arc," one of the scantily-clad women gushed. "I love your new gryphon shifter book."

"I read that one too," one of the dark-bonneted women said, ignoring the scowls of her neighbors. "When is the next one coming out?"

"You can save your questions for inside because I'll be moderating this panel," Bianca said. "Unfortunately, we had a late cancellation from Venus due to the side effects of accidental ethanol poisoning—"

"She's too hung over," Geoffrey said, stepping up beside Bianca. "I'll be filling in."

"Who are you?" one of the women demanded.

"Geoffrey Harstang," he introduced himself, receiving blank looks in return.

"He was the model for the Abraham character in *Mercenary Hearts,*" Bianca told them, and a number of the older women nodded in recognition. "Is it time yet, Julie?"

"Flower has taken to keeping the door locked until everybody who was in the last session has had a chance to leave through the exit on the other side," Julie said. "Is it true that at regular cons everybody tries to leave and enter through the same door at the same time?"

"Pretty much," Geoffrey said. "Flower is nothing if not innovative."

There was an audible click, and the door opened on a largely empty room, though a few women from the last session were apparently interested in seeing how the Amish versus Alien Abduction panel would play out.

"Where are all of the other panelists?" Julie asked the two authors, as the audience filed into the room and segregated themselves into ankle skirts on the left, more skin than cloth to the right.

"No doubt they're running late," Bianca said. "Whatever possessed Flower to put massaging recliners in the Green Room and have bots circulating with gourmet chocolates? I stopped in before my first session and I was tempted to just stay there the rest of the day myself."

"When I was a small boy my father told me that schools and houses of worship on Earth used to paint bathrooms a nasty green color so that people wouldn't be tempted to dawdle," Geoffrey said. "I used to wonder if the green-room moniker really derived from that or from the green lights used for directing traffic. Then I did some research and apparently it came from a famous old theatre in London where the waiting room for actors happened to be green. In any case, it sounds like management may have misunderstood the concept."

"Flower?" Julie subvoced.

"I heard," the Dollnick AI replied. "You can't expect me to get everything right on my first outing and I'm waking the authors up now. The champagne was probably overkill, but they requested it."

"Flower is waking them up," Julie reported. "She served them champagne and they're going to be late."

"I have an idea," Bianca said. "Why don't you take my place as moderator until they get here and ask the two of us questions? It's better than just making everybody wait."

"She has a point," Geoffrey said. "They're probably going to need a coffee before they're ready to face an audience. Besides, from what I heard about your performance last night, it sounds like you're over your stage shyness."

"Flower hid the audience with a hologram," Julie muttered, but she took the center chair that Geoffrey indicated and pitched her voice to reach the back row. "MultiCon apologizes for the mix-up today, and your scheduled panelists will be here as soon as possible. In the meantime,

I'm going to ask Geoffrey and Bianca a couple of questions, and then we'll open it to the audience."

"Aren't you going to do introductions?" one of the women in the audience demanded.

"We covered that in the corridor, but I'm the seventh in the D'Arc line, and he's the one-and-only Harstang," Bianca said. "Most of you know my books, but the closest he's ever come to writing a romance was the time that a scout pilot in his *Galactic War College* series crashed on an alien planet and—do you want to tell them, Geoffrey?"

"I'd rather not," the older author said. "Writing male leads for men and writing male leads for women are two different things."

"Can you elaborate on that?" Julie surprised herself by asking.

"Well, men who read action science fiction don't want to hear about their hero's inner thoughts on intimate relationships, and when it comes to sex, quality takes a back seat to quantity."

There were giggles from the Alien Abduction fans and clucks of disapproval from the Amish readers.

Julie turned to the other author. "I finished your gryphon shifter book last night, Bianca, and I could barely breathe during the mating flight. How do you write a scene like that without being able to fly yourself?"

"Ah, there's a story behind that, actually. A few years, well, more like two decades ago, for a tenth-anniversary present, my parents babysat the kids and sent us on a weeklong vacation to a lunar resort. The hotel had atmosphere retention fields installed over a surprising number of craters, and they rented them out privately, along with Frunge wing sets. My ex-husband and I decided to splurge, and all I'm going to say is that it was memorable enough to make writing the gryphon mating scene a snap."

Julie saw a number of women on both sides of the center aisle surreptitiously getting out their tabs and swiping menus, though where the Alien Abduction fans could possibly have hidden the devices was beyond her. For a moment she worried they had lost interest, but then she caught an image of a gryphon in flight on one of the tabs as a woman showed it to her neighbor, and she realized they were all ordering Bianca's book.

"I believe I heard that you've started on a new book after a ten-year hiatus," Julie said to Geoffrey. "Can you share any details?"

"I'm embarrassed to tell you it's actually closer to twenty years," the author said. "Before my unplanned retreat from civilization, I'd been struggling to keep myself motivated, and most of my work was for anime or the immersives, often uncredited. You see, I'd been writing military science fiction for over three decades, and at some point, I began to question whether the galaxy really needed another book about the last survivors of an alien invasion escaping on an obsolete battleship and overcoming enemies who underestimate the plucky humans."

"Oh, I didn't realize it was so formulaic," Julie said. "So what are you writing now?"

"I don't want to give the whole plot away, but it starts with a retired captain from Earth's fleet escaping from the insane asylum where he's been involuntarily committed after uncovering a plot by corrupt politicians to divert military funding for personal use. He smuggles himself back into space on board a—let's just say he ends up with a crew of misfits and they manage to steal a mothballed destroyer and set about saving the universe."

"That's not a bad setup," Bianca said. "Sixth told me that you had a way with recycling your personal misfortunes into plots."

"This is a work of pure fiction," Geoffrey deadpanned. "Any resemblance to actual events or persons, whether living or deceased, is purely coincidental."

Both authors laughed, and most of the audience joined in on hearing the disclaimer they were all used to seeing, at least in printed novels.

"The funny thing is, fiction disclaimers really have no legal purpose," Bianca said. "If a person who the author has written about can prove libel, which is the written form of slander, a few sentences at the start of a book claiming that the characters are inventions isn't going to hold up in court."

"What about violation of privacy?" Julie asked.

"I don't think there is a right to privacy in the sense that you're thinking. Defamation of character, which encompasses both slander and libel, doesn't just require that a character in a book be identifiable as a real individual. The author has to write something nasty about the person that is both demonstrably false and could be mistaken for the truth."

"Can you give us an example?"

"Well, let's use Geoffrey, since he's the only man in the room," Bianca said with a wicked grin. "Say I write a novel about an old curmudgeon who had a long career writing science fiction before disappearing from the scene for a decade, and in my story, the character is also a plagiarist who steals all of his books from aspiring writers who seek his opinion on unpublished works. Even if I changed his name and physical description, if it was obvious I was writing about Geoffrey, he could sue me for libel."

"And Bianca would hire a good lawyer who could keep the case tied up in court longer than I'm going to live, so I wouldn't bother," Geoffrey interjected.

"But if instead of having my character doing something plausible, I wrote about him having a thousand wives on a hundred planets, he couldn't sue because nobody in their right mind would believe it was true."

"So you're saying that an author actually has to harm a person in some way, beyond just stealing details of their life," Julie summarized.

"I'm not a lawyer, but that's pretty much my understanding," Bianca said. "Otherwise, successful authors would spend more time sitting in court than writing. All that said, it would be incredibly lazy of an author to simply use friends and family as characters without at least changing enough details to make them unidentifiable."

"Changing the species of a character based on a person is a pretty good safeguard against getting sued," Geoffrey added.

"That's right, though a friend of mine once accused me of borrowing his personality for the witch's familiar in our—"

"*Witches Who Love Vampires* series," one of the scantily clad women call out. "You're talking about Percy the Cat, aren't you?"

"Guilty as charged," Bianca said. "Any progress on our missing panelists, Julie? Shall we just open up to questions from the floor?"

"Ooh, yes," a number of voices chorused.

Julie pointed to her ear. "Flower?"

"They won't get out of the massaging recliners," the Dollnick AI reported, sounding not a little frustrated. "I don't want to send my maintenance bots to pry them away because it sets a bad precedent."

"Have you tried cutting off the power?"

There was a brief pause. "They still aren't moving. I think some of them have fallen asleep again."

"Maybe we could just reschedule the panel and break it into two sessions," Julie suggested. "And I'm sure if you sent some of those Green Room chocolates this way it would make up for any disappointment."

"Good idea. I obviously can't keep the chocolates here," Flower replied.

Julie waited for Bianca to finish answering a question about positive reinforcement conditioning in her gryphon book, and the author's click-training story was even funnier the second time around.

"So here's the update," Julie told the audience. "We're going to reschedule the Amish Romance and Alien Abduction Romance sessions separately, and the ship's AI is sending a bot with a special treat to apologize for the confusion. But we do have this room for another forty minutes, so if you want to stay and ask questions…"

"I have a question," a familiar voice said, and Julie gaped as the head librarian stood up, dressed in an Amish outfit.

"You read romance?" Julie couldn't help asking.

"On paper, never on screens," Bea answered in a dignified manner. "And only when the books are set in farming communities or the Scottish Highlands. I have my standards."

"Oh. And what's your question?"

"It's for Bianca. In number two hundred and thirteen of the jaguar shifters series, Noble Pack goes to war with Mountain Pack, and Esmeralda is forced to cancel her engagement with Mario. But in number two hundred and sixteen, she tells Choa that she's never really been in love."

"Wait a second, Bianca," Julie said. "What do jaguar shifters have to do with Scotland or farming, Bea?"

"Did you think that all of those drugs the Mountain Pack traffics just appear out of thin air?" the librarian countered. "I read the books for all of the useful information about coca farming."

"I like to get the details right, but I wouldn't suggest that anybody try to set up a drug cartel based on my descriptions," Bianca cautioned the audience. "Besides, the Mountain Pack shifters are definitely the bad guys. As to Esmeralda's engagement, she was only interested in Mario as a way to get away from Scar, the old leader of the Noble Pack who had his luminescent green eyes on her, despite the distinct possibility that he was her great-great-grandfather."

"You're right," Bea said, suppressing a shudder at the possibility of the relationship. "As I get older, I can't remember more than twenty or thirty books back in any series. How do you keep from making continuity errors?"

"With great difficulty," Bianca said. "Is anybody else interested in hearing about the perils of being a line author?"

Every hand except Geoffrey's shot up, and Julie distinctly heard him mumble, "There goes the rest of the session," but his voice didn't carry past her.

"All right. Just for background, you should all know that I'm the seventh in the D'Arc line. If any of you are familiar with our backlist, you'll notice that I don't try to keep every old series alive, though my eventual successor will probably choose one of those to revive just to put some separation between us. I mainly focus on the jaguar and bear shifters because those were always my favorites, so I've read the entire corpus, but I'll let you in on a little secret. I always do a continuity pass on my old teacher bot before—"

"What?!" several voices interrupted.

"Yes. Not many people realize it, but the same teacher bots supplied by the Stryx when they royally interfered with Earth's education infrastructure also have a spelling and grammar checker that's intended to help young people develop writing skills. If you dig down into the menus, there's an option to chain text files together—

"I've seen that," another woman said.

"Yes, and if you chain a number of files together in sequential order you can request a continuity check," Bianca explained. "It doesn't happen immediately, so the service is related in some way to the updates that get pushed to the teacher bots over the Stryxnet once a day, the same way students can get questions answered. Sixth actually told me about this, and she got the idea from Fifth, so it's been around for quite a while. It does a phenomenal job catching contradictions, but my super-fans are better at telling me when I remember something that's not there."

"What do you mean by that?" Julie asked.

"I send my pre-release manuscripts to a group of super-fans who call themselves the Dark Shifters, a word-play on D'Arc. They know my style so well that they'll catch me if I bring back a character who I think has already been introduced in the series I'm writing on, but who is actually from a different series, or somebody I've never written about."

"You mean, you could have a character enter the action without explaining how he got there because you mistakenly think that he was in a previous book?"

"Bingo. Once I solved a tricky plot by having Elizabeth's older brother show up and give her just the artifact she needed to overcome a curse and revert to human form after she got stuck as a bear. Well, several Dark Shifters pointed out that I must have been thinking about Richard, the older brother in…"

"*Runes of Time*," a woman on the underdressed side called out. "He was an artifact hunter, and he had a younger sister, Liz."

"So you can see how I could get confused, but my super-fans were right on it."

"I thought that teacher bots were only available to children," a woman from the Amish-fan section spoke up.

"I looked into it once," Geoffrey said, jumping on the chance to finally insert himself into the discussion. "Teacher bots are actually available to everybody with an interest in learning, and a number of the alien manufacturers make them for humans under a license from the Stryx, who subsidize the cost. I think as far as the Stryx are concerned, we're all children, at least in terms of our educational achievements. But the bots don't teach anything that we haven't already learned for ourselves as a species."

"How does that explain their ability to do continuity checking on a multi-hundred book series?" Bianca asked him. "I always get the results back the next day, so I can't imagine that the teacher bot is contacting a remote supervisor who sits down and reads them all."

"Somebody once told me that all of the teacher bots are a project of one of the Stryx librarians, so I guess when they call home for help, there's a near-omniscient AI answering the questions that aren't appropriate for the local support network of other users."

"Does that mean a Stryx somewhere has read all of my books?" Bianca looked disturbed. "I don't know if I should feel complimented or scared."

Seventeen

"You're working too hard," Harry admonished his wife while delivering the cup of tea she had requested. "How long have you been on your feet?"

"Just since breakfast," Irene said, and took a grateful sip from the tea. "Compared to the holiday rushes we used to experience at our bakery back on Earth, this is nothing. It's not like we've been retired for that long."

"No, it's not like we've been retired at all, seeing how Flower put us both to work."

"You're working, I'm volunteering," she corrected him. "And speaking of the bakery business, how is the pastry supply holding up?"

Harry glanced back toward the dessert buffet he had just come from while fetching his wife's tea. "All present and accounted for. We could have used a couple of those four-armed bots in the shop back on Earth. One for the counter and one for the kitchen would have done the job nicely."

A woman pushing a rollator spotted Irene's volunteer smock and used Harry's foot as a chock to halt her forward progress. "Excuse me," she said. "Is this the hospitality room for ElderCon?"

"Yes, it is," Irene replied with a bright smile. "It's also the common room for Flower's Paradise, where some of us take our meals, attend lectures, knitting circles, and enjoy all sorts of community activities. Are you interested in the independent living cooperative?"

"My smart badge keeps on nagging me about it so I thought I'd take a look," the woman said. "It doesn't seem like a large enough room to feed the number of retirees I was told live on this deck. Do you have to eat in shifts?"

"Flower's Paradise has a full cafeteria that seats over five hundred, and there are three other independent living cooperatives on this deck, all with their own facilities. But when we started a year ago with just a few dozen members, some of us got into the habit of eating in this room, and Flower is very flexible about such things."

"Doesn't sound like any independent living place I've ever lived in," the woman said skeptically. She lowered her voice and asked, "Do you also have people living here who are..." she let go of the grips with one hand and made a swirling motion around her ear with an index finger.

"Cuckoo?" Irene guessed. "Why do you ask?"

"When I got off the elevator, somebody dressed as a giant insect tried to give me a piece of paper," she said. "Of course, I ignored him."

"That's Dave," Harry told her. "He's not crazy, just a good salesman. He's passing out flyers for M793qK, the Farling doctor. Do you know what the special is today, Irene?"

"It's either same-day hip replacements or a central nervous system cleanse with myelin replenishment," his wife said. "The doctor has been trying different promotions for conditions that are common in our age group. He took over one of the small classrooms down the corridor to set up a field clinic for the duration of ElderCon."

The woman stood up a little straighter between the handles of her rollator. "Do you think he could do something about these?" she asked, indicating her legs with a bob of her chin.

"I don't want to make any promises, but he does consider human biology to be trivial," Irene said. "I haven't heard of much he can't fix, other than old age itself, and some people say that's only because we aren't mature enough as a species to deal with longer lives."

As the woman backed her rollator off of Harry's foot and turned it in the direction of the classroom, Irene added, "When you pass the man in the costume, grab a flyer for a discount. And don't be startled when you meet the doctor. Farlings look rather like giant beetles, and M793qK is on the large side."

A cheerful ding sounded over the public address system, and Nancy's voice announced, "The next presentation about retiring to Flower's Paradise will begin in five minutes in our common room. If you are already here, please take a Danish and a hot drink and find yourself a seat."

"I guess I should get ready," Harry said. "When I got drafted for the board, nobody told me that I'd be attending so many meet-and-greets. And all of the men keep coming up to me and asking where I got the sword cane I use on *Everyday Superheroes*. Who knew that people our age even watch anime?"

"At least Jack and Nancy only asked you to be here for two sessions a day, compared to the six that they're doing," Irene said. "With Maureen and Brenda taking turns in the rotation with you, it spreads the load across the board members."

"Dave is on the board and he's a much better salesman than I ever was."

"It's too much work for him to get in and out of the costume," Irene said and turned to answer a question for a couple who had just arrived. Harry slipped away and joined Nancy and Jack, the latter being an athletic man retired from a Dollnick ag world who served as the cooperative's president.

"How are we doing for numbers?" Harry asked.

"Maureen said that our close rate was almost twenty percent, and if that holds up, we'll double the size of the cooperative before the con is over," Nancy told him. "I wish I could claim that it's all a result of our brilliant programming, but it's pretty clear that the pricing is what closes the deal for most people. Judging by the reactions, I'll bet we see at least an additional ten percent of our guests making the move to Flower in the next year or so, but they have to get out of their current situation first."

"What's so hard about packing up and moving?" Harry asked. "It's not like living on Flower takes us out of touch with our families, and there's something to be said for distance making the heart grow fonder."

"A lot of the independent living facilities on Earth are set up like condos, so people have to sell their unit to recover their investment when they leave. In some cases, if you stay there until you pass on, the facility commits to buying back the unit for ninety percent of the original purchase price, but that's hardly what I'd call a good deal in the real estate business."

"We changed our presentation this morning and it worked well for the first two sessions so we're going to stick with it," Jack told Harry. "Rather than each of us talking for five minutes, we'll just do a brief intro while taking questions, and then break everybody into little groups so they can talk to cooperative members one-on-

one. We had so many volunteers this morning that we've had to turn some away."

"It's probably the pastries," Harry said. "I get the feeling that Flower is cheating on everybody's dietary plans for the duration of the con."

"Do you want me to introduce you as the genius behind Harry's Fruitcakes or as the geriatric fighter on *Everyday Superheroes*?"

"Please stick with the baking," Harry said. "I'm planning to hang up my sword cane as soon as they can write me out of the plot. I never get any good lines, and there's no chance I'm ever going to defeat the evil Farling mastermind."

Nancy looked over towards Irene, who gave her the thumbs up. "No stragglers in the corridor," Nancy told her husband. "Do you want to begin?"

Jack stood up and gave the piercing whistle he had learned while working for the Dollnicks, a handy technique for calling any assembly to order, even when it included the hard-of-hearing. "Thank you for coming to our presentation about living and working in Flower's Paradise," he began. "Please feel free to ask questions at any time. I want to make clear right at the start that even though this is a retirement community with a minimum age limit, the majority of our members find themselves working part-time, and everybody on board Flower is subject to a volunteering requirement."

"So are you running this place, or is it really the ship's AI in charge?" demanded a man who was either dressed as a pirate or who had lost an eye and was unwilling to accept an alien prosthetic.

"The board of Flower's Paradise is in charge of vetting membership applications, programming activities, and managing the cooperative, which is ultimately a self-governing entity with regular town meetings," Jack explained. "Flower is our landlord, and she works closely with the ship's crew in the matter of scheduling our stops and required activities."

"So the ship is going to keep waking us up every morning and insisting that we stand out in the corridor and stretch?"

"In a word, yes."

There was the sound of chairs scraping back and about a third of the people stalked or shuffled out of the common room, depending on their physical condition. Jack waited patiently until the noise died down and then turned back to the audience.

"I suppose I could have put that a little more diplomatically," he continued, "but the truth is, we've been getting more applicants than we can process lately. I'd rather winnow out the field before we talk pricing, because at least two dozen of you will decide to stay on board for that reason alone, whether or not independent living suits you."

"Do you mean that retirees on a fixed income can afford to rent apartments on Flower, just like the younger residents?" a woman asked.

"While most of the adults on board are indeed working full time, relatively few of them work directly for Flower, though that number has been rising with her recent forays into entertainment and packaged foods. There is a minor pricing advantage to living in the cooperative because we rent in bulk and are good customers for add-ons like food service, laundry, and cleaning."

"But you're saying that rather than committing to joining your cooperative, we could just rent an apartment on the main residential deck?"

"Of course, but what makes the cooperative special are the activities and social opportunities. My wife, Nancy, who I met after moving to Flower's Paradise, coordinates our educational programs, and we also have multiple group activities going on every day, including music and dance classes. We aren't here to sell you on the concept of joining an age-restricted independent living cooperative, just to present ourselves as an option. And for the record, there's no commitment beyond your first and last month's rent."

"Will our children be able to visit us here?" a different woman asked.

"Absolutely. We maintain a number of guest cabins just on the other side of this common room, but most visitors prefer to stay on one of the outer decks where they weigh approximately the same as on Earth. I suspect the ship's AI informed you all before you exited the lift tube that your weight on the independent living deck is a heart-healthy eighty percent of Earth normal, which is why the independent living cooperatives are located here rather than further out from the core."

"Do we have to pay extra for visiting other parts of the ship if we join?" a serious-looking man asked.

"No, and while I know you're going to find this hard to believe, the included meal plan is a la carte. I think everybody living in the cooperative takes the majority of their meals either here in the common room or in our main cafeteria, but if you prefer to prepare food in your cabin or eat out at any of the hundreds of restaurants on board,

Flower refunds the price of every meal you skip from your monthly plan."

There were cries of disbelief from the audience, and a number of arguments immediately began between those who suspected they were being sold a bill of goods and others who assumed that Jack was having a senior moment.

"So do we have to save all our receipts to turn them in?" somebody in the front asked after the initial hubbub finally died down.

"That's not necessary. While we don't live under the sort of full surveillance society you find on Stryx stations, Flower does keep track of our locations through a combination of thermal imaging and voice recognition. If nobody has pointed it out to you yet, as long as there isn't a great deal of background noise and you aren't worried about privacy, you can speak directly to the ship's AI and she'll answer via the nearest speaker. In addition, our meals are served by the ship's bots, and they have built-in imaging capabilities that allow Flower to recognize everybody by name."

"You're saying that if we don't show up for meals, we don't pay, and there aren't any penalties or repercussions?"

"We're not living in an adversarial relationship with Flower," Nancy said. "Rather the opposite. She appears to be more interested in filling cabins than earning a profit, which is why the prices are what they are."

After a few more incredulous questions about costs, Nancy gave a brief rundown of the current classes and group activities, and then Jack introduced Harry, asking him to talk a little about working on board.

"I don't know how many of you have heard this story," Harry began, "but we started our independent living cooperative after a number of us lost a significant part of our savings due to a scam. Flower offered anybody who wanted to remain on board part-time work that would cover their expenses, but one way or another, I found myself working more hours than I expected, baking for aliens and creating recipes for a new packaged food business."

"There are real aliens living on board?" a woman asked. "I assumed the ones I saw were just people in costumes for the con."

"You may have been right as the population of aliens is low, but a number of them work in the bazaar or run small businesses. The doctor who set up his clinic down the corridor to offer free health screenings during ElderCon is an alien."

"You're Gerryman from *Everyday Superheroes,* aren't you?" a man asked in an accusing tone.

"I didn't think I was that recognizable," Harry muttered.

"Where'd you get the sword cane?" a number of the older men called out.

A few minutes later, Jack announced that they would be breaking into small groups for personalized tours of the deck provided by volunteers, and Geoffrey slipped out of his seat and headed for the exit.

"Not even tempted?" Irene asked him at the door.

"I only stopped in because Flower wouldn't let me hear the end of it, but I have other plans," the old science fiction author explained. "I really came because I have to see the doctor anyway."

"I hope it's nothing serious."

"Just paperwork," he assured her, and navigated his way to the Farling's temporary clinic. As Geoffrey entered through the bank of diagnostic scanners, he heard the doctor berating an elderly woman about her prescriptions.

"You asked for my advice and I'm telling you," M793qK thundered through his external translation device. "Throw them all out. Half these prescriptions interact with each other and the other half are unnecessary. Why are you taking a drug to lower your blood pressure?"

"Because it's high," the woman said stubbornly. "It's always been high."

"It's low," the doctor contradicted her. "The reason you feel dizzy is because you aren't getting enough blood to your brain. If you ever had high blood pressure, which I suspect was just a matter of defining down the criteria, you don't any longer. And you're taking both a diuretic and an anti-diuretic. Does your family own stock in a failing pharmaceutical company that you're trying to support single-handedly?"

"You don't have to shout, there's nothing wrong with my ears."

"It's what's between your ears that worries me," M793qK told her. "Are you on board for another week?"

"I'm going back Sunday."

"I'm going to keep all of these," the doctor said, sweeping her collection of prescription containers into a plastic sack, "and for each one I'm taking away, I'll give you a free supply of my own brand of placebos. Do you have a favorite pill color?"

"Blue is nice, and pale yellow."

"Blue and pale yellow." M793qK pulled a dozen pill containers off a shelf, seemingly at random, and put them in a clear bag for the patient. "The detailed instructions for taking the pills are printed on the labels, but if you get it wrong it won't impact their efficacy," he told her. "I'll see you next Monday if you have any questions."

"But I told you I'm going back Sunday."

"I'm prescribing another week on board. Flower will modify your travel arrangements. And take your oxygen cart with you. Next!"

Geoffrey stood aside as the woman minced past him with her stash of placebos. He waited to speak until she was out in the corridor. "You know, Doctor, you can catch more flies with honey."

"And what would I do with flies?" M793qK demanded. "That woman purposely left her oxygen cart behind after I cleaned the gunk out of her lungs. I know she heard me tell her to take it but she plays deaf when it suits her." He examined the author through multifaceted eyes. "Have you ever thought of taking up scuba diving? I'll make you a deal on an oxygen tank."

"I'm here because I need some forms filled out for a lawsuit back on Earth," Geoffrey said. "Flower's lawyer, Brenda, said I needed to get my patient records from you to document the condition I was in when I arrived."

"I don't keep patient records. It's not like any of you have interesting enough problems that I could publish a paper."

The author blinked. "Well, I wasn't that enthusiastic about being called to testify in court. Without a record of the cocktail of drugs that weren't fully flushed from my system I doubt we have a case."

"If it means that much to you," the Farling grumbled, and rubbed out a high pitched squeal on his speaking legs. "There. I sent a Human-style medical transcript to Flower and she'll print it for your attorneys."

"But you just said you don't keep records."

"You've been on board less than two cycles, my memory isn't that bad. If your case is still in court two millennia from now we may have a problem."

"You and me both," Geoffrey said. "And Brenda wanted you to include your degrees."

"Celsius or Fahrenheit? Not that I see what my body temperature has to do with your legal proceedings."

"Your medical degrees, to establish your credentials as an expert witness."

"Ah, credentials. I have a lot of those," M793qK said, and stared off into space as he accessed his heads-up display. "Drazen, Frunge, Horten, Dollnick, Vergallian. Humans aren't sufficiently challenging to rate your own specialty, but my Stryx certification as a large mammal veterinarian should impress the court."

"Veterinarian?"

"Right. Now can I interest you in any of my upcycled merch?" The beetle indicated a number of modified walkers and rollators parked along the wall which had obviously been abandoned by patients who no longer needed them after being treated. "I have moveable shelves, a fine folding chair with wheels if you ever find yourself working on set again, and I've modified that one on the end to hold produce when you do your marketing."

"You lashed two boards to the walker for shelves and you haven't done anything at all to the rollator that you're calling the folding chair."

"I adjusted the brakes so they're always on. There's nothing worse for older Humans than going to sit down and having the chair move away."

"No and no," Geoffrey said, passing over the first two offerings. "How does the shopping assistant work?"

"When you unfold it, these canvas sacks I added automatically open, and there's a quilted cooler section in the bottom for your cold drinks or frozen foods."

"That's actually pretty handy," the author said. He carefully crouched to examine the cooler, which turned out to have been repurposed from a transplant organ shipping bag. "I've been doing a little shopping just to have something in my cabin and I was thinking of buying a rolling basket like the old folks took to the market when I was a kid."

"This is better," M793qK said. "You've got the parking brake, it can take more weight than you could possibly push, and it's only five creds."

"Sold," Geoffrey said, forking over a coin. "I have to say—"

"No you don't," the doctor interrupted. "Next!"

Eighteen

"We must be the only people here who aren't wearing costumes," Bill said in dismay. "Do we have time to run home and get them?"

"I just assumed that the cosplay finalists would be the ones who dressed up," Julie said. "They've been running elimination rounds all day, and then there was a two-hour break before the finals. Let's just stay in the back row where nobody notices, and then I'll go change into my Refill costume before the ball."

"I'm going to the ball as a short Dollnick," Bill said. "Flower loaned me a prosthetic arm set, the kind that some people on Dollnick open worlds wear to play paddle-cup-mitt-ball. I just didn't want to carry them around any longer than necessary."

"Why not?" Flower inquired over his implant. "Four arms are better than two."

"I think it's two heads are better than one," he replied out loud, then mouthed "Flower" so Julie would know who he was talking to.

A Grenouthian hopped out onto the stage, followed by a slow-footed Verlock carrying a large bag. Although the bunny was a head taller than Bill, and Grynlan was twice as wide, they both looked like a child's exotic pets from the back row.

"I wonder if we're in the theatre with the live show or if we're looking at a holographic projection from one of the other stages," Julie said.

Bill shrugged. "Flower?"

"You can't tell the difference?" the Dollnick AI asked over both of their implants.

"Not really," Julie said. "Maybe if somebody in the audience threw something and it went right through them."

"I estimated that forty-two thousand people would attend the cosplay finals and these theatres only seat five thousand each. It was either spread the audience over all ten theatres and broadcast holograms to nine of them, or hold the event in an open area, but then the deck curvature would have been an issue."

Jorb and Rinka slipped into the back row, the latter moving carefully so that her long dress, which was reminiscent of a nun's habit, wouldn't catch on anything. Jorb was wearing some sort of military officer's uniform with his tentacle tucked down the back of his jacket, and Rinka had cleverly disguised her own tentacle as a scarf.

"Why aren't you wearing costumes?" Jorb asked.

"We didn't know," Bill said. "We'll get dressed before the ball. You guys look really human," he complimented the Drazens. "Are you competing for the prize?"

"You mean for Best Human?" Rinka asked. "We wouldn't even come close. There are always plenty of the lower-caste Vergallians who can pass as Humans without a costume, and I saw a Dollnick with a fake second head and an extra set of legs who's posing as a man giving his wife a piggyback ride."

"So the two of you just dressed for the ball early?"

"We're finalists in the classic entertainment category for skits," Jorb boasted. "Can't you tell who we are?"

"A prince and a maiden from a fairytale?" Julie guessed.

"Close," Rinka said. "Captain and Maria von Trapp. We're doing *The Sound of Music*."

"Your 'Doe, a Dollnick' song?"

The Drazen girl nodded. "I taught Jorb to harmonize. He's really not that tone-deaf for a male."

"And don't forget I'm treating everybody to a LARP on Union Station before we depart in two days," Jorb said. Then the lights in the theatre dimmed somewhat, though not to the point that they couldn't see their neighbors. The audience quieted down, and a spotlight came up on the masters of ceremony.

"Welcome to the first MultiCon cosplay contest," the large bunny announced. "I'm Grynlan."

"I'm the Grenouthian," the Verlock said ponderously.

"So we're starting with the awards for Best Grenouthian and Best Verlock, and obviously, the two of us are the winners," the Grenouthian said. "I want to—"

"I demand a reveal," somebody in the audience shouted. "You're not in costume at all. You're just lying about which one of you is which to steal the prize!"

The Grenouthian motioned to the Verlock, who shuffled up close so the bunny could dip his paw in the paper bag. It came out holding a ripe tomato. "Any more objections?" the Grenouthian inquired in a steely voice. "Then I just want to say how it warms my heart to see so many Humans aspiring to be something better."

"Like other species," the Verlock put in.

"Right. Or at least displaying a little more fashion sense than usual. We'll run through the rest of the Best Species awards quickly and then get to the character cosplay that I'm sure you've all been waiting for. The award for Best Farling goes to Dave, from Flower's Paradise."

Dave waddled out onto the stage in his beetle costume and accepted a tomato from the Verlock. He showed off how all of his limbs worked by waving to the audience and then waddled back off.

"Impressive multi-faceted eyes," Grynlan observed.

"Yes, amazing what Humans can do with too much time and money. Next up is Best Drazen, and the winner is Vivian, from Union Station.

An attractive Drazen walked onto the stage, waving to the audience with both of her six-fingered hands, and she accepted the tomato from the Verlock using her prosthetic tentacle. The audience gave her a big round of applause.

"I can't believe how good she's gotten with that tentacle," Jorb said. "We'll have to meet up later."

"You know her?" Bill asked. "Is she really a Drazen pretending to be a human in disguise?"

"No, she's a friend from Union Station, and she's the most connected Human I know. Her mother is a co-owner in InstaSitter and helped subsidize Flower. Vivian's father runs EarthCent Intelligence, her aunt owns the Galactic Free Press, and her fiancé is the EarthCent ambassador's son. A few of us always ate lunch together at the Open University, and if you ever need a ship rental while you're here, my friend Marilla is part-owner in Tunnel Trips."

"Oh, I met her with Bianca," Julie said. "She's really pretty."

"Marilla?" Rinka glared at Jorb. "Isn't that a Horten name? You were friends with a Horten woman at the Open University?"

"Did I say 'My friend?'" Jorb backtracked and began to stammer. "I meant 'Our friend,' and it wasn't like that at all. I mean, she's dating the Horten ambassador's son, and..."

"I'm just teasing, Jorb." Rinka giggled and rolled her eyes. "Males."

"Incoming ping from Bianca," Flower announced over Julie's implant.

"I'll take it," the girl subvoced, and pointed at her ear. "Bianca?"

"Flower told me where you are, and I brought somebody I want you to meet, but it looks like you might be on a date."

"Oh, you mean Bill?" Julie asked as she stood. "We just came to see what it's like—we aren't even wearing costumes. When we go to the ball together later it will be a date."

"If you're sure. We're just inside the doors at the end of your aisle."

"I don't see you." Julie squinted in the dim light past a couple of cosplayers. "Are you behind the pair of jaguars—that's you?"

"We'll be right outside."

"Bianca wants me to meet somebody," Julie excused herself, while on the stage, the Verlock awarded a tomato for the Best Frunge to a woman with what looked like a sculpted shrubbery on her head. "I'll ping you if it's going to be a while."

"Don't worry about us, but you're not getting out of our date later," Bill said. "Jorb has been teaching me how to dance."

"This I have to see," Rinka commented under her breath.

When Julie got out into the corridor, she was immediately struck by the family resemblance between the two cosplayers, or at least, their costumes. They looked as much like jaguars as people could look without being down on all fours, but one was definitely older than the other, almost like a mother and a daughter.

"That's an amazing makeup job," Julie said. "I can't even tell which of you is Bianca. Did you get it done in one of the workshops?"

"We both have a lot of practice with Horten cosmetics from decades of going to cons," the younger jaguar said, and Julie recognized Bianca's voice. "This is Sixth," she introduced the other woman.

"You mean, Bianca the Sixth?"

"Pleased to meet you," the older jaguar said, pulling in her claws as she extended a paw to shake hands. "Seventh has told me so much about you."

"She has?"

"And that you've been working with Geoffrey," the younger Bianca said. "Do you have time to grab a coffee from one of the pushcarts? There won't be any wait time with everybody in the theatres, and Sixth and I have been on our feet all day."

"Sure," Julie said. "By the way, I didn't know that everybody would be wearing costumes for the cosplay finals. I spent the day handing out prizes at the art show and taking down the unsold works to prepare them for shipping back to the artists who couldn't attend."

"Seventh told me that you have a talent for organization," the older jaguar said as they headed for the temporary food court. "I went through the art show just before you started breaking it down. I would have gotten here earlier, but I had some loose ends to tie up on Earth."

"It was my first con and Flower helped a lot," Julie told her. "And when neither of us knew, I could always ask Geoffrey or Bianca. I mean, Seventh."

The two jaguars exchanged a look, and Sixth's tail twitched. "He didn't bite your head off?"

"Geoffrey? He's a little gruff if you catch him while he's doing something, but he knows more about cons than Flower. He's too old to work full-time according to Dollnick rules, but I think he put in as many hours as me during the con, and he really helped with the addicts."

"Addicts?" Sixth asked.

"Didn't I tell you about Flower buying the contact list for ConAnon?" the younger Bianca said to her senior. "It worked out really well in the end, but some of the hard-core panel warriors got a bit high on the whole thing and needed to be talked down."

"Geoffrey brought a whole group of them to the art show and I gave them a guided tour," Julie said. "I couldn't believe how much they all knew about science fiction and fantasy characters. I thought that most of the pieces in the show were straight from the imaginations of the artists, but it turned out that half of them were fan art. There was even a collection of paintings somebody did based on one of Geoffrey's series, but he didn't say anything about it himself until one of the ConAnon crowd pointed it out."

"I'm surprised he didn't make a big deal out of it to blow his own horn," Seventh said. "Was he upset?"

"The woman who recognized the characters said something about smelling a lawsuit in the works, but Geoffrey just laughed it off and said that if somebody wanted to portray his characters in oil paint, it was an honor."

The two jaguars exchanged another look. Then the three women arrived at the band of empty tables that extended in a narrow strip all along Flower's circumference between the area that was now being cleared for the ball and the end section of the deck where the merchants and art show had been located. A young waitress in a cute bunny outfit arrived just after they sat. She hopped the final few steps to their table.

"Is the contest over already?" the girl asked. "I thought we had another hour to get ready for the rush. If you want something hot I have teabags, but we haven't even started brewing coffee yet."

"Do you have any juice?" Sixth asked.

"Fresh squeezed. We have orange, apple, grapefruit, pear, grape, lemon—"

"Apple for me."

"Regular tea," Seventh requested.

"I'll have the same," Julie said and tried not to giggle as the waitress hopped off. "I hope she doesn't try that carrying our drinks."

"Not a fan of cosplay yourself?" Sixth asked.

"I'm not sure I even knew what it was a couple of months ago. I can't get over how realistic the two of you look. If I had seen you anywhere other than at the con, I would have taken you for a species that crossed humans with cats."

"I'm just glad that zombie cosplay went out of fashion. I went to a con around forty years ago where—now that I think about it, I'd rather not."

"I took the liberty of discussing the plot we talked about with Sixth and she thought it had real potential," the younger Bianca said. "Then we got to reminiscing about how I became her understudy. I was about ten years older than you are now, but I wasn't really that much further along as a writer."

"No, what impressed me was your level-headedness and how you could be enthusiastic about the characters without getting them confused with reality," Sixth said, and turned to Julie. "I'm the last person who would tell my readers how to live, but some of the most enthusiastic ones can be a little scary, if you know what I mean. Once at a con, a group of women who fancied themselves shifters actually asked me to move to their den and become the alpha female. I excused myself to go to the bathroom and didn't look back until I was on the train home."

"I can see where that would be uncomfortable," Julie said. "Geoffrey told me a story about some ex-mercenaries who returned to Earth and tried to talk him into traveling to one of those little countries where the population really crashed after the Stryx opened Earth. They wanted to stage a coup and start an empire with him at the head."

"We were still together when that happened," Sixth said. "I can't help thinking that if they had asked him six months later he might have taken them up on the proposition."

"I've never gotten that feel from him, maybe he's just mellowed a lot as he aged," Julie said. "Have you seen him since you got here?"

"I haven't seen him in fifteen years," Sixth replied. "I spent a number of years away from Earth, and when I returned, there was a long hand-written letter from him waiting for me. It detailed his plans to buy an old country estate and convert it into a retreat for authors and artists. He invited me to join him in setting it up, and I really didn't know what to think, it was so unlike him. I, well, that's all water over the dam, but I would like to ask him what happened."

"Geoffrey was pretty wrapped up in himself when I first met him," the younger Bianca explained to Julie. "I can't really believe the change myself, and I keep waiting for him to slip up and show his true colors."

"Like now?" a man's voice inquired dryly, and the women all looked up to see Geoffrey standing there in a jacket with two extra sleeves sewn across the front in the style of humans living on open worlds who emulated their Dollnick landlords. "Flower sent me as a messenger, Julie. Your Drazen friends are two acts away from getting on stage to sing."

"I really don't want to miss that," Julie said. "Will you still be here in ten minutes?"

"I think I'd like to see it too," the current Bianca said, giving Julie a wink as she rose from her seat. "We have two teas coming, Geoffrey. You can drink them."

"We'll be back," Julie promised Sixth, and the two younger women headed for the theatre.

"You're supposed to put your arms in the top sleeves so you can still move them," the older Bianca said to Geoffrey. She watched in amusement as he gingerly sat down, being careful not to push the chair away with the backs of his legs. "You're wearing that thing like a straitjacket."

"It's symbolic. You heard about my being committed?"

"Seventh told me, though she didn't know much about the details." Bianca the Sixth examined his face and sighed. "You've finally aged, Geoffrey."

"You haven't changed a whisker," he said gallantly. "I'll bet the male jaguars won't leave you alone."

"What really happened? I got one letter from you, the best damn thing you ever wrote in your life, and then I spent years trying to hunt you down. It was as if you had vanished off the face of the Earth. In the end, I paid a very good law firm to look for you, but the best they managed was a confirmation that you were still alive and collecting your annuity. Every road of inquiry dead-ended on patient confidentiality laws and I couldn't find anybody with legal standing to get through them."

"It was Sonya's kids," the old man said sadly. "I never met them before she died and I don't know how they could have hated me so much. I guess seeing an old man talking about philanthropy when they didn't have any money of their own pushed them over the edge. Maybe they even convinced themselves that I'd be better off locked up. I've stopped second-guessing them."

"And you're not pursuing it?"

"Not with a vengeance. Flower set me up with a lawyer who is trying to recover as many of my assets as possible, mainly the old book rights, and I'm part of a lawsuit against the so-called hospital where I was locked up. I'd like to think that with the kids, it was a crime of passion, but the owners of that facility knew exactly what they were doing. Now tell me, how have you been?"

"You really have changed, Geoffrey. Twenty years ago, you wouldn't even have asked."

"The thing I can't figure out is why you were ever with me in the first place," he said. "I hope you didn't worry too much about my disappearance, but I—" he paused as the waitress in the Grenouthian costume returned and placed the juice and two teas on the table. If she was at all surprised at Julie and the younger jaguar being replaced by an old man in an improvised straitjacket, she didn't show it. "I'll get this," Geoffrey told the waitress, struggling to free one of his arms.

"You goof," Sixth said, and gave the girl a five-cred coin. "Keep the change."

"Thank you." The girl dropped the coin in her pouch and then helped Geoffrey out of his jacket, which wasn't that difficult since the front wasn't closed.

Geoffrey laughed and slipped his arms into the regular sleeves of the Dollnick-inspired jacket. "I would have had it in another second," he said. "I put it on by myself."

"Wherever did you get the idea?"

"I asked Flower to help me out with a costume so I should have expected something with four arms. The idea of wearing it as a straitjacket just came to me. Maybe I'm getting better at laughing at myself."

"It's about time." Sixth took a sip of her juice. "This really tastes fresh-squeezed. I thought the waitress was trying to be funny."

"This ship is like the Garden of Eden without the snake," Geoffrey said. "I plan to spend the rest of my life here."

"And the letter you sent me? Have you changed your mind?"

"As soon as the lawyers finish their wrangling, I'm going to assign whatever royalty stream I have left to a foundation. Depending on how much there is, I'm thinking of splitting it between creating a colony for working writers and artists on board, and giving the rest to Flower to maintain some older authors less fortunate than ourselves at one of her independent living cooperatives. You wouldn't believe how inexpensively you can live here."

"There's a difference between cheap and free. And if you give up all of your royalties, how will you pay the bills?"

"My annuity will let me live like a king on Flower." He blew on one of the steaming teas, took a tiny sip, and set it down again. "If you didn't come all the way from Earth just to go to a con, the colony has a position open for a jaguar queen."

"I write children's books now, Geoffrey. The cosplay is just for old time's sake."

"And I'm part of those old times."

"You're definitely old," she said with a sigh. "Of course, I'm old too, and after you walked out, I swore off living with mutts. But between the vision you laid out in that letter and what you said now about helping young writers, I suppose I'll have to stick around and keep you to it."

Nineteen

"Mac's Bones," Jorb instructed the lift tube and lowered his noodle-axe to the floor. "Sam and Vivian are going to loan us their LARPing gear so you guys don't have to rent, but they're both at work, so we're picking it up from his brother-in-law, who runs a ship's chandlery. If we're lucky, Kevin will even have some enchanted bags-of-holding he can let us use because Sam's sister brings them home from work."

"Enchanted bags-of-holding?" Julie asked.

"So you can pick up all kinds of loot and not get weighed down. There's a Terregram mage on board who does the magic stuff for SBJ Fashions."

"That's the same business that sponsors Colonial Jeevesburg, where Razood has his blacksmith's shop," Bill said. "I met Jeeves the first time we stopped at Union Station. He came on board Flower to audit the craftspeople and make sure they weren't just pocketing his subsidies."

The capsule door slid open and Jorb led the group out into the corridor. "Hold up," he said. "This place looks familiar but it's not the way to Mac's Bones. Don't tell me—"

"Welcome to Union Station," a voice announced from behind them, and they all turned to see a floating robot of the simplified form taken by Stryx AI during their youth. "I have a proposition for you."

"If it has anything to do with those experimental sensory deprivation pods you came up with for the educational LARPing course, forget it," Jorb said.

"You haven't even heard the proposition yet," Jeeves scolded mildly, winking the lights on his casing. "We were approached by a Drazen consortium about providing holographic services of a confidential nature. It's all very hush-hush and I just got everything ready for a beta test."

"No," Jorb said, and turned to his friends. "I took an Open University course with Sam, Vivian, and Marilla a couple of years ago. Jeeves kept putting us in these alternative realities that were more like tests than games. In the last one, we were able to keep adding abilities, like being able to fly, and without doing any work, I could suddenly understand musical notation for the first time in my life."

"You entered some sort of immersive alternative reality with that Horten girl?" Rinka demanded.

"Yes. I mean, not with her, but the four of us."

"Except the two Humans are engaged to be married."

"They weren't then," Jorb said, unconsciously tightening his grip on the noodle-axe in case he needed to defend himself from Rinka, whose tentacle was now rigid. His shoulders sagged. "If you want to do this, I guess it could be fun."

"And it pays," Jeeves informed them. "One hundred creds for a maximum of four hours of work."

"You mean we could finish quicker?" Julie asked.

"Theoretically," the young Stryx said, though he didn't sound very convincing. "It's just in here. I have sensory deprivation pods set up that will levitate your bodies so they won't feel any external contact. This only works because the four of you already have high-quality implants to provide the neural interface for stimuli. As the pods interfere with external signals, I'll let Flower know what's going on so she doesn't worry."

Bill helped Julie into her pod and then lay down in his own, while Jorb and Rinka did the same. The covers closed simultaneously, and there was a swell of orchestral music. Even though the test subjects couldn't see each other in the darkness, they were somehow aware of one another's presence. There were some strange flashes of light, a couple of clunks, and they all heard the young Stryx's voice somewhere in the background saying, "Oops. Third time's the charm."

"Huh?" Bill said, looking around. "Where are we?"

"Standing in front of your café," Flower's voice responded through the closest speaker grille. "Are you feeling all right?"

"Jeeves said that you wouldn't be able to talk to us," Julie said. "Maybe we've been teleported back, like in all those science fiction…" her voice trailed off as Bill turned her way and she saw his face. Her hands went to her own face and she stifled a scream. "What happened to my skin?"

Bill turned pale. "I think something went wrong," he said. "Jorb, tell Jeeves to let us out of here."

"It's just an illusion, don't trust your sense of touch," the Drazen reassured them. "I don't know what this LARP is intended to do, but going by the new rings on my tentacle, I think it's projecting us about fifty years into the future."

"You look almost as old as Geoffrey," Julie told Bill, her voice coming out in a whisper.

"And you must be around Bianca's age now," he said, and then hastily appended, "The younger one."

"Are the two of you really going to age this fast?" Rinka asked. "It seems so unfair."

"JB's Café," Jorb read the sign above the empty café. "That must be Julie and Bill."

"And the Singing Dojo is ours?" Rinka grabbed Jorb's elbow and pointed. "I'm almost afraid to look inside."

"Can't say I didn't warn you," Jorb said, then he squared his shoulders and strode toward the dojo.

The doors slid open and a small Drazen girl rushed out crying, "Poppa! Poppa!" She leapt in the air and thudded into Jorb's chest, wrapping her tentacle around his neck. "Borl took my gryphon doll and he won't give it back!"

"Who's Borl?" Jorb asked reflexively.

The little Drazen girl was so surprised that she stopped crying and pulled her head back to examine Jorb's face. "Borl. My older brother." She turned towards Rinka. "Momma? What's wrong with Poppa's memory?"

For a moment Rinka looked like her legs were going to fail her, but then she steeled herself and held out her arms. "Let me have her, Jorb. You better go check and see what trouble your son is getting himself into."

The little girl laughed as she was transferred from one parent to the other. "When Borl's good, he's your son," she said to Rinka. "When he's bad, he's Poppa's."

"You better check behind our counter," Julie urged Bill, as Rinka followed Jorb into the dojo. "I'm too frightened by what I might see."

"Do you think I'm going to find our kids hiding back there?" he asked and gave a nervous chuckle. "If we do have any, I hope they're living on their own by now." Still, he couldn't help hesitating as he entered the café. "Anybody here?"

A young boy, perhaps ten, popped his head up over the counter. "Dewey made me do it."

"Made you do what?"

"Eat the last piece of chocolate cake. I told him that if you and grandma wanted me to have it you would have said something."

"Dewey?" Bill called cautiously.

A devastatingly handsome man who appeared to be in his early forties came through the swinging door that led from the kitchen. He was carrying a tray of fancy pastries made from the translucent dough favored by Hortens so they could see the fillings.

"Thanks for the loan of the kitchen," the stranger said. "I'm sure you know what picky eaters the Hortens are, and I wouldn't want to start the intelligence conference off on the wrong foot." He placed the tray on the counter, ruffled the boy's hair, and then looked past Bill at Julie. "What are you staring at, Jewels?"

"Jewels?" she repeated the unexpected nickname. "Is that really you, Dewey? Did you buy a body and become an artificial person?"

"This old thing?" the AI said, framing his face with his hands. "I've had it for fifty years now. Next you're going to ask me if I'm still running the Human Empire's intelligence service."

"I have to sit down," Julie said, collapsing into a chair at one of the café's tables. "I need something to drink."

"Milk," Flower suggested via one of the overhead speaker grilles. "Why don't you bring them both a glass, Harry?"

Bill and Julie both stared at the swinging door, watching for a hundred-and-twenty-year-old man to emerge, but it was the boy who came out from behind the counter with two glasses of milk on a tray.

"Your parents named you Harry?" Bill asked.

"Mom said you insisted," Harry told him. "The same with my sister Irene. Are you really not mad about my eating the last piece of chocolate cake?"

"How could we ever be mad at you?" Julie asked, her voice choking up as her eyes began to water. "You're like a little angel."

"I hope you recorded that, Flower," the boy said to the ceiling. "I'm going to be asking you to play it back for grandma—a lot." He looked over as a Drazen boy entered the café. "Did you get it, Borl?"

"Poppa said I could go and he gave me ten creds for the rides."

"Great. See you later, Dewey. And don't you guys forget about my school play tonight." As Harry rushed out after his Drazen friend, Bill distinctly heard him say to Borl, "Grandparents. If you don't remind them all the time, they forget."

"I've got to get going too," the artificial person said. "After I finish with the Horten delegation, I've got a hot date with an artificial person who joined Flower when we stopped at Chintoo. Wish me luck."

"Good luck, Dewey," Julie and Bill chorused reflexively as he exited with the tray of Horten pastry. Then they each took a swallow of milk and stared at one another, trying to process what had just happened.

"Well, aren't you going to tell her?" Flower prompted.

"Tell her what?" Bill asked.

"Don't play dumb with me. You've been planning this for months."

"You have?" Julie asked, looking at him suspiciously.

"I don't know what she's talking about," Bill said.

"I'm going to have to ask M793qK to come by and look you both over," the Dollnick AI said. "You're acting very strange."

"Just tell us," Julie said.

"Then don't blame me for ruining the surprise. Bill always felt bad about not being able to afford a nice engagement ring when he originally proposed so he bought one for your fiftieth anniversary. Check your pockets."

Bill rooted around in his pants and came out with a small jeweler's box. He peeked inside, began to pass it to Julie, and then pulled it back.

"Did you change your mind after fifty years?" Julie asked.

"Not one bit of it," he said, getting up from his place and then going down on one knee. "Julie. I know that this is just some sort of beta test, but it will probably be another fifty years before I can afford a ring like this, and—"

"Did you fall, Bill?" interrupted a middle-aged woman dressed like a female George Washington in a Revolutionary War uniform complete with a three-cornered hat. She rushed up behind the elderly suitor and lifted him back onto his feet. Then she did a double-take at the jeweler's box. "Is it your fiftieth anniversary already? Flower told me she was planning a surprise party and—damn, I just did it again, didn't I?"

"Em?" Julie asked. "Lynx's little Em? And you're still wearing those purple glasses the Farling doctor gave you?"

"You know that I dug them out to wear last year when I became captain and found out that children were afraid of my uniform. The eyeglasses soften the whole effect, and it drives Flower crazy that I wear them," she added with a chuckle. "Hey, as long as I've already ruined your special moment, I'm dying for a coffee."

"I'll get it," Bill said, pocketing the jeweler's box and moving around the counter. "Julie probably wants a little time to think it over in any case."

"Think what over?" Em asked. "The two of you are acting strange. And why is this place so empty? Did young Harry switch the sugar for the salt again?"

"We, uh, do you remember the last fifty years?" Julie asked her.

"Are you trying to get rid of me? Better make that coffee to go, Bill. I think your wife has been reading too many of her own time-travel romances. I'm boycotting D'Arc books until she gets back to the gryphon shifters."

"I'm just trying to figure out how real this is," Julie protested, but Bill had already brought the coffee in a takeout cup. "Wait. Are you saying that I became the eighth Bianca D'Arc and I'm still writing?"

"Okay, you got me," the captain said, giving them both a wink. "I hope I still have a sense of humor when I get to be your age." She brushed past Jorb and Rinka as they entered the café together.

"Jeeves tricked us," Jorb said immediately. "It's our second level test."

"Is that like an Open University thing?" Bill asked. "I haven't even finished my remedial preparation course yet."

"You're preparing for university?" Julie asked.

"I was going to tell you if I passed the entrance exam."

"Not a test for you, a test for us," Jorb said. "It's our second level compatibility test, and that Drazen consortium Jeeves mentioned has to be the one in which my family are the majority stakeholders. They must have spent a ton of creds to get Jeeves to interfere in our courtship."

"But all of this—it's too real," Julie said. "Do the Drazens have this level of technology?"

"We don't," Rinka told her. "A standard second-level compatibility test involves a long period of fasting and meditation, followed by hallucinogenic drugs and hypnosis. The whole family on both sides has to fill out endless questionnaires so that the professional surrogates can act the required parts. It's half-scripted, half-improvisational theatre."

"You look pretty happy about it," Bill observed. "I don't remember seeing you holding hands like that before."

"We passed," Jorb said. "My family will probably disown me for finding my own match, but I never wanted to join the consortium anyway."

"Just ten more years now and Jorb can officially propose," Rinka said happily. "I don't know what I'm going to wear."

"Ten years!" Julie and Bill said together.

"That's the minimum wait. Besides, now that I've had the experience of actually being a parent for a few minutes, I know how much preparing I have to do. Ten years is barely enough time to study up."

"So while we were meeting future versions of people we know, you were taking a test?" Bill asked.

"Meeting people is the test," Jorb told them. "Once I figured out what was going on, I said to Rinka, 'This is the future I want for us.'"

"And I said, 'This is the only future I will accept,' and everything on our side of the corridor just faded away," Rinka explained. "A voice told us we passed and to come and get you."

"This is the future I want for us too, Julie," Bill said, and he dug the jeweler's box out of his pocket again.

"It's a good future," Julie agreed, reaching for the box. Jorb and Rinka disappeared, replaced by a little old lady who looked like the kind grandmother from a holiday immersive.

"Who are you?" Bill demanded. "What happened to our friends?"

"They're getting out of the sensory deprivation pods now, but I told Jeeves to give me a private minute with the two of you. I'm the Union Station librarian, and I provided all of the characters for your immersive experience."

"So it wasn't an official Drazen test?"

"It was for Jorb and Rinka," Libby replied. "I'm simply taking advantage of the opportunity to step out of the background and introduce myself to the two of you."

"What's so special about us?" Julie asked.

The old lady gave them a warm smile. "I think the two of you are very special people, but of course, I have a weakness for Humans who empathize with artificial intelligence. I wanted to speak with you about Flower."

"Are you the Stryx mentor she's always talking about?"

"Yes. Flower has been a bit of a special project for me. She was totally devastated when her crew rejected her, and for a long time, it wasn't clear whether she would survive, or worse, whether we would have to terminate her."

"Terminate her? What did she ever do to anybody?"

"Dollnick AI isn't built around stable solutions to the equations of artificial intelligence, and in the absence of a mission, it can go off in very bad directions. Finding work for Flower as EarthCent's circuit ship has provided her with a new focus, but she's still very fragile in some ways. Without violating the confidentiality of the mentoring relationship, I can tell you that Flower has a great deal of affection for you both."

"Was she participating in this?" Julie asked.

"No, that was me playing Flower's role. Jeeves told you the truth about your implants being unavailable to her while you were in the sensory deprivation pods. And I want to apologize for sending the future version of Em to interrupt your proposal. I know this may sound outlandish, but it would negatively impact the trust Flower has in me if you visited Union Station and returned home engaged. She couldn't help but feel that I stole the match from her."

"So you want me to propose again when we get back?" Bill asked.

"I hate to impose, but if you delay for a week, at least until Flower reaches her next stop, she won't feel like she's splitting a prize with me. I run a matchmaking service on Union Station and it appears that she's trying to emulate me. It happens sometimes in mentoring relationships."

"Then why did you put the ring in my pocket in the first place and have your version of Flower push me to propose?"

"Jeeves contracted with the consortium to provide a realistic immersive experience of what the future might hold for the participants in fifty years. He subcontracted me to build the alternative reality for you, as it's a bit beyond his scope, and I did my best to be accurate."

"You must have a lot of information," Julie said.

"Flower and I talk frequently," Libby replied. "We gave her unlimited Stryxnet access for that purpose. But unlike artificial intelligence, your time isn't unlimited, so I should return you to your friends."

"Just a second. How come you sound just like the teacherbot I had growing up?"

The old lady's eyes twinkled, and then the illusion faded and Julie found herself watching the lid rise from her sensory deprivation pod.

"Did you guys stay to finish your milk or something?" Jorb asked as he helped her out of the pod.

"It was strange," Julie said. "I'm going to need time to think about everything that happened."

"Thank you for your cooperation," Jeeves told them. "That didn't take nearly as long as I thought, so I'm going to get back to the office before a certain employee spends all of my money. Here's your fee for participating," he added, extending a pincer and dropping a one-hundred-cred coin in Julie's hand.

"How about mine?" Bill asked.

"Check your pocket." Bill did as he was told and his fingers closed on a small box. "An alternative payment from my parent that I'm assured is worth well over a hundred creds," the young Stryx said. "Now if you'll follow me to the lift tube, this deck is off-limits to biologicals without an escort. And don't forget to check the Libbyland attractions while you're on Union Station. We're running a discount in honor of MultiCon."

Twenty

"...nine for Jorb, seven for Razood, and two for Brynlan," Lume concluded. "Do any of you have any objections to the final count?"

"Humans are too impatient," complained the slow-spoken Verlock who had finished last in the competition to recruit new intelligence sources at the con. "Next time I'll know to make my pitch in lift tube capsules where my targets can't run off before I can get to offering them money."

"Why don't you start with what it pays?"

"We have very explicit rules on that subject," Brynlan explained. "The Verlock Intelligence Service has been collecting data for millions of years, and our statisticians have determined that the sources who are offered a money-first pitch are more likely to invent facts in order to get paid."

Jorb slapped a coin on the table in front of the Vergallian agent whose cover job was her finishing school for teenage girls. "Here's my twenty creds, Avisia, but if we do this again, you have to agree up front not to use your pheromones on men. It's not fair to the rest of us."

"I'll have you know I didn't even consider moving to chemical warfare," the impossibly beautiful Vergallian retorted. "I just stopped by the con wearing my Battle Royale costume for a few hours every evening and the young men lined up to pledge their loyalty to the Empire of a Hundred Worlds. And I didn't have Flower sending me prospects like she did for Yaem."

"You know I was working around the clock on the con and Bill handled my recruiting effort," the Sharf protested. "It's going to take me another week to catch up on my sleep."

"M793qK ran a close second with a Human doing all of his recruiting," Lume commented as he paid the Vergallian. "Dave really knows how to close a deal."

"The Farling uses his stand-in for intelligence work?" Avisia seemed to be contemplating something, and then she shook her head. "No, the girls in my finishing school are too young for that sort of thing."

"You didn't do that badly, Director," Razood said to the Grenouthian. "How many did you say you recruited? Sixteen?"

"I would have doubled that easy if I wasn't so focused on expanding our anime production business," the Grenouthian grumbled. "Still, I have to admit that some of those Humans who presented short features they created without access to professional studio equipment have real potential. If you'd let me add the new production hires for Flower Studios to my total for new intelligence sources, I'd have won."

"Does anybody want to bet on how many different shows Flower has up for awards next year?" Jorb asked. He looked over to the entrance of the alien cafeteria as the third officer entered. "Hey, Lynx. Do you want to get in on our new pool?"

"Maybe later, but I'm here on business," the captain's wife said. "Flower wants me to conduct an exit interview with all of you who were involved in the con so we can see what needs to be improved for next time around."

"We need to work on sending the guests home," Yaem said immediately. "When I finally got out of bed an hour ago, I stopped down on the con deck to get my coffee mug back from the temporary office. Based on the number of people I saw in costumes, it looks like somebody forgot to tell them that it's over."

"I invited everybody who attended to remain on board," Flower announced via an overhead speaker. "I thought that some cosplayers would make an interesting addition to the theatre district, and I'm thinking of permanently rebranding it as a con deck. Many of the attendees had to get back to their jobs or families, but the retention rate among the ConAnon members was nearly a hundred percent. Perhaps I'll start advertising the deck as a residential option for anybody who likes wearing costumes around the clock."

"Do you mean like a theme park?" Lynx asked. "You'll get EarthCent in trouble with the Grenouthians because they've already licensed the exclusive rights to human-derived theme parks."

"Not a theme park, a permanent con. There should be a better name than that, but I suppose we'll just have to invent one ourselves. PermaCon? Con Living?"

"And when did you think would be the right time to spring your new idea on the ship's officers?" Lynx inquired acerbically.

"Now seems to be appropriate," the Dollnick AI responded. "Any other feedback about the con?"

"We should have arranged with Union Station ahead of time for the exclusive use of the LARPing studios," Jorb said. "There were some pretty long lines by the midafternoon most days, and the professional league play had priority."

"Did anybody give up and return before they got a chance to try it?" Yaem asked. "I don't recall hearing any complaints."

"The Stryx provided a kind of sandbox studio where I taught basic use of noodle weapons to keep everybody busy while we were waiting," Jorb said. "Couldn't you manage a LARPing studio on board, Flower?"

"I don't quite have the spare processing capacity, but I'm looking into upgrading my support network with commercial 3D rendering engines that could do most of the grunt work," the Dollnick AI said. "I'll keep you posted."

"Do you really think that running a permanent con will serve some sort of a societal purpose for humanity, or are you just looking to fill more cabins?" Lynx asked.

"Is there a difference?"

"You mean you're filling cabins for the greater good?"

"I like to think that we're all in this together," Flower said. "More residents equal greater utilization of my facilities, which translates into higher efficiency and lower operating costs. In addition, a higher population makes us a more attractive destination vacation for visitors at our regular stops, which supports our primary mission. Greater numbers of visitors translates into a better chance for us to recruit people to fill our various needs. It's win-win-win."

"Did you manage to recruit any employees for your shipyard scheme?" Yaem asked. "I heard back from my boss at Sharf Intelligence, and they located the intellectual property owners of the old two-man trader design. The basic tooling is still in mothballs, and the owners are willing to lease it to us, I mean, to you, with the stipulations that the ships you produce are sold exclusively to Humans, and that you buy all of the fuel packs and drive units from Sharf manufacturers."

"Excellent. I was able to hire a number of Humans with somewhat relevant design and manufacturing experience during the con, and I hope to be able to start taking orders for new two-man traders when I host the next Rendezvous."

"Since when did you talk the Traders Guild into having it here?" Lynx asked. "Would it kill you to keep me in the loop?"

"It's not a done deal yet, but I've offered them free docking for all comers if they hold Rendezvous on board," Flower said. "One of the guild's new council members owes us his life, so I expect it's in the bag. If I don't have room for all their ships, I'll just have to set up an outside parking area and remain in one place for the duration."

"Why do I get the sneaking suspicion that all of this has to do with your wanting to join the Conference of Sovereign Human Communities? You're trying to get in good with the Traders Guild so they'll support you for CoSHC."

"If the Traders Guild wants to express their appreciation for my restarting production of affordable two-man traders by sponsoring our membership bid for CoSHC, that's just an example of one pair of hands washing the other."

"She means it in the singular sense," Bill said, setting an enormous salad on the table. "I'll be back with the side dishes in a minute."

"I didn't even see him come in from the kitchen," the Grenouthian director muttered to Yaem. "Have you been teaching him infiltration and surveillance techniques?"

"Haven't had the time," the Sharf said. "He must have picked that up on his own. The captain gave him a book to study."

Razood returned from the mini-bar with a bottle of expensive single malt Scotch and a small tray of shot glasses. "I want to propose a toast for Jorb's passing his second-level compatibility test," the Frunge said as he began pouring shots. "Couldn't have happened to a nicer Drazen."

"Do try to use your new influence with Rinka to persuade her to come and teach my girls," Avisia begged Jorb. "I get a sore throat just trying to sing scales with them. An hour twice a week would be a huge help."

"Bring Harry out here," Lume instructed Bill when the young man returned with the side dishes. "We're congratulating Jorb on moving one step closer to marriage."

Lynx followed Bill back to the kitchen, and asked in a low voice, "How are things progressing with you and Julie?"

"Almost there, I think," Bill said. He hesitated, remembering the Stryx librarian's words, and attempted to stretch himself as an actor. "I want to make the proposal special, so I'm going to ask Flower for help."

"Of course I'll help you," the Dollnick AI said. "I knew that you and Julie were right for each other as soon as you joined the ship."

"Where is Julie now?" Lynx asked. "I should get her feedback about the art show. Is she back to working at the library?"

"She's at The Spoon with the Biancas and they just ordered," Flower replied. "It's a business lunch, so let the exit interview go until later."

"Thanks, Renée," Julie said, handing the three menus back to the waitress. "How are your classes at the Open University going?"

"Good, I think. They don't have tests in the regular sense, but there are competency exams before you can move on to the next level."

"Do you mean you could spend a whole year in class and not even know whether you're passing?"

"Students who can't tell whether or not they understand the material probably don't," Sixth said, and the younger Bianca nodded her head in agreement.

"The competency exams are super practical," Renée told them. "I already aced the waitressing one for advanced credit in the hospitality program. Speaking of which, I'll get your orders in and your drinks right out."

"I wish there had been an Open University campus on Earth," Seventh said. "I was lucky that a Verlock magnet academy opened in our city when the children were just old enough to start, but they were so well prepared when they went to college that they found it boring."

"They weren't willing to leave Earth for university?" Julie asked.

"Both of them finished the magnet academy at sixteen, and I wasn't comfortable letting them go off on their own at that age," the younger Bianca said. "That was before I traveled all over the galaxy doing Guest Human spots at cons, so I didn't know that they would have been safer on a Stryx station or a Verlock open world than on Earth. But they seemed so young to be on their own."

"I understand that you went the teacherbot route," Sixth said to Julie. "I never went to a real school myself, though some of the parents took turns helping us with reading and math."

"I thought you—" Julie began, and then clamped her jaw shut.

"You thought I went through school before the Stryx opened Earth?" Sixth chuckled. "I'm not *that* old. Seventh went to a private school, and you can see it come through in some of her books."

"All that stuff about mean-girl cliques and boys getting pushed into lockers was real?"

"Unfortunately," the younger Bianca said. "That's one reason I jumped at the chance to send my children to the Verlock academy."

"Two milks and one coffee," Renée said, placing the drinks on the table.

"I ordered coffee too," Julie and Sixth said at the same time.

Renée pointed at the ceiling and retreated with her tray.

"Drink half of your milk and I'll top you off with the good stuff," Seventh said to her senior. "Does this mean you went for your physical exam to determine the options for your required team sport?"

Sixth nodded. "The Farling said that my bone density is too low, and if I didn't want to pay for the treatment, I should move to a lower gravity deck and drink more milk."

"Was the treatment that expensive?"

"It was cheap. I just don't go in for a lot of doctoring. But if it means being able to order coffee..."

"You're both staying on board?" Julie asked.

"Her, not me," the younger Bianca said. "I have public appearance commitments and my daughter is expecting my first grandchild back on Earth. But I'm going to talk to both of my children about moving to Flower. It's better to plan for the future than to just let it happen."

"Which is the perfect segue to what we wanted to discuss with you," Sixth said to Julie.

"I've only been to the independent living cooperative a few times, though I guess I know a lot about living on Flower in general," the girl guessed at the older Bianca's meaning. "You'll get used to things like the morning calisthenics, and the whole team sport concept is pretty flexible. I started in theatre and ended up with a paid acting job on *Everyday Superheroes*."

"I meant that we want to discuss your future with us, but I'll let Seventh make the pitch."

"How would you like to be my understudy and eventually take over?" the younger Bianca asked Julie. "It would only be part-time for the next few years, doing research, writing scenarios, and learning how to edit for the D'Arc style. After that, I'm hoping to slow down and maybe write the occasional gryphon book, so we'd be splitting the load until I retire."

"But I still haven't finished writing a complete novel on my own," Julie protested. "What makes you so sure I have any ability?"

"Craft can be learned, and it's clear from our conversations that you have an excellent imagination," Sixth said. "Seventh told me that you don't like talking about your life before you joined Flower, but I dug up an interview you did with the Galactic Free Press. All authors end up mining their pasts for characters and ideas, and putting some of your bad memories to good use may help you exorcise any remaining demons."

"I'm not sure it's ethical to profit from having worked for a drug syndicate."

"Knowledge is knowledge. If we all threw out the things we learned from people we didn't approve of we'd be even more ignorant than all the aliens think we are. Most romance writers I've known struggle to write realistic bad men, because at most, they've met a few pimps or pushers at parties. You have more real-life experience with the day-to-day operation of organized crime than any paranormal romance writer who's ever put pen to paper."

"I never thought of it that way, but it seems like a really big jump," Julie said. "If I try this, are you going to be available to help after, uh, Seventh returns to Earth?"

"You've already figured out our nefarious plan," Sixth said with a laugh.

Renée brought out salads for the Biancas and a burger with fries for Julie. The two older women looked longingly at the French fries, and Julie moved her plate to the center of the table. Seventh pushed it right back.

"No," she said. "I save all of my spare calories for chocolate."

"I start the day with chocolate and then see how much room I have left for food," Sixth said, and then her eyes shifted to something over Julie's shoulder. "Look what the cat dragged in."

"Biancas," Geoffrey greeted them. "Julie."

"We're planning to make it three Biancas, unless you poach her to write Geoffrey Harstang books."

"The space marines genre changes too rapidly for line authorship to be much benefit," he said, pulling up a chair and helping himself to a couple of Julie's fries. "May I?"

"What are you doing here, Geoffrey?"

"You know I've always been a diner fan, and this is the first place I ate after coming on board Flower. I finally arranged to meet with the captain to repay the favor, but it seems that I'm here twenty minutes early."

"Which is unbelievable in itself," Sixth said. "I'm going to have to find the people who ran that hospital where you were locked up and offer to pay their legal expenses. You could be their poster boy for the most improved patient."

"Never get on her bad side," Geoffrey advised Julie in a stage whisper. Then he continued in his normal voice, "Has Lynx done your exit interview yet?"

"My what?" Julie asked.

"Flower has her going around asking everybody involved in planning the con how they think it could be improved. She'll probably be after you too, Seventh."

"Already got me," the younger Bianca said. "I pointed out that only a male would have tried combining Amish and Alien Abduction Romance into one session."

"Yaem's an alien," Julie pointed out. "How could he know?"

"Males are all aliens when it comes to romance," Geoffrey said. "If the females of the galaxy ever decide to unite and take over, all they'd have to do to distribute their plan secretly is to publish it in romance novels."

"Maybe we already have," Sixth said, artfully raising a single eyebrow.

"What did you tell Lynx in your exit interview?" Seventh asked Geoffrey.

"That I thought it was all around the best con I've ever attended, and if Flower wants me to participate in a more limited manner the next time around, I'll be honored," the author said. "But I don't have the energy I used to, and the colony project that I'll be collaborating on with Sixth is going to take up all of the time that I don't spend writing."

"And treating me to dinners," the older Bianca said.

"You mean the writers colony you were talking about before?" Julie asked.

"Ach, don't call it that!" Geoffrey said, putting his hands over his ears. "Some writers think there needs to be a possessive apostrophe hanging on after the 'S' and it makes me crazy. I've rewritten whole books to avoid adding possessive apostrophes to plural words that any fool would understand in context."

"He's exaggerating, as usual," Sixth said.

Julie and Seventh finished their meals before Sixth made it halfway through her salad, thanks to the unending banter the two older authors kept up. The younger Bianca eventually gave Julie a wink and a nod that they should leave the pair of former lovers alone. Seventh insisted on paying the check and invited Julie to head over to the con offices to go over the D'Arc understudy contract on their tabs.

"I have bots breaking down the offices as we speak," Flower said over Julie's implant. "I suggest the library instead."

"Flower says the con offices are gone and we should try the library," Julie told the younger Bianca.

"I may sound old-fashioned, but isn't talking discouraged in libraries?"

"The reading room has audio suppression fields over all of the tables. It's become the preferred place for our local Galactic Free Press reporter to do interviews."

"Then the library it is."

Bea was at the main desk when they entered, and to Julie's surprise, the head librarian rushed out to meet them with a hardcover copy of Bianca's latest release.

"I picked it up after your session since you didn't bring books to sell," Bea explained. "I wondered if you would mind..."

"I'm happy to sign it," Bianca said, setting the book on the checkout desk. "If everything goes right, soon you'll be asking Julie to inscribe D'Arc books."

The head librarian gasped and grabbed Julie's hand. "You're going to apprentice to Bianca? You have to let me proofread for you."

"We're about to look over the contract. I don't see how I can turn it down."

"Flower will be so pleased," Bea said. "Now we'll have two of the top romance line authors living on board."

"Do you mean me and Sixth?"

"I mean Bianca D'Arc and Isla Stuart," the head librarian said. "She has a cover job working as the receptionist at the print on demand publisher just up the corridor, but she spends most of her time writing the most delicious Highland time travel books."

"I had no idea she lived on board," Bianca said. "I haven't seen Isla in at least five years so I'll have to stop in and surprise her."

A man who looked like an immersive action hero carried a stack of books behind the circulation desk and began rapidly placing them on shelves.

"Who's the hunk?" Bianca asked Julie.

"Maybe my replacement for while I worked at the con?" she ventured, and then did a double-take when he turned and she recognized him from her experimental LARPing experience. "Dewey?"

"Do you like it?" the newly minted artificial person asked, patting both hands on his chest. "I had enough saved up to manage the body without a mortgage, though I have to admit I miss my old shelving attachment."

"Whatever you paid, it was worth every cred," Bianca told him. She pulled Julie close and whispered. "And I think I just had an idea for another series."

"But you look exactly like you did when I saw you—" Julie caught herself just before spilling the beans about her encounter with the future on Union Station and substituted "—in a dream, Dewey. And you said that you were working as the head of intelligence for the Human Empire."

"I met several of the artificial people working for EarthCent Intelligence while I was picking up my new body on Union Station. They tried to recruit me, but I'm sticking with Flower," Dewey said. Then to Julie's surprise, he laughed, and it looked and sounded completely natural. "Human Empire. I guess somebody has an ambitious subconscious after all."

My special thanks to Bianca D'Arc (the first) for allowing me to use her name.

You can help keep Flower open for business even if you were born too early to grab the space elevator up for her next stop at Earth and shop in the bazaar. Tell a friend about **Independent Living** and the **Union Station** series.

If you like science fiction without wars, you should also enjoy my AI Diaries trilogy, which starts on present-day Earth with **Turing Test**. You can sign up for e-mail notification of my new releases on the **IfItBreaks.com** website or ping me at e_foner@yahoo.com and I'll add you manually. I'm also online at: Facebook/E.M.Foner/

About the Author

E. M. Foner lives in Northampton, MA with an imaginary German Shepherd who's been trained to bite central bankers. The author welcomes reader comments at e_foner@yahoo.com.

Also by the author:

Independent Living
Assisted Living
Freelance on the Galactic Tunnel Network
Date Night on Union Station
Alien Night on Union Station
High Priest on Union Station
Spy Night on Union Station
Carnival on Union Station
Wanderers on Union Station
Vacation on Union Station
Guest Night on Union Station
Word Night on Union Station
Party Night on Union Station
Review Night on Union Station
Family Night on Union Station
Book Night on Union Station
LARP Night on Union Station
Career Night on Union Station
Last Night on Union Station
Soup Night on Union Station
Meghan's Dragon
Turing Test
Human Test
Magic Test

Made in the USA
Monee, IL
23 May 2022

96944044R00152